SEDUCED BY THE SCOT

Perks of Being an Heiress, Book 3

By Jillian Eaton

DRAGONBLADE PUBLISHING, INC.

Dragonblade Publishing, Inc. is an imprint of Kathryn Le Veque Novels, Inc.
P.O. Box 7968
La Verne CA 91750
ceo@dragonbladepublishing.com

Produced in the United States of America

First Edition July 2021
Print Edition

ARE YOU SIGNED UP FOR DRAGONBLADE'S BLOG?

You'll get the latest news and information on exclusive giveaways, exclusive excerpts, coming releases, sales, free books, cover reveals and more.

Check out our complete list of authors, too!

No spam, no junk. That's a promise!

Sign Up Here

www.dragonbladepublishing.com

Dearest Reader;

Thank you for your support of a small press. At Dragonblade Publishing, we strive to bring you the highest quality Historical Romance from the some of the best authors in the business. Without your support, there is no 'us', so we sincerely hope you adore these stories and find some new favorite authors along the way.

Happy Reading!

CEO, Dragonblade Publishing

Additional Dragonblade books by Author Jillian Eaton

The Perks of Being an Heiress Series

Bewitched by the Bluestocking

Entranced by the Earl

Seduced by the Scot

You are the star of each night
You are the brightness of every morning
You are the story of each guest
You are the report of every land

No evil shall befall you
on hill nor bank
In field or valley
On mountain or in a glen.

~ Gaelic Blessing

CHAPTER ONE

L ACHLAN SMELLED HER perfume before he saw her.
It was a delicate, intimate scent. Difficult, if not impossible, to discern from the wild pink roses that surrounded the gazebo in a tangled sprawl of pale pink and deep green. Had he not held her in his arms, or pressed his mouth to the sensitive stem of her neck, or slept beside her when the only two things she wore were moonlight and that intoxicating perfume, he might have missed it.

But Lachlan had done all those things. And more. Which was why his nostrils flared and his eyes darkened with recognition the instant *before* he stepped around the side of Hawkridge Manor and saw her sitting in the gazebo, looking as pretty as a picture with her paintbrush in hand and her golden hair swept back from her countenance in an elegant coiffure.

She was the epitome of an English lady. Fair coloring, high cheekbones, a long, willowy frame. A top lip that was ever-so-slightly heavier than the bottom and curved in the shape of a cupid's bow. Hazel eyes, flecked with green, which could go as sharp as a scalpel or as soft as lamb's wool, depending on her mood. A faint dusting of freckles, so slight as to nearly be invisible, across the bridge of her nose.

In his humble opinion, Lady Brynne Weston was the most beautiful creature that God had ever seen fit to create. Was it any wonder he had fallen in love with her when he was a lad of sixteen? And had remained in love with her these eleven years past as he'd grown from a bairn into a man.

He'd loved her every month, every day, every second.

For Lachlan, it was always Brynne.

Which was why he had finally returned to claim her. To apologize for his wrongs, and to make her remember–she *had* to remember–how good they'd been together before he allowed secrets to tear them apart.

His boots sank silently into the grass as he approached the gazebo. Growing up in a rambling castle with a father whose hand had been heavy and vicious, particularly after a night of drinking, Lachlan had learned at a young age to walk without making a sound.

He stopped at the bottom of the steps and, for a moment, he simply allowed himself to drink in the sight of her. This was the closest they'd been in a year. And it had been eighteen months of torment. Eighteen months without hearing her laugh, or seeing the shape of her smile, or tasting the sweet nectar of her lips.

Surely there was no greater torture contrived by man than being kept from the woman he loved. Give him the rack, or the wheel, or that horrific metal box with the spikes in it. He'd take them all, gladly, if it meant never having to go another day without seeing his Brynne.

Her face was obscured by the large easel, but she'd stretched her legs out in front of her stool as she worked, affording him a tantalizing glimpse of her slender calves enclosed in silk stockings.

Not so very long ago, he'd peeled those stockings off of her...with his teeth. He would like nothing better than a repeat performance of that *very* memorable night, but he had a feeling that Brynne wasn't going to be nearly as happy to see him as he was to see her...considering the last time they were together she'd pointed a pistol at his nether regions and told him, in no uncertain terms, that if he ever dared approach her again she wouldn't hesitate to pull the trigger.

Feisty lass.

"Could you step to the side please, Mae?" she said without bothering to glance up from her canvas. "I fear you're in my light."

Her voice, as lilting and musical as chimes in the wind, was like a balm to his soul.

"Is this better?" he drawled, moving slightly to the left.

Blue paint splattered across the gazebo's white floorboards as the paintbrush she'd been holding fell from her fingers. Lachlan unconsciously held his breath as Brynne rose to her feet, and released it on a spill of air from the corner of his mouth when her shocked, furious gaze met his.

"Get out of here," she whispered, pointing in the direction of the drive where his belongings, unbeknownst to her, were being unloaded and carried into the manor as they spoke. "Before I pick up that brush and stab you through the heart with it."

Like the roses her perfume reminded him of, Brynne's thorns were buried out of sight. Which made them all the more painful when they drew blood. Not that he'd been expecting a warm welcome with open arms (he was an optimist, not an idiot), but he *had* held out hope that they'd moved beyond death threats. Although considering what he had done to his beloved's fragile heart, a brush stabbed through the middle of his chest wasn't any less than what he deserved.

"Now, Bry, me love," he said with an admonishing cluck of his tongue. "Is that any way tae greet yer husband?"

Her eyes narrowing, she took a menacing step towards him with her fists clenched, as if she were a boxer capable of knocking him out with one mighty swing instead of a tiny slip of a lass whose head barely reached his chin.

"You're no husband of mine, Lachlan Campbell," she spat.

He arched an auburn brow. "The priest who married us might have a word or two tae say about that."

"Our marriage should have been dissolved a year ago." A beam of sunlight slid beneath the gazebo's domed roof and surrounded Brynne's head in a halo of glowing light as she lifted her chin. With the sun in her hair and fury in her eyes, his wife was half ethereal fairy, half wrathful sprite…and he desired all of her.

Even when they were little more than children, there'd always been two sides of Brynne. The obedient daughter who had diligently listened to every rule her governess set, and the rebellious lass who had snuck out her window at night to meet him underneath an alder tree where he'd carved their initials into the rough bark. The elegantly composed lady who had entertained everyone from princes to esteemed foreign dignitaries, and the seductive minx who had run away to Gretna Green to marry a brutish Scot.

"On what grounds would ye call for an annulment?" he drawled, his second eyebrow rising to join the first. "In case ye forgot, our union was consummated. *Several* times." As his mouth curved into a wicked, wolfish grin, twin blooms of color flooded Brynne's cheeks.

"On the grounds that you're a boorish lummox and I never should have married you!" Her shout was loud enough to spook a pair of nesting doves out of a nearby bush. They took to the air as she took another step towards him but, in her anger, she misjudged the depth of the stair and her foot slipped.

Lachlan lunged forward and caught her before she could fall, his arms wrapping around her slender frame like two steel bands as he settled her on her feet. And for an instant…just an *instant*…she leaned into him, the weight of her head on his chest as light as a feather on the wind. But it was there. He felt it as clearly as he felt the sun on his face and the ground under his legs. Then she made a ball with her hand and drove it into his gut, and he felt that as well.

"Bluidy hell," he grunted, letting her slip out of his embrace as he doubled over. "Ye knocked the wind right out of me, love." Stretching upright, he gazed at her flushed countenance with some amusement.

"Have ye ever considered stepping intae the ring? Ye would do some serious damage with that right hook."

Brynne's hands went to her hips. "Do not call me that. I am not your 'love'."

"Ye were once," he reminded her. "Not so long ago."

"A *lifetime* ago. What are you doing here, Lachlan? What do you want?"

It was the first time he'd heard her say his name in a year, and he savored the sound of it on her lips as he would the first sip of a vintage scotch straight from the oak barrel.

"Ye," he said roughly, dragging a hand through his tangled mane. Loose from the leather tie he normally used to bind them, the auburn locks brushed his shoulders. "I want *ye*, Bry. That's why I've come. That's why I'm here. Tae win ye back."

The color drained from her cheeks, leaving her as pale as the white sheets he'd seen flapping in the wind on the far side of the manor. Slightly alarmed by her lack of pallor, and the way she suddenly swayed on her feet, he reached an arm to steady her, but she slapped his hand away.

"*No*," she said forcefully. "No to all of it. I do not know what possessed you to think anything has changed between us, but nothing has. Nothing *will*. All you've done by coming here is waste your time and tire a good horse." The flecks of emerald in her eyes intensified with her heightened emotions, giving the illusion that her irises had shifted from brown to green.

From personal experience, Lachlan knew they only did that when she was genuinely furious…or in the midst of lovemaking.

"We can change it if we want," he said with a Scot's bred-into-the-bone stubbornness. Unable to help himself, he closed the distance between them with a single stride and cupped her cheek in his large palm. She glared up at him, a she-wolf ready to bite. "I made a mistake, Bry. I should have told ye the truth–"

"Yes," she interrupted. "You should have. About a lot of things. But you lied, Lachlan. *You* lied. And you ruined us."

"I'm many things, *mo lean nan.*" As his temper flared, he unconsciously slipped into the native Gaelic that he'd learned at his grandmother's knee. "A liar isna one of them."

"What is an omission, if not a lie that hasn't been spoken yet?" Deftly, she twisted her head to the side and ducked under his arm. "You may not have lied outright, but you didn't tell me the truth, either. If you had–" She stopped short. Gave a clipped, irritated shake of her head. "It doesn't matter. The past cannot be changed, and there is no possible future where we are together."

He'd been expecting this reaction.

Had braced himself for it.

But it still hurt like a bloody son of a bitch.

Especially since he couldn't help but compare how they were now to what they'd been. To *who* they'd been. Two young, naïve lovers ready to tackle the world and all the troubles it contained. Never guessing that the troubles on their own doorstep were far larger than any ills that awaited them beyond it.

"There are things we need tae discuss," he said roughly. "Matters that need to be handled. If we could sit down and have a civil discussion over tea and biscuits–"

"Tea and biscuits?" she said incredulously. *"Tea and biscuits?* There's no amount of tea in the world that would fix what you broke, Lachlan. And the only thing that needs to be *handled* is our annulment. Which can be done through our solicitors. I'll send a letter to London in the morning."

He gritted his teeth. "I dinna want an annulment."

"And I do not want to go through this again. I refuse. Do you understand me? I *refuse.*" Her chest rose as she took a deep breath, and fell as she released it. "You need to leave."

"Little songbird–"

"Leave!" she cried, and the glitter of tears he saw in her eyes stopped him cold.

His Bry never cried.

Never.

Lachlan knew he was a right bastard for bringing her this pain again. But he wasn't the only guilty party...and she wasn't the only one hurting. There were two sides to this Shakespearean tragedy, and while he may have shouldered most of the blame for what had happened to them, he didn't lay claim to all of it.

"Right then," he said. "I'll go. There are some supplies I need in the village."

"Supplies?" A line of bewilderment creased her fair brow. "Supplies for what?"

"Why, for me stay." At her blank stare, his smile hardened. "Ye didna think I came all this way tae just turn around and leave again, did ye? Ye're my wife, Lady Brynne Campbell. I'm yer husband. And it's high time we shared the same roof...and the same bed."

Her eyes widened, her lips parted in outrage, but before she could muster a reply, he turned on his heel and loped away.

BRYNNE'S LEGS FELT as if they were carved from wood as she staggered into the manor. One look at her, and Mrs. Grimsby, the housekeeper, ushered her straight into the parlor and nudged the door closed behind them.

Soft and plump with a merry smile and a perpetual twinkle in her brown eyes, Mrs. Grimsby was the eldest daughter of the previous housekeeper, a dragon of a woman who had often sent Brynne scurrying away in terror. She had a husband, who worked as the head groundskeeper, and three daughters of her own, all grown with families. Both she and Mr. Grimsby had begun discussing their retirement, but they were loyal above all else, and loath to leave the family they'd served so diligently for more than two decades.

"Sit down and drink this," Mrs. Grimsby said gently, pressing a cool glass of water into Brynne's numb hands. "That's it. Slowly now. Good, good. Head between your knees if you're feeling faint, just as we talked about."

Wordlessly, Brynne lowered her forehead towards the ground as the housekeeper took the glass and then began to rub her back in large, soothing circles.

"My poor dear," Mrs. Grimsby clucked. "I haven't seen you in such a state in ages. Deep breaths, my lady. Deep breaths."

Years, Brynne thought silently as she inhaled through her mouth and exhaled through her nose, just as Mrs. Grimsby had taught her. It had been years since she'd had an Episode. So long that she thought they were a thing of the past. Why, she hadn't even had one when she walked into the bedroom and saw Lachlan–no. Best not to think about that now. Or ever again, if she could help it. Which was why she'd buried that brief period of time in a box, and she'd put the box in a trunk, and she'd locked the trunk with a key.

For eighteen months, almost to the day, she'd kept that key tucked away and the trunk closed. For eighteen months, she'd avoided dwelling on what she had seen that day when it all came crashing down. Her life, her love, her happily-ever-after. Like wooden blocks knocked asunder by a child's clumsy hand.

Except Lord Lachlan Campbell was no child.

And a shattered heart was no easy thing to rebuild.

Thus, she'd made the decision to pretend it had never happened. Their secret engagement, their giddy elopement, their blissful honeymoon, everything that had come after...all of it, gone. She had carved it out of her mind, and out of her memory, and put it in that damned box. Where the feelings and emotions couldn't be seen, or heard, or touched. Then she had gone on with her life as if nothing was amiss. As if she really *had* been on holiday in Bath, which was the excuse she'd given everyone to explain her absence. They'd believed her because...why wouldn't they? She was Lady Brynne Weston, after all.

Perfect, pristine, practical Brynne.

And she'd done such a good job at concealing her hurt, her shame, her brokenness, that no one–not even her twin brother, Weston–had suspected that her entire world had been tilted on its axis and all of its contents dumped out, leaving her to pick up the pieces without anyone being the wiser.

Which was why it was so important–vital, really–that she *not* have an Episode.

And she hadn't.

Until today.

When Lachlan had strolled back into her life looking as devilishly handsome as the day she'd married him. The bastard. But he hadn't just unlocked the trunk and released the memories she had tried so hard to forget. Oh, no. Her estranged husband wasn't nearly that subtle. Instead, he'd smashed it open with a hammer, wrenched the box out, and proceeded to stomp it into smithereens.

Now she couldn't breathe.

She couldn't *breathe*. Courtesy of strict tutelage, she was fluent in six languages, could perform a curtsy with a glass bowl resting on top of her head, knew every step to every waltz ever created, and could play the piano with such proficiency as to nearly be considered a master. But she was unable to breathe. The most basic of all subconscious human actions, and she was struggling to remember how to do it. Because of *him*. Because of what his reappearance meant. Because of what he'd unleashed inside of her.

"A cold compress," she murmured, pinching her throbbing forehead between her thumb and index finger. "If you please, Mrs. Grimsby."

"Right away, my lady." The housekeeper dashed from the room. In the silence left by her departure, the ticking of a longcase clock in the corner of the parlor tolled as loudly as church bells on Sunday morning.

Wincing from the sound, Brynne reclined all the way back onto the sofa Mrs. Grimsby had guided her to, and dragged a pillow over her face.

In and out, she reminded herself. *In and out. Like waves upon the shore.*

By the time Mrs. Grimsby returned with a damp cloth that she draped across Brynne's temple before whisking the curtains closed and quietly excusing herself, Brynne had managed to regain control of her racing pulse. Such a small thing, but a step in the right direction nevertheless.

As her breathing evened, the weight sitting on her chest began to subside, and her fingers tingled as sensation returned them, like the tiny prick of a hundred little needles. Eventually, the shadows in the corners of her vision receded, and her heartrate steadied, then slowed.

Goodness, but she hadn't missed that. Years since her last Episode, and yet it was exactly as she remembered it. Just as she still recalled the first time she'd ever had one. Of course, back then, she hadn't known *what* was happening. Or if she would even survive it.

She'd been fourteen. The same age, minus seven minutes, as Weston. Their mother had died birthing them. Their father had left them to be raised by a handful of rotating nannies and governesses. Mrs. Grimsby was just a scullery maid, and the housekeeper–Mrs. Pembroke–was to be avoided at all costs.

In a household of servants and no parents, Weston was the constant in Brynne's life.

Her brother was her rock. Her most trusted confidant. Her best friend.

And as she had watched his carriage, destined for Eton, roll away, something inside of her had snapped, like a clock screw twisted a tad too far. At least, that was the best way she could describe the terrible, suffocating feeling of having the air suddenly thin and her heart race and the awful, awful pressure gathering somewhere deep inside of her chest.

Panicked and gasping for breath, she'd clawed at her throat as she had dropped to her knees, and then collapsed onto her side. Until she opened that bedroom door and saw Lachlan sprawled on the rumpled bedspread, it was the single worst moment of her entire life.

The parlor had swirled. Her vision had dimmed. And just as she'd been about to slip into unconsciousness, Mrs. Grimsby—who back then was simply Lucy—had come rushing in. She'd immediately called for a doctor, and then helped Brynne sit up.

"Breathe," she had said urgently. "You must breathe, Lady Brynne. In and out, in an out. Slower. Slower."

"I–I *can't*," Brynne had gasped, but Lucy—stalwart and dependable, even then—had refused to accept such an answer.

"You can and you must," she'd insisted. "Think of…think of waves on the beach. Rushing up to the shore, then falling back into the ocean. Up and back. Up and back. There. There you are."

The doctor had arrived within the hour and he'd examined Brynne quite thoroughly before reaching a diagnosis.

"I've only seen this once before, when I first began my practice," he'd said as he returned his stethoscope—a curious wooden instrument in the shape of a stick with a circle at each end—into his black medical bag and snapped it closed. "In a woman with a newborn baby who had just received news of her husband dying on the battlefield. Horrific business, war. How fortunate we are that Queen Victoria has proven herself to be such an excellent diplomat and has kept us from conflict."

"Did the woman have a disease of some sort?" Although shaky and pale, Brynne had managed to stay upright in bed through sheer force of will…and the mountain of pillows Lucy had placed behind her.

"A disease? No, no, nothing like that. There is not a name for it, I am afraid. Too rare. As I said, you're just the second case I've ever seen." He'd stroked his salt and pepper moustache. "But the symptoms—dotted vision, heart palpitations, cold sweat—are almost exactly the same. Too similar to be a coincidence, at any rate. You, my dear child, have suffered from what I shall refer to as an attack of anxious mannerisms in my research paper."

"An attack of anxious mannerisms," she'd repeated. "What—what is that? How do I treat it? Is there medicine? Or a tonic?" Her nose had wrinkled. "My brother had to take a tonic once when he was ill with a cough. I tried a spoonful. It was very bitter."

"No medicine," said the doctor as he'd put on his coat and gone to the door. "No tonic. This is a simple case of mind over matter. If you start to feel this way again, tell yourself not to."

"Tell myself not to?" Puzzled, she had shaken her head. "But—"

"I've another patient waiting in the village. Drink plenty of broth and get lots of rest," he'd advised. "You should feel better in the morning. If there's been no improvement within twenty-four hours, ring for me again and perhaps we'll try a tonic."

That was the last time Brynne had called for the doctor.

Over the course of the next few months, she had two more attacks of anxious mannerisms. Or Episodes, as she and Lucy began to call them. Once, when she received a letter from Weston that he would not be returning home for Christmas. And again, when she'd missed an entire sequence of notes during practice for her piano recital and her instructor labeled her as "completely hopeless".

With time, she came to realize that the Episodes were tied directly to her emotions. When she became too mentally overwhelmed, whether it was due to the prospect of facing a holiday alone, or failing to reach the high bar her tutors had set, her mind was unable to process the additional pressure. Almost like a tea kettle that began to whistle and blow steam after being left too long on the stove.

Not surprisingly, the doctor's suggestion—that she merely tell herself *not* to have an Episode—had little effect. But with practice, and

Lucy's unique breathing techniques, she was able to keep her symptoms to a minimum. As she grew older, and learned how to exert more control over herself and her emotions, they occurred with less and less frequency.

Finally, much to her relief, the day came that the "attack of anxious mannerisms" stopped altogether. She'd truly believed they were behind her. A relic of a miserable adolescence that she'd done her best to forget...along with her horrible mistake of a marriage. But while she had successfully managed to sweep her lonely, unpleasant childhood under the proverbial rug, it seemed large, arrogant Scots were too big to fit beneath carpets...or inside trunks.

In hindsight, it was foolish–if not downright naïve–to believe that she'd seen the last of Lachlan Campbell. Like a bad penny, it was inevitable her husband would show up again. The husband she despised. The husband who had betrayed her. The husband she was still madly...irrevocably...completely in love with.

CHAPTER TWO

Eleven Years Ago
Hawkridge Manor

WHEN BRYNNE HEARD the wheels turning on the stone drive, her young heart pattered with excitement. Weston was home! Four weeks prematurely, as it so happened, but with no other visitors scheduled and their father in the wind, who else could it possibly be but her brother, returned early from Eton?

How she'd missed him. With the exception of a brief–and intimidating–visit from her grandfather, the Duke of Caldwell, she had spent the last month in relative isolation. Which wasn't anything new, in and of itself. Brynne and Weston were often alone. But they were alone *together*. A distinction that became notable only after she found herself roaming the whitewashed walls of Hawkridge without her twin by her side.

She had the servants, of course. Lucy, in particular, was a comfort, especially since Brynne's newest governess, Miss Hardgrave, possessed all the warmth of an iceberg.

But it wasn't the same.

That didn't matter anymore, however.

Because Weston had returned.

Except when she burst out the front door (ignoring the sharp call of her governess that ladies did *not* run) and took the steps two at a time to meet the shiny black coach before the prancing pair of chestnut geldings had even come to a full halt, it wasn't her brother's face peering out the square window, but an unfamiliar boy with a spill of red hair and an arrogant smirk.

"Who are *you*?" Brynne demanded when he hopped out of the carriage without bothering to wait for the footman to bring the mounting step around.

Taller than her by several inches, with a broad frame that needed to fill out in places and a face that was all jutted angles and peaks, the boy stuck out his hand and grinned at her. "Lachlan. Ye must be West's sister, Lady Brynne. Please tae meet ye."

Scottish, she thought silently as she regarded his hand with some suspicion. And a student at Eton as well, as evidenced by the coat of arms on his navy blue jacket. Three lilies on the bottom, a golden lion on the upper right hand corner, and a *fleur de lis* on the left. When she attended Cheltenham Ladies' College next year, a boarding school for girls of distinguished families, she would have a similar insignia.

"What are you doing here?" she asked as she touched the very tip of his fingers in a quick, fleeting handshake before tucking her arms behind her back. She peered past him into the carriage, hopeful that her brother was sitting within but, to her disappointment, the seats were empty. Her gaze returned to her unexpected visitor, and she frowned. "Where is Weston?"

Instead of answering her questions, Lachlan rocked onto his heels and let a whistle pass between his lips as he stared up at the front of the manor. "Now I see why West is so high in the instep."

"My brother isn't 'high in the instep'," Brynne said defensively. Already resentful of this stranger who should have been her twin but wasn't, she followed the direction of his gaze as her frown deepened into a scowl.

While most admired the stately country estate for its sheer size, she'd always considered it to be more of a prison than a palace. The outside may have been beautiful with its walls of ivy crawling up gray sandstone, a solarium encased in glass, and matching chimneys in red brick, but there was no cheer to be found within.

Her mother had died here.

Her father had abandoned her here.

And her childhood–what remained of it–was withering here. Like an apple left too long on the branch, she remained glossy on the surface, but she could already feel herself slowly hardening on the inside.

Without family, without friends, without anyone that genuinely cared for her well-being (who wasn't being paid to, that is), how long would it take until her dreams, and aspirations, and hopes for a future beyond this place rotted and fell to the ground?

Now, she had this *boy* to contend with.

Whoever he was.

In the single letter she'd received thus far, Weston hadn't mentioned anyone by the name of Lachlan. And she found it difficult to believe that her stern, serious brother would have anything to do with a rude, contentious Scot.

"I think there has been some mistake," she began. "This is *Hawkridge* Manor. Your driver must have gotten confused, and brought you to the wrong place."

"Oh, I'm in the right place." Lachlan slid his hands into the pockets of his coat before he slanted her a sideways glance and grinned, revealing a roguish dimple in the middle of his cheek. "West failed tae mention what a bonny lass his sister is."

Brynne blushed.

She couldn't help it.

Stuck in that indeterminate phase between adolescence and adulthood, she was too tall, too gangly, too thin, too everything wrong and nothing right. But this boy–this Lachlan with the devilish grin and arrogant way about him that made her want to gnash her teeth with annoyance even as part of her was quietly thrilled by it–thought she was *bonny*.

"What are you doing here?" she repeated.

"Suspended from school for fighting," he said cheerfully, as if such an admission was something to be proud of instead of ashamed by. "Two weeks until I can return. Yer brother invited me tae stay here instead of making the trek all the way back tae Glenavon. By the time I got home, I'd just have tae turn around again."

Brynne didn't even know where to start. But if Lachlan *was* an invited guest (and she had no reason to believe he was lying), then it fell upon her, as the only Weston currently in residence at Hawkridge, to be a gracious host.

This was what she'd been trained to do. While boys were raised on arithmetic and philosophy and war history, girls were taught how to properly manage a household and when to bring out the good silver and the correct order to serve tea in accordance with the guidelines set forth by the all-important social hierarchy. Dukes first, then marquesses, earls, viscounts, and so forth and so on.

"Why don't you come into the parlor for a glass of lemonade," she said with the polite poise of a lady twice her age. "The staff will see to it that a bedchamber is readied, and your personal belongings are put away. If you need anything during your stay, you have only to ask me or the head housekeeper, Mrs. Pembroke."

Lachlan's grin widened. "Aye, yer grace," he said, bending forward in an exaggerated bow that brought a fresh flush of heat to her cheeks.

"I am not a duchess. You–you can just call me Brynne." It wasn't proper to encourage such familiarity, but if it was to be just the two of them over the next fourteen days, surely there was no harm in addressing each other without the pomp and circumstance of their titles.

"Brynne. That's Celtic, ye know. A form of Brenna." A swath of auburn hair fell across his brow as he canted his head to the side. "Do ye have Scots blood in ye, Bry?

She bit the inside of her cheek, an anxious habit her governess had not yet been able to quell. "Not–not that I am aware of. And it's *Brynne*."

Mischief and a glint of something else, something she wouldn't come to understand for a few more years yet, gleamed in Lachlan's eyes. Framed with lashes a shade darker than his hair, they were amber with a hint of copper, and reminded of her of a lion. Come to think of it, *all* of him reminded her of a lion. Lanky and lean and not quite grown, with a sleek auburn pelt instead of gold, but a lion nevertheless.

"I like Bry better," he said, tossing his hair out of his eyes. "It suits ye."

And she liked the way he said it. Soft, and husky, as if they were sharing a secret. But even as butterflies hummed in her belly, a warning tickled in her ear. Her governess had told her about boys like these. To watch for them, and be wary of them, and to avoid them at all costs. For even though Brynne wouldn't have her Season debut until she turned sixteen, it was imperative that she learn early on which type of man would make a proper husband, and which ne'er-do-well to steer clear of...no matter how charming he might have been.

Why, no doubt Lachlan flirted with *all* the girls. She wasn't special. But then, she didn't need a rogue-in-training to tell her that.

If she were special, her father and brother wouldn't have left her here. If she were special, she wouldn't have been kept sheltered. If she were special, she wouldn't have been forgotten. Because special things weren't hidden away to collect dust while life continued on without them. They were polished, and proudly displayed, and talked about.

One day, she told herself. One day, she'd escape Hawkridge, and she would never–ever–come back. She'd be the toast of London, and everyone would want to be her friend, and she'd be invited to so many balls and soirees that she would lose track of them all.

But until that day came, she was stuck here. In the middle of the countryside. Like a princess in an ivory tower waiting for her prince to swoop in and rescue her. Except instead of a prince, she'd gotten Lachlan the Lion.

She swallowed a giggle.

They'd both come up with their own monikers for each other, it seemed.

Although she thought hers was far cleverer.

"Who did you fight with that you were suspended?" she asked as she led the way into the manor. They entered the foyer first, a massive rectangular room with a grand staircase in the middle and parlors off to either side. Further down the hall there was a drawing room, and a music room, and a library. The kitchen had its own wing, which attached directly to the servants' quarters. There was the solarium, a more recent addition, and a scattering of terraces and balconies. Upstairs held no less than twenty-seven bedchambers spread across two stories and half a dozen washrooms, three of which had recently been renovated with pipes that carried hot water! A form of magic, as far as Brynne was concerned.

"Lord Archie Wheeler. The dunce." Handing his jacket and gloves to a footman, Lachlan turned in a slow circle, his gaze drawn to the gold chandelier dangling above their heads. "Are those real crystals?"

"Yes. What makes Lord Wheeler a…you know." Unable to say the word allowed, she gestured with her hand.

"Dunce?"

She nodded.

"He's a blowhard and a bully." Lachlan dropped his chin and raised his brow. "Goes after the smaller boys who canna defend themselves. Ye would have boxed his ears, tae, I wager. Ye strike me as the sort who wouldna stand for the antics of a tyrant."

To date, it was the finest compliment that Brynne had ever received.

"Is that what you did?" she asked, fascinated despite the fact that a young lady should never condone any form of violence. Particularly of the common schoolyard brawling variety. "You boxed his ears?"

"Aye. Twice."

"*Twice*," she breathed, her eyes widening. "Then what happened?"

"He fell tae the ground and cried for his mother. Bullies are tough until they're the ones being picked on. Would have given him a shiner, tae, for what he did tae Tommy Helms. If his friends hadna pulled me off, that is. Cowards, the lot of them."

"What did Lord Wheeler do to Tommy Helms?" she asked.

"Cornered him in the middle of the courtyard and yanked down his trousers for the whole school tae see, then made fun of the size of his dobber."

Brynne's brow furrowed. "Dobber?"

"Pecker. Ye know what a pecker is, don't ye?"

She shook her head uncertainly.

"Lobcock. Plug tail. Thomas." He looked at her in exasperation. "Penis?"

"Oh." Her cheeks heated. "*Oh.*"

Yes, she knew what a penis was. The library at Hawkridge was enormous, covering a variety of topics from edible herbs and plants to the rise and subsequent fall of the Roman Empire. Naturally curious, and bored with her embroidery, Brynne had tasked herself with reading through the vast collection of books whenever she could manage to sneak away from her studies. She'd started in alphabetical order, and after making her way through *A Study on the Principles of Sufficient Reason* had stumbled upon *Anatomy, Physiology, and Hygiene* by Benjamin Mussey.

She hadn't understood a lot of the words, having never heard them before, but there had been pictures. Diagrams. Of the female *and* the male body. Which was how she knew what–and where–that particular part of the male anatomy resided.

"I...I didn't realize it had so many different names," she said.

"Do ye want tae hear more?" Lachlan asked with some enthusiasm.

"No," she said hastily. "I think I've heard quite enough, thank you. But if Lord Wheeler did that to Tommy, why were *you* suspended? That doesn't seem very fair."

"Because Wheeler's father has deep pockets. Probably why his son is such a little shite. If it were left tae him, I would have been booted out of Eton on the spot. The headmaster thought a two week holiday was a more fitting punishment." Grinning, Lachlan spread his arms apart. "And here I am."

Brynne blushed again, although this time she didn't know why. Lachlan was loud, and brash, and violent–everything she'd been kept away from. How odd, then, that she actually...maybe...a tiny bit...*liked* him. And, now that her initial shock at his unannounced arrival had subsided, she was glad that he had come to Hawkridge. At the very least, he'd provide interesting company, in addition to helping the time pass more quickly until Weston returned.

"The receiving parlor is this way," she said, indicating a set of French doors with a stained glass inlay. "I'll have a maid ready us some lemonade. Are you hungry? We've anything you could want. Cold meats or salmon for a sandwich, and–"

"*Lady Brynne.*"

As the sound of her governess' voice cracked through the foyer like the slash of a whip, Brynne winced and instantly squared her shoulders. Miss Hardgrave was a stickler for proper posture, and whenever she caught her charge slouching, Brynne would have to walk up and down the hallway with a book balanced on her head.

Ever since she'd outgrown the nursery and become too old for a nanny, Brynne had been kept under the care of a governess. Six of them, to be precise, each one lasting for a year or two before they were removed and replaced for reasons that were never explained to her. Miss Hardgrave was the seventh, and by far the worst.

Strict, stern, and unforgiving, she ruled over every aspect of Brynne's life with an iron fist and a disapproving frown. From monitoring what Brynne ate, to enforcing what time she went to bed, the governess seemed to take unique pleasure in the control she yielded.

Brynne despised her, as did Weston. He wanted them to drive Miss Hardgrave out (as the twins had been known to do on occasion), but what if her replacement was even worse? Brynne didn't dare risk it. Especially without Weston here to look after her.

"Who is this?" Miss Hardgrave's steely gaze raked across Lachlan with visible contempt. Tall and thin as a pencil, her brown hair was pulled back from her face with such force that it stretched the skin at the corners of her eyes. A confirmed spinster approaching her fortieth year, she'd graduated Blakeshire's Governess Academy with top honors and had been employed by some of the most prestigious families in all of England before she'd come to Hawkridge.

"Lachlan Campbell," he said with an insolent smirk.

Miss Hardgrave's lips pinched so tightly together they all but disappeared into her pale, wan face. "You must be the new footman. Servants are to use the side entrance, not the main foyer. You'd also do well to watch your tone, Mr. Campbell. Impudence is not a quality that Lord Dorchester seeks in his servants."

At that, Brynne stepped forward.

"Lachlan isn't a servant," she explained earnestly. "He is a guest. Weston has sent him to stay with us while he is…ah…on temporary leave from Eton."

"A guest?" asked Miss Hardgrave, visibly thrown off guard.

"Aye," said Lachlan, his voice cooling as his face hardened, giving a glimpse at the man he'd soon become. Rough, intimidating, and one who didn't suffer fools–or tyrannical governesses–lightly. "And it isna mister, it's lord. Lord Campbell. Ye would do well tae remember that."

The governess' face puckered, as if she had suddenly bitten into a lemon. Her elevated position in the household put her far above a footman, but she was still well beneath the aristocracy and, as such, would have to keep her obvious disdain for Lachlan in check. "I...I apologize for my error, *Lord* Campbell. I can assure you that it will not happen again."

As her gaze traveled from Miss Hardgrave to Lachlan and back again, Brynne barely managed to suppress a smile. It appeared as if the governess had finally met her match. If her expression was any indication, she wasn't pleased about it.

"I was just about to offer Lord Campbell some refreshments in the parlor," Brynne said tentatively. "After that, I thought a tour of the grounds–"

But Miss Hardgrave was already shaking her head. "You are late for your French lesson. Mrs. Pembroke is more than capable of showing our guest around. I will let her know that he is here, and that the maids should ready a room in the East Wing."

"The East Wing?" Brynne echoed in dismay. "But that's all the way on the other side of the–"

"Your lesson," Miss Hardgrave said firmly. "Tardiness does not become a lady. Leave our guest's accommodations to the staff. I am afraid that your schedule is such that you'll not have the ability to be in Lord Campbell's company outside of dinner. Even then, I'm sure your studies will preclude you from lengthy conversation."

As Brynne was ushered away, she cast a helpless glance over her shoulder and met Lachlan's amber gaze. He winked at her, and mouthed something she couldn't hear...but which she understood nevertheless.

A silently passed message that left her feeling strange and warm and fluttery, as if she'd been standing out in the sun for too long without a hat.

"I'll see ye soon, Bry."

CHAPTER THREE

L ACHLAN KNEW THAT he was supposed to be remorseful for what he'd done to Lord Wheeler. At least, that's what the headmaster had told him.

"A two-week suspension from your classes," the old bugger had croaked. *"So that you may think upon your actions and what you can do to improve yourself. This is not your first incident, Lord Campbell. But it shall be your last, lest I inform your father that your schooling at Eton has been permanently terminated."*

Truth be told, Lachlan *did* feel a wee measure of contrition.

If he had to do it over again, he would have hit Wheeler a hell of a lot harder.

The prancing roaster.

Wheeler had deserved to be laid out on his arse, and Lachlan was glad to have been the one to put him there. Suspension or no suspension.

Gits like Wheeler needed to be taught that just because they came from a wealthy and powerful family didn't mean they could get away with torturing the small and the helpless. Wheeler and his band of bullies were no better than children with magnifying glasses pointed at a hill of ants on a sunny day.

Lachlan shouldn't have been punished for knocking the sniveling little viscount down a peg or two. He should have been bloody *commended*. Yet here he was, stranded at a stranger's estate for the next fourteen days while Wheeler got to sleep snug in his own bed.

At least the scenery was pretty to look at.

And he wasn't just thinking about the gardens.

Lady Brynne Weston really *was* bonny. The bonniest a lass as he'd ever seen. Not that there were many lasses in the tiny village of Glenavon. Bonny or otherwise. A few at the local pub, but the only time he went there was to drag his father home before he drowned himself in a tankard of ale.

Lachlan wasn't the first Campbell to be suspended from Eton. He heralded from a long line of proud, violent Scots with an eye for pretty women and a penchant for drinking. On the day he'd arrived at the prestigious boy's finishing school, the headmaster's eyes had all but rolled into the back of his skull.

"Not *another* one," he'd muttered before ushering Lachlan inside.

Lachlan couldn't blame the old bugger for his trepidation. But he wouldn't mind an apology. After all, three years into his schooling and he hadn't burned down a building (as his grandfather, Robert Campbell II, who was now deceased, had famously done), or gotten pigs drunk on ale and set them loose in the dormitory (his father, Robert Campbell III), or chucked all of the Duke of Ashbury's belongings out a third story window into the lake (his brother, Robert Campbell IV).

Why, aside from the little skirmish, Lachlan was a bloody paragon of virtue!

But courtesy of his last name, he was labeled a mischief maker before he'd ever stepped foot through the gates. That was the trouble with reputations...sometimes you made them, and other times they were made for you. Either way, they were difficult things to change. People saw what they wanted to see. And even though Lachlan was different from his father and four brothers in any manner of ways, he'd already been painted with the same broad brush.

The headmaster had probably been *itching* for a reason to toss him out since he first walked in the door. Handing Wheeler his well-deserved comeuppance was just the excuse the school was waiting for to rid itself of another Campbell, albeit temporarily.

If Lachlan managed to stick it out another year, he'd be the first man in his family to actually complete all of his courses and attend convocation. As a general rule, Campbells enjoyed starting things–fights, business endeavors, marriages–but they were shit all at finishing them. Which helped to explain why Lachlan and his brothers all had different mothers...and why the once mighty and world-renowned Glenavon Distillery had been run straight into the ground.

But Lachlan had plans for that.

Not for the multitude of women his father had bedded, wedded, and either lost in childbirth, divorced, or simply forgotten about. There was nothing he could do about *that* particular family disgrace. As for the abandoned distillery, however...suffice it to say he had big plans for the whisky company that his great-great-grandfather, the very first Robert Campbell, had started under the cover of darkness in caves off the coast to avoid the bloody British and their excise taxes. And his children had subsequently bankrupted it through poor business practices.

Namely, they'd drank all the whisky and never gotten around to making more.

Before any renovations could begin, however, Lachlan needed to survive the next two weeks so that he could get back to his studies, finish school with high enough marks that he'd be able to secure a private loan, and hire an architect willing to work for the promise of what was to come.

It was a tall order.

Some might say impossible.

But in addition to their less desirable traits, Campbell men were also determined and stubborn to a fault. It wasn't a matter of *if* Lachlan would see his dreams realized. It was a matter of *when*. In the meanwhile, he'd serve his suspension. A punishment that was feeling a lot more like a reward now that he had a fair-haired companion to pass the time with.

He just needed to figure out a way past the dragon at the gate...but Lachlan was nothing if not inventive.

T*AP.*

Tap tap.

Tap tap tap.

Blinking groggily, Brynne sat up in her bed and drew off the covers. The floorboards were cold beneath her bare feet as she padded to the window and peered out, cupping her hands on either side of her face in an attempt to see through the darkness of a quarter moon.

Tap.

On a gasp, she leapt back from the sill when a small stone struck a glass pane. Given that her bedchamber was on the second story, she had been expecting a branch, or an owl, or some other naturally occurring nighttime noise that was responsible for rousing her from a heavy sleep. But there was nothing *natural* about a rock being twenty feet off the ground.

Someone was throwing pebbles at her window.

And she had a sneaking suspicion of who it might be.

Careful not to rouse Miss Hardgrave, whose bedchamber shared an adjoining wall, Brynne quickly swept a wrap over her nightgown and tiptoed out of her room and down the stairs. She didn't know what time it was. Somewhere after midnight, as that was when she'd set aside her book and fallen asleep, and before five, as that was when the servants woke and began readying the household for the day ahead.

Regardless of the exact hour, she should *not* have been out of bed. The knowledge of which caused a tiny tingle of excitement between her shoulder blades. She, Brynne Weston, follower of rules and sufferer of anxious mannerisms, was being *rebellious*.

Miss Hardgrave would have an absolute fit if she found out. This was, by far, the most disobedient act that Brynne had ever committed. Which, depending on how one viewed it, was either very good or very sad.

She hesitated on the bottom step, her toes curling over the smooth wooden lip as her practical mind urged her to return upstairs with all haste while her rarely explored adventurous spirit cried for her to keep going. After a brief internal struggle, the latter side won out and, with a wide grin, she dashed across the foyer and into the kitchen where the servants' entrance provided her the most discreet pathway out of the house.

Her bedroom overlooked the rear of the estate which meant she had to go all the way along the length of the solarium, careful not to turn her ankle on the freshly dug piles of earth that were being used to build staggered flower beds, and around the back terrace before she reached the enormous alder tree that had stood guard beside her window long before even her father had been born.

Its massive canopy had obscured her view from above, but now that she was on the ground and her eyes had adjusted to the slivers of moonlight dancing across the rolling lawn, she picked out Lachlan's shadowy frame with ease.

"Took ye long enough," he said, stepping out from behind the alder's trunk.

"I thought it was you," she said smugly.

He cocked a brow. "Is there anyone else that would be throwing rocks at yer window in the middle of the night?"

"Well, no," she admitted.

"Didna think so."

They stared at each other. The volatile, hotheaded Scottish boy who had been suspended from school for fighting and the quiet, introspective English girl who had never met a rule she didn't follow.

They shouldn't have ever met, let alone been standing together in the darkness. Yet here they were. Two lonely souls who were (unbeknownst to even themselves) desperately seeking a connection with someone who understood them in a way their families could not.

"Want tae see something neat?" Lachlan asked.

"Yes," Brynne said, and this time there was no hesitation. "Very much."

"Come with me, then." He took her hand, his fingers sliding between hers until they were locked in a firm grip and, together, they plunged into the night, following a narrow trail lined with chipped marble.

She didn't ask how he seemed to already know the grounds surrounding the manor as well or mayhap even better than she did. Lachlan struck her as the adventurous sort, and it was easy to envision him exploring the paths, and the outbuildings, and the gardens that made up the estate while she'd been stuck inside practicing how to pour tea out of a long-stemmed teapot.

"Where are we going?" she asked breathlessly when they passed the stables and entered the woods. A thorn bush snagged at her nightgown. She gave it a yank, and winced when the fabric tore. But there was no time to stop and examine the damage done, not with Lachlan galloping ahead at full speed.

They twisted their way through the forest, leaping over exposed roots and jumping across logs. Twice, she nearly fell and, twice, Lachlan was right there to catch her, almost as if he instinctively sensed when she was in trouble even before she did.

Finally, they tumbled out of the woods and into a meadow. Despite having spent every summer and half of the winter at Hawkridge since she was born, Brynne had never visited this particular spot before. Filled with wavy grass that gleamed in the moonlight like an ocean of silver, it sat high on a knoll surrounded by trees.

"Here," said Lachlan, pulling her towards the center. "Stand right here and close yer eyes."

Brynne followed his instructions obediently. Her feet were smarting from running along the rough forest trail, a sticky layer of perspiration clung to her forehead, and the hem of her nightgown was in tatters, but none of that mattered. Despite their rough start this morning, she trusted Lachlan. As much as she trusted Weston, the person she loved most in the entire world. Which was strange and bewildering, especially considering she'd known her brother since the minute she was born and Lachlan for all of ten hours.

But the wonderful and wise thing about being young and naïve was that she still trusted herself. The world hadn't had time to break her heart or make her hard. Thus, when that little voice inside of her spoke up and said that she was safe with Lachlan, and that he'd never do anything to harm her, she had no reason to doubt it.

"All right," he said, his warm breath tickling the wispy curls at the nape of her neck as he stepped behind her, "now drop yer head all the way back and open yer eyes."

Again, she did as he asked. Slowly, bit by bit, as if it were Christmas morning and she wanted to savor every second of joy that came from walking into the drawing room on that special day and seeing the mountain of presents piled beneath the tree, Brynne tipped her face to the heavens and opened her eyes.

"Oh," she gasped, stunned by the sight that awaited her. "It's...it's *beautiful.*"

She'd seen the night sky before, of course.

Countless times.

But not like this.

Never like this.

It was...it was *infinite.*

A sprawling cloak of black velvet dotted with millions and millions of stars, each one shining brighter than the last. There was nary a cloud to be seen. Only the sliver of the moon, a crescent of alabaster carved out of the abyss that glowed with its own special source of light.

"Here," said Lachlan, patting the space beside him as he folded his legs and lowered himself to the ground. "Ye can see it better when ye're laying down."

Slipping out of her wrap, she gave it a quick shake and then placed it on the grass like a blanket before sitting next to Lachlan with her knees drawn to her chest. Their shoulders bumped. Accidentally at first, and then on purpose when he gave her a playful nudge.

"See that?" he said, raising his arm and pointing to a section of sky straight above their heads. "Where the stars come together tae form a line with a spoon at the end. That's called The Plough. It's a constellation."

"A constellation?" she repeated, unfamiliar with the term.

"Aye," he said, sounding surprised that she didn't know what it meant. "We've a massive telescope at Eton. It has its own room and everything. Havena ye looked through one before?"

Shyly, she shook her head.

Dresses and embroidery. Teapots and dancing. Such silly, useless things when compared to the vast openness of the universe and all of the wisdom it contained. While she was learning how to be a perfect wife, Lachlan was looking through telescopes.

She knew that young girls weren't meant to be curious.

But all Brynne had were questions.

"Can you teach me?" she asked. "About the constellations."

Resting her head on Lachlan's shoulder, she followed the direction of his finger as it swerved from one cluster of twinkling stars to another.

"There's Aquarius. The first I ever found. And that one, there. The zig-zag? That's Cassiopeia. Over here we should have...aye, there it is. Leo. It's my favorite because it looks like a–"

"A horse," she said, her eyes shining as she traced invisible lines between the cluster of stars.

Lachlan grinned. "I was going tae say lion."

"Who named them all?"

"Greek astronomers, for the most part."

"Is that what you hope to be one day? An astronomer?"

His shoulder lifted her head ever-so-slightly as he gave a small shrug. "I like tae look at the stars, but I'm meant for other things. My dreams are here, on the ground. What about ye, Bry? Where are yer dreams?"

"Everywhere. And nowhere." Her lips twisting in a rueful smile, she sat up straight and hugged her legs more closely to her chest. "My future is already planned out for me. Next year, I'll attend Cheltenham, and then make my debut in London Society. If all goes according to plan, I'll be engaged before Christmas and married in the spring. Children will follow after that. Two boys, preferably."

"And is that what ye want?" Lachlan asked, studying her closely.

No one had ever asked her that before.

What *she* wanted.

Not even Weston.

Perhaps because there was no point.

What else *could* she want from her life, other than what was already planned for her?

Were she a man in possession of her own fortune, she might have been an astronomer. Or a doctor. Or a philosopher. Even a detective. Or nothing at all. Instead, as a girl on the brink of womanhood, her path was clearly marked. She was to become a wife and then a mother. With no way to make her own fortune (even her dowry wasn't her own), there weren't any other avenues available to her. No other achievements to be made. No other dreams to pursue.

Oh, she might always choose to be a spinster. Live alone in a cottage on the sea with her knitting and her cats. Except even then, she'd be relying upon the generosity of her father and brother. They'd never go so far to turn her out into the cold. But she would live with the knowledge that she was a disappointment to them, and that she hadn't done as she was meant to.

"I don't know," she said honestly, scratching her fingernail at a spot of mud on her skirt. "I should think that I would like to be a wife, someday. Maybe. I guess. And a mother after that. But is that what I want because I've been *told* that is what I should want? Or do I want it because it is something I really do desire?"

Lachlan frowned. "Ye should never do something just because it's expected of ye."

"No, I suppose not." She was quiet for a moment. "I'd like to travel. I've never seen much of the world. London, and Bath, and Sussex. A bit of Scotland. But I'd like to see Paris and Brussels. New York and Boston. Egypt and Mumbai."

"What would ye do there?"

"Paint," she said impulsively. "That's what the great artists do. They travel the world and they paint what they see for those who cannot go where they've been. But I don't want to spend my life staring at the proof of someone else's adventures. I want to make my own."

Lachlan nodded, as if he understood. And she felt as if he truly did. As if he were the only person who could. Because surely a boy who studied the stars knew what it was like to want more from the universe than what it had given you.

"If ye want tae be a traveling artist, then that's what ye should be." Plucking a long piece of grass, he stuck the end between his teeth and spoke out of the corner of his mouth. "What's stopping ye?"

She giggled at the absurdity of the question.

Where to even begin?

"Miss Hardgrave, for one. Being just fourteen, for another."

"That old bat," he snorted. "She's all bark and no bite. Leave her tae me. And ye willna be fourteen forever. Soon ye'll be full grown, and then what?"

"You ask a lot of questions," she noted.

He spat out the grass. "Because I'm interested in the answers."

Did that mean he found *her* interesting? She liked to believe that it did. Thankful for the darkness as a rosy blush unfolded across her cheeks, she returned her attention to the sky.

"Do those have a name?" she asked, pointing at a collection of stars in an unusual pattern.

"Aye. That's Ursa Major." Shifting closer, he gently moved her arm to the left. "And there is Ursa Minor."

Side by side, they gazed at the galaxy until dawn.

CHAPTER FOUR

"LADY BRYNNE, YOU *must* stop yawning," Miss Hardgrave scolded. "With your mouth open that wide, you resemble a masticating cow."

Brynne snapped her teeth together with an audible *click*.

"I am sorry, Miss Hardgrave."

The governess' eyes narrowed. "Were you up late reading again?"

"Yes." It may not have been the entire truth, but it wasn't a lie. She *had* been reading…before she fell asleep and Lachlan woke her by throwing stones at the window.

They'd managed to sneak back into the manor just before daybreak. She was fairly certain Lucy had seen them, but the maid wouldn't say anything. After stashing her stained, ruined nightgown under the bed, she had climbed beneath the covers and pretended to sleep until her lady's maid had woken her to get dressed.

She had hoped to see Lachlan at breakfast. To share a mischievous glance over sliced ham and broiled eggs. But there was no sign of him, and she'd eaten alone before being whisked off to her studies.

French first, and then German, a language that had undergone a resurgence in popularity since Queen Victoria married Prince Albert of Saxe-Coburg and Gotha, a German dynasty that could trace it roots all the way back the 10th century. While Prince Albert was fluent in English, it was rumored that he and Queen Victorian often spoke in his native tongue while they were in private. With an influx of German nobles currently populating the court, it was only natural that ladies of the *ton* were expected to learn their language.

Once those lessons were concluded, Brynne had gone straight the music room where she'd rehearsed her major scales in preparation for the recital she would be giving over the Christmas holiday when her brother and father returned to Hawkridge.

The piano was followed by embroidery in the parlor, and then tea in the drawing room where Miss Hardgrave had found her yawning over a plate of scones smothered in raspberry jam.

"You will ruin your eyesight with those books of yours," said the governess, her mouth thinning in disapproval. "Not to mention all of the silly nonsense they fill your head with."

"The book I was reading is a study in the historical significance of the industrial revolution and what it means for our future as a–"

"The industrial revolution?" Miss Hardgrave scoffed. "What need do *you* have to know anything about that? As I said, silly nonsense. If you insist on reading, I have the latest issue of *The Englishwoman's Domestic Magazine*. There is an excellent article on the durability of porcelain dinnerware."

Brynne muffled a sigh. "It sounds enlightening."

Clearly unable to tell whether her charge was being satirical or not, Miss Hardgrave held Brynne's gaze for a moment longer before she sniffed and pulled the plate of scones out of reach. "I've noticed your dresses have been ill-fitting as of late. Best limit your sweets."

Brynne, too, had noted the subtle changes in her body.

Curves where there used to be straight lines.

Soft, plump hills where there used to be flat, bony meadows.

Her hips and chest, in particular, seemed to be the worst culprits.

Not for the first time, she felt a distant longing for the mother she'd never known beyond a portrait hanging in the library above the fireplace. A mother who could explain what was happening to her with kindness instead of shame. A mother who would foster her thirst for information instead of actively seeking to destroy it.

Instead, she had Miss Hardgrave. Possibly the very *worst* person in the history of existence to guide her as she blossomed from an uncertain, gangly young girl into an uncertain, shapely young woman.

"I fear you are right, Miss Hardgrave," she said abruptly. "Reading at night has strained my eyesight, and now I have a terrible headache. I–I need to rest."

"Rest? But your dance instructor is–"

"You should eat those." She glanced down at the scones, then back up at her governesses. "I've noticed your dresses have been ill-fitting as of late."

Miss Hardgrave's eyes widened. Her face flushed a deep, blotchy red. But before she could muster a sharp retort, Brynne leapt from her chair and ran from the room, her heart thumping wildly at her daring impudence.

Except she didn't go upstairs to her room. Before her rare surge of rebelliousness abandoned her, she darted outside in search of Lachlan.

LACHLAN GRINNED WHEN Brynne, out of breath and pink-faced, dropped down beside him in the middle of the same field that they'd sat in the night before. The stars were hidden in the light of day but the sky, clear and cloudless, remained pleasing to look at.

Almost as pleasing as Bry.

Today, she was as pretty as a spring daffodil in a yellow dress several shades darker than her hair. Swept off her temple in a braided twist, it shone as bright as gold in the afternoon sun. He was tempted to touch it. To stroke a loose tendril just to see if it was as soft as it appeared. But while he was *practically* a man full grown at sixteen, Brynne–as she'd shared last night–was two years his junior. A child, really. Barely out of the nursery. And his head ought not to be filled with lustful thoughts.

"I was wondering when ye were going to escape the witch," he said by way of greeting.

"You...you shouldn't call her that," she puffed. "Or a...a bat, either."

"Why not? She's both those things and then some."

"She is also my governess. I may not like her, but I should be respectful."

"Well she's not *me* governess, and I think she's a bluidy bat witch."

The corners of Brynne's mouth gave a tiny, betraying twitch. "What are your teachers like at Eton?" she asked. "Are they nice? In his letter, Weston said they were nice."

"That's because yer brother is a goody two-shoes."

"He is not!" At Lachlan's stare, she dropped her chin and muttered, "All right, maybe he is. Maybe we both are. But that's only because we were raised to follow the rules."

"Aye, and what has that gotten ye?"

He was equal parts fascinated and repulsed by what he'd glimpsed thus far of Brynne's upbringing. The poor lass was like a bird in a cage. A well-fed bird. A well-groomed bird. But a cage was a cage, even when it resembled the largest, bloodiest estate he'd ever clapped his eyes upon.

By contrast, Lachlan and his brothers had grown up without a single rule to abide by. Well, that wasn't completely true. They weren't to kill or otherwise permanently maim each other or anyone else. But other than that...other than that they were left wild and reckless.

The first–and only–nanny he'd ever had had run screaming out of the castle before her second day was through. His father, long distracted by drink and women, hadn't bothered to hire another. Which left Lachlan to care for himself. And then for his three younger brothers, as Rob, the heir, was as useless as tits on a boar, and all of the boys' mothers had either perished in childbirth (as Lachlan's had) or fled.

Mountainous and rugged, the Scottish Highlands weren't for the faint heart on the best of days. Add in a drafty old castle, a drunk laird, five rambunctious boys (the youngest of whom was in nappies), and the petite, pretty wives that Robert Campbell kept coaxing in from London couldn't leave fast enough.

At exactly forty years of age, Lachlan's father had been a widower twice over, divorced thrice, and was currently courting his sixth bride-to-be. If it went anything like his previous five marriages, he'd have her with child before the year was out and Lachlan would soon be saddled with another squalling brother to look after.

In short, the world he lived in was as different from Brynne's as night was from day. But even as tumultuous as it could be, he vastly preferred the chaos to this cold, orderly existence of rules and restrictions.

"Miss Hardgrave is raising me to be a proper lady." As she spoke, Brynne self-consciously pulled the hem of her skirts to cover her ankles even though her feet were properly covered today in stockings and shoes. "She's stricter than my past governesses, but she is only doing the job my father has hired her to do."

"Then he's tae blame," said Lachlan, canting his head.

Her smooth brow furrowed. "To blame for what?"

"Imprisoning ye here."

"I'm not…I'm not in a *prison*."

"Can ye leave?"

"Not without permission, but–"

"Then it's a prison," he said smugly. "A fancy one, I'll give ye that. But satin curtains or stone walls, a prison is still a prison. Which makes ye a prisoner." He scratched his leg. "I bet ye have a schedule tae follow from the second ye wake up tae the second ye go tae bed."

Brynne's chin jutted, revealing a hint of stubbornness that he'd not seen before. With a gleam of obstinance in her gaze and wildflowers at her feet, she reminded him of a woodland fairy princess sprung straight from the pages of the old fairytales that his grandmother used to read to him.

"You've *no* idea what you are talking about."

"Maybe." His shoulder lifted in an amicable shrug. "Maybe not. Care tae prove it?"

"That I am not a prisoner?"

"Aye. That ye're free tae do as ye please. That ye can make yer own decisions."

"I can make my own decisions," she said defensively.

"Prove it," he taunted. "Or are ye even more of a goody two-shoes than yer brother?"

She mulled it over for a moment.

He could almost hear the gears clicking in her mind.

Part of her, he was almost certain, wished that she'd never come out to find him. That she remained tucked safely away in that marble monstrosity of a manor, learning how to wave a fan or curtsy or whatever it was that girls were taught to do. But there was more to Lady Brynne Weston than met the eye. And if he could use his time here to coax her out of the gilded cage they'd trapped her in, then he'd consider it time well spent.

"All right," she said after a lengthy pause. "What do I have to do?"

A grin split Lachlan's face from ear to ear. Picking a nameless flower with white petals from amidst the stalks of grass, he twirled it between his fingers before he held it out to her. "It's simple, really…"

As THE WAGON jostled over a dip in the road and the blanket draped over her head threatened suffocation, it occurred to Brynne, somewhat belatedly, that taking Lachlan up on his challenge was not the *best* choice she had ever made.

Or even a good one, for that matter.

But it was too late now.

Tucked in the back of the dry supply wagon as it made its way towards the village to stock up on flour, grain, oats, and other necessities that would fill the kitchen for the next week, there wasn't anything she could do but keep her head down and pray that she wasn't discovered.

Beside her, Lachlan's teeth flashed white in a mischievous smirk as they struck another rut in the road and the entire conveyance rattled. Unlike Brynne, whose palms were damp with sweat and shoulders were tense with nerves, he actually seemed to be *enjoying* himself.

"How are ye doing?" he whispered, sliding his hand across the roughly hewn floor of the wagon to grasp her fingers.

"How do you think I'm doing?" she retorted even as his touch helped to lower the intensity of her unease. "This is a horrible idea."

"Ye agreed tae it."

Yes, she had. In some misguided attempt to prove that she wasn't a captive in her own house (which she absolutely was, or else she wouldn't have to sneak out underneath a *blanket*), she had agreed to accompany Lachlan into the local village, someplace she was never allowed to go without a proper chaperone.

The wagon was her idea. She'd thought it rather clever. A secret means to escape Hawkridge without Miss Hardgrave being any the wiser. But she hadn't taken into account how bumpy it would be. Or how stiflingly hot. Or how guilty she'd feel for breaking the rules.

Lachlan was right.

She *was* a goody two-shoes.

Even more so than Weston.

Except...except to her knowledge, her twin had never defied their governess by sneaking out of his lessons in the middle of the day. And he'd almost certainly never gone into the village when he wasn't supposed to. And he'd definitely *never* hidden inside of a supply wagon. Did that make her braver than him? Or just more foolish?

She really didn't know the answer.

"What are we going to do now?" she hissed, wedging her foot against an empty crate to prevent herself from moving as the wagon took a sharp left hand turn and then slowed. From outside the blanket draped over them, she could hear the sounds of harnesses jingling and people talking and the toll of a church bell. Given that the only church within twenty miles was the one that sat in the middle of the village square, she knew, that for better or worse, they'd reached their destination.

Lachlan winked at her. "Whatever we want. Just be ready tae jump."

"Jump?" she said, horrified. "What do you mean, be ready to–"

"One, two, three–*JUMP!*"

He grabbed her arm and, together, they rolled out of the back of wagon and landed in a cloud of dust and tangled limbs. Laughing, Lachlan pulled her to the safety of the pavement just as another carriage, pulled by a matched pair of prancing chestnuts, came breezing past. The driver hollered something, but Brynne was unable to make out what it was above the dull roaring in her ears.

"Well done," Lachlan said approvingly, giving her hearty slap on the back.

Gasping for air, Brynne doubled over and clutched her knees. Her hat, silk taffeta over wired buckram, slipped off and plopped onto the ground. "I–I cannot believe I did that!"

"Ye mean ye've never leapt out of a moving wagon before?"

She straightened and stared at him incredulously. "You have?"

"At least half a dozen times."

"Half a *dozen–*"

"The trick is in the landing." Bending down, he grasped her bonnet and gave it a light shake before returning it to her. "Ye have tae keep moving so ye dinna get run over."

"I'll keep that in mind for next time," she said faintly as she accepted her hat.

Clearly, Lachlan was what Miss Hardgrave disparagingly referred to as a "ruffian". That is, a man (or in this case, a boy) of mischievous character intent on committing various misdeeds. In short, he was *not* the sort of company that a young girl on the brink of womanhood should be keeping. Especially one who needed to maintain an impeccable reputation. And yet...and yet she was having *fun*. Real, honest-to-goodness fun. Well, except for almost being crushed to death by a carriage. But Lachlan had protected her. And Miss Hardgrave thought she was immersed in her French tutoring (when in actuality, she'd sent off a letter first thing in the morning telling her instructor, Monsieur Dubois, that she was ill). Which meant...which meant she was *free*. Free to have all of the fun that she wanted.

"We should go in the confectionary shop," she said, her eyes lighting. "I'm never allowed, but my father has an account with every merchant in the village, and we can buy whatever we want."

Half an hour later, they emerged from the shop, their arms overflowing with an assortment of twisted barley sugar sticks, strawberry drops, caramels, and–Brynne's favorite–lime fruit, which consisted of a slice of dried lime dipped in lemonade and then rolled in sugar.

They carried their bounty to a bench in the middle of the square, and sat beside each other in the dappled shade of a large oak tree.

"Trade ye a strawberry drop for a caramel," said Lachlan, speaking around a sugar stick jammed into the side of his cheek.

Brynne studied the candy she'd arranged in neat piles on her lap. "One strawberry drop for two caramels and the last barley stick."

"*Two* strawberry drops for one caramel," he countered, "and we'll split the last barley stick."

"All right. What?" she asked when Lachlan shook his head at her as he accepted the candy. "What is it?"

"Ye need tae learn how tae drive a harder bargain." He popped a strawberry drop into his mouth and bit down with a loud *crunch*. "I would have given ye the whole barley stick."

"Well, why didn't you?" she asked in exasperation.

He shrugged. "Because ye gave in."

"Miss Hardgrave says that a gentleman should always make every effort to appease a lady."

"Never said I was a gentleman." Cracking the barley stick into two pieces, he offered her half. Reluctantly, she accepted the stick and handed over two strawberry drops.

"But you must be. A gentleman, that is. Or else you wouldn't be at Eton."

"I'm at Eton because that's where me brother went, and me father, and me grandfather." Shoving the remainder of his candy into the pockets of his trousers (he wasn't wearing a coat), Lachlan linked his hands together behind his head and leaned back. "But ye can trust me when I say there's never been a Campbell who has ever been accused of being a gentleman."

"Then you won't attend the London Season?" Brynne didn't know why that should give her a twinge of disappointment. Even if Lachlan *did* go to London, and they *did* happen to meet at a ball, their social circles would never intersect. In all probability, this was the closest they were ever going to be. Trading candy on a bench in the village square. And that made her feel more than disappointed.

"I've another year of schooling, and then I'll make me...what do ye women call it?"

"Our formal debut."

"Aye." His dimple flashed as he smirked. "I'll do that."

"I don't know if men *can* have formal debuts."

"Why not?"

Her mouth opened. Closed. She thought it over. "I do not know, actually."

"Ye'll be the talk of the *ton* when ye do it. Make yer debut, that is. Blokes will be stumbling over themselves tae put their names on yer dance card."

"Do you really think so?" she said, pleased. Wasn't that exactly what she wanted? People to notice her. People to *want* to spend time with her. People to make her feel special and important.

"Aye," he said flatly, and even though she was fairly certain he meant it as a compliment, he didn't seem particularly pleased. "Ye'll have half a dozen proposals before the first week is out."

"Will yours be one of them?" She'd meant it as a jest. A little teasing. Not something to be taken seriously. But when Lachlan's eyes darkened and his gaze flicked, just for an instant, to her lips, she instinctively sensed that there was nothing the least bit humorous about the sudden electrical charge she felt pulsing in the air.

At fourteen, Brynne knew nothing of passion or desire beyond the books she had stashed beneath her mattress. Books written by the likes of Jane Austen and Emily Brontë and her sister, Charlotte. Books that made love seem like such a complicated, difficult endeavor that she wasn't at all sure if it was something she wished to partake in. But when Lachlan looked at her like that, as if she were…as if she were the most delicious strawberry drop he'd ever seen, she wondered if the books weren't on to something after all.

"The second-born son of a Scottish laird offer marriage tae the daughter of a marquess?" With a snort, Lachlan sprang off the bench. "Yer father would laugh me out of drawing room."

"He wouldn't," Brynne protested.

If only because he probably wouldn't be *in the room*, she added silently.

"Aye, he would." A swath of auburn hair tumbled across Lachlan's brow as he stretched his arms up and grabbed on to a low-hanging branch. After adjusting his grip, he lifted himself off the grass and gave a few experimental swings before kicking his legs out, spinning in midair, and landing in rather spectacular fashion.

Brynne clapped politely, then shook her head.

"All right," she admitted, smiling. "Maybe you would not be my father's *ideal* candidate for a husband. If I am to follow tradition, I'll marry an earl, or a marquess, or maybe even a duke. They'll be practical, and proper, and perfect in nearly every way."

Lachlan wiped his hands off on his trousers, then regarded her with a lifted brow and a mocking tilt of his mouth. "Aye, but can they climb a tree?"

"I'm quite sure they will have never tried."

"Sounds like a bunch of boring lunkheads tae me."

"Maybe." Her brow creased. "But when the times comes, *I'll* get to choose who I marry. No one else."

He snorted again. "Because ye are so free tae make yer own decisions."

"I came here, didn't I?" she said, proudly lifting her chin.

"That ye did." His gaze softening, he held out his hand. "Should we strike a bargain, Lady Brynne Weston?"

She eyed his hand dubiously. "The last time I struck a bargain with you, I lost out on half a barley stick."

"In ten years, if ye havena married some wealthy bounder, we'll meet back here, at this very spot. And we'll marry each other."

She started to giggle.

Stopped when she realized he was serious.

"Oh. *Oh.* But…" Her mind whirling, she stood up slowly, and as if from a faraway distance, watched her palm slide tentatively along his until their hands were clasped together. "Ten years."

"Ten years," he said solemnly. Then he grinned. "Have ye ever been in a pub before?"

"Of course not. Why do you ask?"

"Come on." Rolling his eyes, he gave her arm a tug and, together, they ran across the village square.

ELEVEN DAYS LATER, as she watched Lachlan's carriage drive away, Brynne realized two very important, life-altering things.

Firstly, she desperately wanted to be more than what she was

46

becoming. While Miss Hardgrave, and her father, and even her brother believed that her entire destiny was to marry well and have children and preside over an estate just like this one, Brynne wanted *more*. More happiness, more fun, more leaping out of wagons and gazing at the stars and sneaking into pubs. She'd lived more in these fourteen days than she had in fourteen years. And she'd *laughed*. How she'd laughed. She wanted to laugh like that again. She wanted to *be* like that again. The person she was when Lachlan was near. Which brought her to her second life-altering realization.

She, Brynne Weston, at all of fourteen years of age, was in love.

With Lachlan Campbell.

And even though it was a child's love, a sweet love, a love born of innocence and wonder, it was real. It was strong. But most importantly, it was true.

Until it wasn't.

CHAPTER FIVE

Present Day
Hawkridge Manor

AFTER PRYING HERSELF off the sofa by sheer force of will, Brynne managed to go about the rest of her day with a modicum of normalcy. With Weston temporarily in London, it fell to her to see that personal notes were sent to every guest that had attended their annual house party, as well as collect any belongings that had been left behind and send them on their merry way. Then the kitchen needed to be restocked, all of the linens refreshed, the bedrooms–all twenty-two of them, not including the master chambers–cleaned. Tasks that would ultimately fall upon the shoulders of Mrs. Grimsby and the staff, but Brynne liked to have a hand in the organization of it all.

She also had a lingering guest to look after.

Well, two.

But only one was human.

Barely.

"It stinks in here," she said, her nose wrinkling as she strode into the library and began flinging open the drapes, letting streams of light in the dim, stuffy room that smelled vaguely of cigar smoke, brandy, and a duke badly in need of a good bathing.

Preferably outdoors.

"I've gone blind," Sterling Nottingham, Duke of Hanover, covered his face with a pillow as sunlight drenched the library in a spill of light gold, revealing that he was wearing the same clothes she'd seen him in yesterday, and hadn't even bothered to remove his boots before drowning himself in a bottle of her brother's liquor and passing out on a chaise lounge that would in all likelihood need to be burned.

"You're not blind." The first time she'd happened upon Sterling in a similar situation, Brynne had felt a stirring of sympathy. A friend of Weston's, who had also become a friend of hers over the years, the duke was, under ordinary circumstances, a jovial, well-kept, gentlemanly individual. But after his mistress was violently murdered–and he became the prime suspect in the eyes of the *ton*–Sterling had sunk into a state of...well, whatever *this* was.

Drinking until the morning. Sleeping until the afternoon. Dragging himself about with disheveled hair and red-rimmed eyes and wrinkled clothing.

It was pitiful.

Embarrassing, really.

And while she was happy to offer Sterling refuge at Hawkridge Manor for as long as he'd like to continue avoiding the vicious gossip that awaited him in London, such destructive self-indulgence was not to be permitted.

"Sit up," she said briskly. "There's a pitcher of water on the table beside you, and your breakfast–while cold by now–is waiting in the solarium. Once you've eaten, you will bathe, and put on *clean* garments. Then a walk is in order, to clear your head."

Sterling slowly lowered the pillow. "Can't I just go upstairs and sleep?"

"No."

"But my head hurts."

Her gazed went to the empty bottle of brandy laying halfway under then chaise lounge, then returned to the duke. "I imagine it does. I am having a locksmith install a lock on Weston's liquor cabinet and the wine cellar. Today."

That got Sterling to his feet.

"You can't," he protested, shoving his hands through his hair, black and tangled, as he stumbled to his feet, toddled to the left, and just barely avoided crashing into a chair before he caught his balance. "What am I supposed to drink?"

"As I said, there is a pitcher of water on the table."

"Water?" he said, aghast. "But that tastes terrible."

She rolled her eyes. "It doesn't taste like anything."

"I know. That's what makes it terrible."

"Your Grace...Sterling...I say this as a friend." She hesitated. "And someone who has experienced the pain of heartbreak. You cannot continue down this path you've set for yourself. Nothing good shall come of it."

His eyes, several shades lighter than Weston's stony gray, hardened. "Are you responsible for your best friend's death?"

"You are referring to your brother," she said quietly. "But you're not to blame for what happened to him."

Sterling's mistress was not his first encounter with tragedy, or with death. Brynne did not know all of the details. No one did, except for the men who had been there on the day of the duel that had taken the life of Sterling's brother...the rightful Duke of Hanover. There'd been whispers, even then. Ridiculous, hurtful stories that Sterling had planned the entire thing in order to inherit the title. A title that otherwise never would have belonged to him, as the second-born son.

And then to be accused in the court of public opinion (perchance even the House of Lords, once they convened) to murdering the woman he'd loved...

It was clear *why* Sterling would want to drink himself into oblivion.

It was even clearer that he'd kill himself in the process.

She could have let it go.

She *should* have let it go.

He outranked her.

There was no blood or romantic entanglement between them.

He wasn't even her friend as much as he was Weston's.

But knowing what it felt like to suffer, knowing the allure of wanting to make yourself so small that you eventually disappeared, Brynne *had* to do something. If nothing else, it would take her mind off her estranged husband...and maybe even save a duke while she was at it.

"You're not to blame," she repeated when Sterling's countenance collapsed into bleakness. "But as long as you keep feeding your demons, they'll keep convincing you that you are."

He rubbed his hands down his face. "When did you grow up to be this wise? Yesterday, you were running around in braids while West and I practiced fighting with sticks so that when we grew up we could be knights and defend our Guineveres." He gave a ghost of a grin. "Mine was much prettier than his."

"Naturally." She pointed at the pitcher. "Drink. Then food, then bathe, then get some fresh air. If you care to join me, I'll be dining at half-past six this evening. Or I can have food sent to your room."

"How can you be this nice when your brother is such a cold-hearted git?"

The corners of her mouth twitched. "I'll see you once you've made yourself presentable."

As she quit the library, she thought–of all things–about glaciers. When she was a girl, she'd sat in this very library and read about them. About how they were formed. How old they were. And how the ones with the least amount of ice on the surface were often the largest and the coldest deep below.

WHEN THE DOOR to the formal dining room unceremoniously swung inward, Brynne looked up from her plate of baked herring seasoned with white pepper, fresh broccoli sautéed in garlic, and scalloped potatoes. But the welcome she'd been about to deliver to Sterling died on her lips as Lachlan, not the duke, sauntered in, appearing every inch as handsome and arrogant as he had this morning when he'd approached her at the gazebo.

She noted that he had changed into formal evening wear; exchanging his casual square cut lapel jacket for a satin waistcoat and trim smoking jacket that hugged his muscular torso. Gray trousers had replaced his breeches, and he'd even made an effort to tame his hair. Freshly combed, it was secured at the nape of his neck in a style that invoked images of Celtic warriors of old when men had charged fearlessly into battle armed only with their swords and the fierce love they had for those they'd left behind at home.

It wasn't difficult to imagine Lachlan as a warrior. Having seen him in the nude, Brynne knew firsthand that he certainly had the physique of one. All hard muscle and sinew with nary an inch of softness to be found...*anywhere*.

"What are you doing here?" she asked, carefully laying her fork down beside her plate before lifting her glass of wine. A rich dark red, it disguised her angry flush as she raised it to her lips and took a measured sip. "I thought I made myself clear: you are not welcome at Hawkridge Manor."

"Do ye know there's a bluidy *sheep* asleep in the parlor?" Instead of answering her question–or even acknowledging it–Lachlan proceeded to seat himself to her left, leaving only a single chair between them.

"Yes, I am aware." She flicked a glance at the two scullery maids waiting in the corner of the room. A subtle nod of her chin and they hurried out, discreetly closing the door in their wake. "Her name is Posy, and she belongs to my brother's fiancée."

Even with the pins and needles dancing under her skin courtesy of the large Scot sitting beside her, it pleased Brynne to say those words aloud. Lachlan's unexpected arrival had overshadowed the joyous announcement of her brother's betrothal, which she'd received via a letter sent from London where Weston and Evelyn Thorncroft, his American bride-to-be, were staying temporarily.

Brynne preferred to think she'd played a large part in their union, as she was the one who had invited Evie to attend the house party in the first place, during which Evie and Weston had fallen in love. She had liked the intelligent, outspoken American from the first moment they'd met, and vastly preferred her to the meek, mild-tempered Lady Martha Smethwick whom Weston *had* been planning to marry.

It was a *bit* of a tangled web as Joanna Thorncroft, Evie's elder sister, was also Brynne and Weston's *half-*sister courtesy of a secret affair that had only recently come to light. A secret affair between Brynne's father and Joanna's mother that had resulted in a daughter raised in another country as the child of another man.

The only thing that had tied the two families together was a sapphire ring (a family heirloom, such as it were) that the Marquess of Dorchester had given Anne Thorncroft before she fled England for a quiet, peaceful life as the wife of a doctor in the small town of Somerville, Massachusetts.

When Weston asked their father for the ring as he prepared to get down on bended knee in front of Lady Smethwick, he was furious to learn that it had been given away years earlier. *So* furious that he'd hired a private investigator to get it back for him. Unfortunately, that meant stealing it from the Thorncroft sisters...which, as it all turned out, was really for the best as it had led to Joanna and Evie setting sail for London in pursuit of the ring...and Joanna's heritage.

Brynne had yet to meet her half-sister. It was something she was looking forward to with immense anticipation. Or at least she had been until Lachlan arrived. As she couldn't very well leave him here at Hawkridge Manor while she flitted off to London to see Joanna and congratulate Weston and Evie in person, she needed him to leave.

Immediately.

"What are you doing here, Lachlan?" More than a decade later, and she was *still* asking him the same question that she'd posed all those years ago when he first came to Hawkridge Manor. So much had changed since then...and yet the words remained the same.

"I told ye at the gazebo," he said, his gaze unwavering. "I'm here tae win ye back."

Her fingers tightening around the slender stem of her wineglass, she met his stare without blinking. No matter what happened, she refused to let him know that he still affected her. That his voice still sent tiny thrills of delight racing across the delicate bumps of her vertebrae. That the heat emanating off his large body still warmed every inch of her. And–worst of all–that she still loved him. That she'd never *stopped* loving him. Even after all that he had done.

To her.

To them.

To any future they might have had.

"You spoke nonsense at the gazebo," she corrected icily. "Pure, unadulterated nonsense. Win me back? I am not a gift that you've misplaced, Lachlan. Nor a lamb at a fair."

"No, ye are me wife." The clenching of his jaw indicated he wasn't nearly as calm as he'd like her to believe with his sauntering gait and slouched, devil-may-care posture. "We've been separated this past year, aye. Tae give ye space. Tae let things calm. Tae allow cooler heads tae prevail. But we are married, Bry. Ye canna deny that."

"*You're* the one who is denying what's crystal clear. We may be legally bound to each other, Lachlan, but you are no more my husband than the butcher down the lane." Half her plate remained, but she feared if she tried to eat another bite her stomach would reject it later. Setting her wine glass onto the table with careful precision–it was either that, or slam it against the wall–she rose to her feet and stared down her nose at the man who'd once owned every piece of her heart...before he stabbed a knife through the middle of it. "It appears I did not make myself clear enough this morning. You are not welcome here. Were Weston in residence, he would see that you were tossed out on your ear."

Crossing his arms, Lachlan thoughtfully drummed his fingers along the sharp line of his jawbone where he'd allowed a layer of scruff, darker and shorter than the mane on his head, to grow.

On most men, the beard would have appeared unkempt. But on Lachlan it only served to heighten his roguish appeal, and Brynne's teeth gritted with annoyance as she resisted her natural inclination to brush her fingertips across his beard and see if it felt as rough as it looked.

No, she told herself sternly, in much the same way she denied herself a second macaroon after dinner.

No, no, no.

"Yer brother toss me out on me ear?" Lachlan smirked. "That I'd like tae see. Ye finally told him about our elopement, then?"

At her blank stare, he chuckled humorlessly under his breath.

"Aye, that's what I thought. Still tae ashamed to claim a half-blooded Scot as yer husband, Bry?"

She stiffened at the accusation. An accusation that stung all the more because it carried a shard of truth. As much as she'd have liked to deny it. As much as she *had* denied it. Both to Lachlan...and to herself.

"I was never ashamed of you." Even as she said the words aloud, her gaze slipped away and she bit her lip.

"Aye." He placed his hands flat on the table. "Ye were. Or ye wouldna have run away with me under the cover of darkness and then hid our marriage from all the world as if it were a terrible secret."

Her cheeks heated. "You *asked* me to run away with you!"

"I did. Because I couldna stand tae not have ye for another second, another minute, another hour. And because that was what we both agreed tae. Ten years," he said, his eyes as flat and unreadable as a

55

blank page of parchment. "Ten years, and if we werena married, we'd marry each other. That was the deal we struck."

"A deal with the devil," she whispered. "I was a child when I made it."

Lachlan's chair clattered to the floor with a loud *bang* as he stood up.

She flinched both from the violent sound and the sudden anger swirling in the depths of his gaze.

"But ye were a woman when ye honored it," he snarled, stepping over the fallen chair and around the edge of the table until the only thing that separated them was an invisible wall of vibrating fury. "Ye made a choice, Bry. I didna force ye."

"I never claimed–"

"And then ye made another choice when ye walked away." He leaned in close. So close that she smelled his scent, an achingly familiar combination of evergreen and peat. So close that she saw the flecks of gold surrounding his pupils. So close that the yearning deep inside of her was almost too strong to ignore.

"Aye," he said huskily when her gaze betrayed her and went to his mouth. "The fire's burning, Bry. It never went out." His hands, impossibly gentle for how large they were, skimmed along the outside of her arms until they reached her wrists. He encircled the tiny bones, thumb and index finger easily overlapping. "Which means ye have one more choice tae make."

Her heart beat like a wild thing inside of her chest. It thrashed against her ribcage, pounding against all of the measures she'd put in place to protect herself from exactly this. From falling back into his orbit, like a star spinning wildly through the galaxy only to become ensnared by the gravitational pull of a planet.

"I cannot." With her eyes, with her heart, with all she had within her, she implored him to understand. To turn on his heel and walk out the same door he'd come in. To leave her to the life she'd made for herself. A life that wasn't perfect. A life that fell far short of the one she'd dreamed of. That they'd dreamed of. But at least in this life...in this life, it didn't hurt to breathe. *"We* cannot. We tried, Lachlan. We did our best. And...and you weren't the only person to make mistakes."

It was the first time she'd acknowledged her wrongdoing.

The first time she'd admitted that some of the fault for their marriage crumbling was her own.

There was a sense of peace in that.

A relief of pressure that she hadn't known she was holding.

But it wasn't enough.

It would never be enough.

For they'd gone too far apart to pretend they could come back together now.

"Thank ye for saying that." His thumbs rubbed light circles on her fluttering pulses. "We might have broke, Bry, but we're not broken. I love ye. I havena stopped loving ye. Not for a bluidy moment."

She was tempted–oh so tempted–to give him what he wanted. To rest her head in the middle of his hard chest and begin again. To let go of all past hurts and heartbreak. To take the easy way out.

But what he *wanted* was not what she *needed*.

And the easiest path was rarely the best.

Slowly, steadily, she extricated herself from his grip. Took one step back, then another, and another, until the length of the room–and all the pain they'd caused each other–stood between them once again. An impenetrable wall that no chisel could break. "If you truly love me...then you'll let me go."

CHAPTER SIX

L ET HER GO? Let her *go?*

Didn't Brynne know that if Lachlan could, he would have?

He'd never liked pain with his pleasure.

If he had the ability to release himself from the spell she'd cast over him when he was but a boy of sixteen, he would have done it gladly. But while a man could live without a limb, he needed his heart. And if he let his Bry go, he'd be wrenching the organ straight out of his chest.

Yet he'd be damned if he begged for her on his bloody knees.

"I'm not keeping ye," he said, gesturing at the door. "But I'm not leaving, either. Not until we've figured this out once and for all."

"There is nothing *to* figure." Her hands went to her hips as temper glinted in her eyes. Temper he was glad to see, as he couldn't abide her sadness...especially knowing he was the cause of it.

"If you will not leave of your own accord, then I shall have you thrown out."

He snorted at that. "Ye and what army?"

"Why are you *doing* this?" she exclaimed, her slender shoulders heaving in visible frustration. "Everything was fine. We were fine. You didn't have to come here. Stirring up old waters best left alone."

"Ye call hiding away in a house that ye hate fine?" he asked.

"I am not *hiding*," she scoffed. "Two days ago this house was filled with over two dozen people and if not for you, I'd already be on my way to London."

"Ye can be standing in the middle of the room with a hundred people surrounding ye and be hiding, Bry. This isna the life ye wanted. Hosting house parties for yer brother, keeping yer gorgeous paintings tae yerself, pretending tae be the perfectionist that everyone expects ye tae be."

"There's nothing wrong with any of that!"

"There's nothing right, either. Not for ye." Couldn't she see? Couldn't she see that she'd flown right back into that gilded cage that they'd made for her when she was a girl? Except this time, she was the one who had closed the door. "Ye wanted more for yer life, Bry. Ye wanted tae travel, and see the world, and experience all it had tae offer."

She pressed her lips together. "I can do that yet."

No, he thought silently. *Ye canna, love. Not without someone there tae break ye free.*

"Once Weston is married," she went on, "I have every intention of traveling. Not that it is any concern of yours."

"And will ye continue tae live here? In this place that ye have always despised?" As he hated the white-walled mansion every bit as much as Brynne did, Lachlan's gaze frosted over when he took a sharp glance around the room.

After his initial two-week tenure here, he'd returned the following summer as a temporary ward of the Earl of Dorchester. His father had recently married–again–and not wanting to overwhelm his young bride with a gaggle of rambunctious boys, had sent as many of them away as he could.

Lachlan was glad–even secretly overjoyed–to return to Hawkridge Manor. He'd thought of Brynne often, and couldn't wait to see her again. But by the time he'd gotten there, she had already departed for Cheltenham Ladies' College.

He had felt her absence keenly. And after the first month of being stuck in that frigid, Godforsaken tomb of an estate, he was already counting down the hours to when he'd be able to return to Campbell Castle.

It may have been in a state of perpetual disrepair with crack in the walls and spiders hanging from the ceiling and a wild pack of hounds gamboling through the halls at all hours of the day and night, but on its coldest day his childhood home was warmer than Hawkridge.

When he'd returned to the manor as an adult, he was surprised to find it exactly as it had been when he was a boy, despite having transferred to Weston's management. Then, it was well-known that Brynne's brother was just as emotionless as her father. And those who didn't know his Bry as he did swept her with the same brush.

On more than one occasion, he'd heard her described as an ice queen. Beautiful, reserved, and utterly untouchable. But he knew better. He knew there was warmth there. Warmth, and humor, and an almost insatiable curiosity for life and all the wonders it contained.

Which was why he couldn't stand seeing her here. Trapped in the very same place that had robbed her of a child's unique freedom and inquisitiveness and joy.

She was a grown woman now.

He knew that better than anyone.

But that didn't mean she wasn't still trapped.

Trapped by a society that benefited from her lack of independence.

Trapped by a series of outdated rules designed to suppress women and elevate men.

Trapped by a family that had never *quite* understood her.

Not even her own brother.

But Lachlan had. Lachlan *did*. Often better than he understood himself. He and Brynne…they were two stars in the same constellation. Two parts that helped to comprise the whole. And when one of them dimmed, they both lost their light.

"Ye need a home, Bry. Someplace tae put down yer roots. Someplace tae return to after yer travels. Someplace tae raise yer children." He walked towards her then. He didn't direct his legs; they moved of their own accord. He half-expected her to run, and he wouldn't have blamed her if she did. But his Bry was stronger than that. She may have been as slim as a willow, but there was steel there.

Steel and softness.

Independence and uncertainty.

Brynne was a maze of contradictions, and he adored every twist and turn that made up the woman he loved. The woman he'd lost due to his own arrogance and their mutual failure to communicate. The woman he'd do anything to have again.

"Tell me ye are happy." He glided a finger along her jaw. Curled it beneath her chin. Nudged her head until there was nowhere she could look but into his eyes. Nowhere she could hide. Not from him. Never from him. "Tell me ye are happy, and I'll leave."

"I..." Her throat convulsed as she swallowed. "I am fine."

"That's not happy."

"Maybe not," she acknowledged stiffly. "But it's a far cry better than miserable, which is what I am with you."

A dagger shoved between his shoulders would have hurt less.

"Bry–"

"This not going to work, Lachlan. It was *never* going to work." Her hazel eyes flashed with a combination of frustration and bewilderment. "Your coming here changes nothing."

"And is that what ye feel for me?" he challenged roughly. "Nothing? Because the goose pimples on yer flesh when I do this"–he trailed his fingers along her neck, traced the coarse pads across the slanted lines of her collarbone, slid down to outline the rounded curve of her breasts with his palms–"say otherwise."

She swallowed again. Skimmed her tongue between her lips. Shifted her weight.

"Physical attraction is not everything," she said after a long, ragged pause.

"Aye," he whispered, watching her eyes drift closed as he rubbed his thumbs across her nipples. Nipples that were hard and swollen beneath the thin layer of her muslin bodice. "But it's not nothing."

Bending his head, he brushed his mouth across hers.

Just a fleeting taste.

A memory of what had been.

A hope for what might be.

Her mouth hardening beneath his, she began to pull back...but then with a tortured, breathy whimper that went right to his loins, she rose up on her toes, grabbed on to the lapels of his jacket, and turned the taste of attraction into a torrent of desire.

"Bry," he groaned, cupping her breasts and slipping his tongue between her lips as a bolt of lightning sizzled through the air and slammed into the ground at their feet.

Fire enveloped them, flames licking up their bodies as they hungrily devoured each other like two poor souls starved. And in a way, they were. Starved for love. Starved for affection. Starved for the connection that had brought them together...and then snapped, leaving them floundering in dark water with no way to kick themselves back up to the surface.

For eighteen months he'd been treading in that obsidian pool of despair, longing for those late nights and early mornings where all he had to do was roll onto his side and Brynne was there waiting for him, a slumberous smile on her lips and passion in her eyes.

He backed her up against the wall. Filled his hands with all those rich, luxurious waves of tawny blonde hair as they deepened the kiss. As they used it as a lifeline to draw themselves out of that damned well and into the light.

Inch by inch, stroke by stroke, touch by touch, they went higher, and higher, and higher. The pleasure of having her in his arms, of feeling her heartbeat against his chest, of knowing she was right where she was supposed to be…it was indescribable. It *was* everything. But just as they reached the edge, just as he thought they might actually have a chance of making it out of that inky darkness…the rope broke.

And down they plunged.

"I cannot," Brynne gasped, wrenching herself free. Shoving away from the wall, she ducked under his arm and stumbled around the edge of the table. Steadying herself on a chair, she wiped the back of her hand across her mouth then clasped it to her belly. "I cannot do that with you without picturing you doing it with *her*."

The "her" Brynne referred to was Allison Adair.

Lachlan's mistress…and the biggest bloody mistake of his life.

His short nails digging into the sides of his temple, he raked them along his skull and hissed out a breath. They'd had this conversation a dozen times. *Two* dozen times. He'd explained, and apologized, and even begged until he was blue in the face.

But it always ended the same.

With his heart bleeding in his hands…and Brynne walking out the door.

"I don't know what else tae say that hasna already been said."

"Sometimes…" she murmured without looking at him. "Sometimes I wish I never saw you and her. In that bed. Sometimes I lay awake at night and wonder where we would be now if I didn't see you then."

"I told ye nothing happened," he said fiercely. "I *never* betrayed ye, Bry."

"There's more than one way to commit a betrayal, Lachlan."

"Aye." As a spark of anger ignited, he glared at the middle of her shoulder blades where a long curl, tugged free from its coiffure, dangled. "There is. And what of the betrayals *ye* committed, Brynne?"

At that, she whirled around. "*My* betrayals?"

"I held secrets from ye." Even now the shame of it heated his cheeks, but he plowed ahead, determined to speak his piece. "I dinna

63

deny that. And if I ever did anything tae encourage Allison tae seek out my bed that night, I'm sorrier for it than ye will ever know. But ye took vows, Bry. Ye promised tae stay by me side as me wife *'Til death comes tae part us asunder'*. Those were the words we spoke tae each other. When ye left me, when ye left *us*, was that not a betrayal?"

"You gave me no choice *but* to leave!" she cried.

"Or maybe there was a part of ye that was never completely there. With me. In that castle." The weight of his words, the truth of them, hung in the air like a guillotine waiting to fall. "Less than half a year, and ye fled in the dead of the night like a bluidy thief. Do ye know what I think?"

"No," she said shortly.

"I think I just gave ye the excuse ye were already looking for tae end what ye regret ever starting."

Her eyes cooled; ice glazing over the top of a pond on the first true cold day of winter. "This discussion is over."

"Aye," he said, his voice clipped and all the more bitter for it. "Run along. That's what ye do, isna it? When things get uncomfortable, ye run back tae what ye know. Like a horse with an entire field at its feet, but instead it returns tae its little square of wood and straw and grain."

"I'm not a horse," she said scornfully.

"Then what are ye?"

"I know what I am not. And I am *not* yours. Not anymore."

As she stormed out, Lachlan couldn't help but ask himself if she ever truly was.

THE NEXT MORNING, Brynne rose with the sun and went straight to her brother's study, where she dashed off a letter to their solicitor in London. The legality of dissolving a marriage that had both been consummated and surpassed its first year would be difficult, if not impossible, but if anyone could tackle such a difficult task, it was Mr. Jacobson.

All things being equal, she'd prefer to avoid an outright divorce. Especially since she hadn't told anyone she was married. Not only that, but such an act would require her to prove that Lachlan had committed either adultery, cruelty, or incest before the Court of Divorce and Matrimonial Causes.

Two of the three were not applicable. She and Lachlan were certainly not related, and while she could argue that he had caused much emotional distress, it did not raise to the level of cruelty demanded by the court.

As for the third…

The third she refused to consider on the grounds that a charge of adultery meant invoking the name *and* the presence of the third party involved. And Allison Adair was the second person on earth she never wanted to see again.

The first being Lachlan.

Naturally.

Which left, to the best of her knowledge, judicial separation. The marriage would remain legally binding, but the court would prevent Lachlan from interfering with her affairs. In short, she would be married but not married; bound to Lachlan legally, but not responsible to him personally. She could own property in her name, control her own inheritance without having to give it to her husband, settle her own debts.

Such an act would prevent her from ever marrying again. It wasn't ideal, but having been spurned once by a man she loved, she had little interest in ever repeating the experience.

There could be no children, which she *did* want.

Someday.

But surely such a sacrifice was worth her independence. Because she *wasn't* a horse in a stable. Whatever Lachlan had meant by that ridiculous analogy. And she *was* going to travel.

Someday.

And if she didn't…if she failed to fulfill the dreams she'd shared on a starlit night with a boy who'd one day shatter her heart….well, there were worse things.

She was financially supported by her family and respected by her peers. What need did she really have to see the world, or paint for anyone besides herself? She was content here. And if she occasionally felt a tug towards something greater, something more meaningful, then she could simply host a charity luncheon for the orphanage or hold a dinner party to benefit the theater or do any other number of things to prove that despite what Lachlan had said, she was happy.

And she'd be even happier once she was legally free of him.

Using Weston's gold letter seal to stamp the wax, she left the study and handed off the missive to the first footman who crossed her path in the hallway.

"Please have this delivered to the village before the mail coach leaves for London," she instructed.

"Yes, my lady. At once."

The footman hurried off to carry out her orders, and she sought quiet refuge in the parlor, her naked fingers–she'd not bothered to put her gloves back on after writing the letter–splaying across the wide wooden sill that shone with a fresh layer of beeswax polish.

She had every confidence that Mr. Jacobson would soon see the matter of her marriage settled. Hopefully sooner rather than later, as the last thing she wanted–aside from Lachlan showing up unannounced–was a long, drawn out affair that would have steam pouring out of the gossips' ears and ink splattering across the pages of the London Caller.

A sardonic smile twisted her lips as she considered the irony. Once, not so very long ago, she'd yearned for a life in the limelight. To be seen, and heard, and *known*. Not in a way that would invoke a scandal. Oh, maybe a *tiny* scandal. The sort where she tripped and flashed an ankle for all to see, or was caught out in the rain and a handsome lord offered her refuge in his carriage. The kind that would get her noticed and acknowledged without ruining her reputation.

But all it had taken was one London Season for her to discover that she did not, in fact, enjoy the attention that had been lavished upon her as the reclusive granddaughter of the Duke of Caldwell. Attention that had always felt artificially sweet, like too much sugar spooned into the tea. While once she'd dreamed of being a social butterfly when she was a little girl yearning to spread her wings beyond the confining walls of Hawkridge Manor, it wasn't long before she began to dread the endless litany of social engagements and public appearances.

The *perfection* that was required of her...it was too much for a single person to maintain. Especially one who already suffered from anxious mannerisms.

Say this, but not that.

Approach that person, but not this one.

Curtsy, dance, smile, laugh, flutter a fan.

She was like a doll in a music box, spinning and spinning on a metal disc...until one night, at the Duke of Hallowell's annual ball which marked the beginning of yet another Season, she spun straight into the arms of Lachlan Campbell.

CHAPTER SEVEN

Six Years Ago
Grotonborough House
Duke of Hallowell's London Residence

THE BALLROOM WAS filled with the *ton's* elite. The Duke of Hallowell's ball was an exclusive affair not be missed, and everyone had turned out in droves in the hopes of starting off their Season with a proverbial bang.

Having successfully completed half her dance card, Brynne was resting her weary feet beside a potted fern. A light sheen of perspiration clung to her upper lip, her shoulders ached from holding them so rigidly during the intricate steps of the increasingly popular Viennese waltz, and there was a blister forming on the back of her heel. But to look at her–calm and composed in her rib-squeezing gown of pale lavender–no one would think anything was amiss. Which was exactly what they were supposed to think.

Of its own accord, her gaze wandered across the vast room with its glittering chandeliers, velvet wall hangings, and marble tile floor (which was not at all conducive to dancing). Courtesy of the two hundred some odd guests swarming about like a cluster of bees buzzing around a hive, the ballroom was stuffy, if not downright suffocating. She yearned to escape to the outdoor terrace, but for as long as she remained under the watchful eye of her chaperone, she might as well have set her sights on the moon.

Her chest pressed painfully against the constrictive confines of her boned corset as she took a deep breath. And then let it out on a stunned *whoosh* of air when her stare caught on a strikingly handsome lord who towered easily over the rest of the guests.

Five years had passed since she'd last seen Lachlan Campbell. Five years since that magical two weeks when they'd shared their dreams and stared at the stars and promised each other their futures over strawberry drops and half a barley stick. So much had changed in that time…and so much–too much–had stayed the same.

She was now a young woman of nineteen; which made him a man of twenty-one. But as soon as their eyes met, her recognition was immediate and absolute.

Oh, he was larger. Wider. His shoulders and chest filled out the emerald green jacket he wore splendidly, and his thighs…well, let's just say she began to use her fan quite rigorously. The hollows in his cheeks were gone. His hair, combed and groomed and tied back from his face in a neat tail, gleamed a dark russet in the candlelight. Even his stance was different. More elegant. Refined. He held a mahogany walking cane as if it were an attachment of his gloved hand, and the lay of his broad satin necktie was beyond reproach.

The change from the boy he'd been to the man he'd become was off-putting and, for a moment, Brynne considered disappearing behind the fern…but then he flashed her a boyish grin, and she was relieved to see that beneath all that polish and pomp, he was still her Lachlan.

"Lady Brynne," he murmured after he'd crossed to her and bowed.

His brogue was thicker, she noted. Swathed in velvet and charred with smoke, the rumble of it against her ear caused her belly to jerk in response. It was the first visceral reaction she'd had to a member of the opposite sex since…well, since forever. This was the beginning of her fourth Season, and the number of suitors she'd been introduced to was bordering on the infinite.

Old, young. Stocky, thin. Bland, charming. Quiet, loud. They'd run the gamut from gentleman to duke and every title in between, but for all their differences, they had a single thing in common: none of them made her breath quicken or her pulse race like Lachlan did.

To have him standing in front of her after all this time...to *see* the man he'd become...when her heart pitched inside of her chest and the narrow ribbon of space between her breasts grew both clammy and flush all at once, she forced herself to inhale through her nose and exhale through her mouth as a familiar–and dreaded–tightening sensation filled her chest.

No. No! She was not going to have an Episode *here*, in the middle of a ballroom, with two hundred of her closest peers looking on. Especially when they were already staring, and secretly judging, and watching her every move with the greedy keenness of a circle of vultures waiting to descend and pick her bones clean if she made a mistake. For while the *ton* adored a respectable lady with nary a blemish attached to her name, there was nothing they loved more than tearing down what they'd propped up.

With a great deal of self-control, she managed to keep her entire body from trembling when Lachlan gently grasped her hand. Brushing his lips ever-so-softly across her satin-clad knuckles, he peered up at her beneath his brow.

"Ye grew up, Bry," he said huskily, his timbred voice intentionally low so that those surrounding them, including her attentive chaperone, the Dowager Countess of Crowley, a longtime friend of the family, couldn't hear. "Ye were pretty enough before. But now ye're as radiant as the sun."

Radiant as the sun.

"I..." Words failed her. She swallowed once. Twice. "You look well."

Propriety dictated that he should have released her hand, but he didn't, and neither did she think to withdraw it from his grasp. For some reason, a flicker of sadness, there and gone again before she could blink, rippled across his countenance. "And ye still look like ye're in the same cage, little songbird."

"Cage?" she said, temporarily drawn out of the moment as confusion marred her temple. "I don't understand."

"I wouldna expect ye tae." His thumb slid slowly across her palm, and her entire arm tingled. "Do ye remember, Bry? When we first met?"

How could he think, in a thousand lifetimes, that she'd forget?

It was the happiest she had ever been.

Brynne had attended a countless number of balls in some of the grandest estates in all of Europe. Watched a parade of magnificent theater productions. She'd had an audience with the *queen*, for heaven's sake. And yet the two weeks she had spent with a half-wild Scottish boy when she was but a girl of fourteen were the most precious memories in her possession.

"Yes," she whispered, captivated by the banked fire burning in his eyes. "I remember."

Lady Crowley stepped in then. A confidante of Brynne's mother who'd never had children of her own, she had offered herself up as Brynne's patroness at the start of her debut Season. Her father, who had no interest in taking part in London High Society, even if it was on his daughter's behalf, had readily agreed, and Lady Crowley had been accompanying Brynne to all of her various social functions ever since.

A generally calm, placid woman, the dowager countess was a remarkable improvement over Miss Hardgrave. Firm, but fair, she endeavored to keep a watchful eye over her charge whenever they were out in public. In private, she helped Brynne organize her social calendar, sort through the massive amount of proposals she continued to receive, and kept gentlemen callers at bay when the interest was not reciprocated (which it almost never was).

The two women rarely discussed anything of a deeply personal matter–Brynne had never told her patroness about Lachlan, for instance–but they maintained a mutual respect and understanding.

With shiny brown hair threaded lightly with gray, serious blue eyes, and a smooth complexion that didn't yet betray her age, Lady Crowley was a comely woman who had received her own fair share of proposals over the years. Without hesitation, she'd turned down every one, because (as she'd once shared with Brynne after indulging in a second glass of wine at a dinner party): "the only way a woman of our means can truly achieve independence is by becoming a widow".

But from the faraway glaze that captured her expression whenever she mentioned her husband, who had perished from an attack of the heart at the tragic age of two and forty, Brynne suspected love also had something to do with Lady Crowley's decision to never remarry. That is, she remained in love with Lord Crowley...a bond that even death itself hadn't managed to sever.

"Might you introduce me to your acquaintance, Lady Brynne?" she asked pleasantly even as her gaze focused with razor-sharp intensity on Lachlan. Like a mother gazelle sniffing the winds and sensing danger was near, she placed her hand on Brynne's elbow, a discreet–but meaningful–measure of protection that did not go unnoticed by Lachlan.

"Lady Crowley, may I present Lord Lachlan Campbell." As subtly as possible, Brynne withdrew her fingers from Lachlan's grip. "A...a schoolmate of my brother's from Eton. Lord Campbell, it is my pleasure to introduce the Dowager Countess of Crowley, my patroness."

Lachlan bowed again. Slightly deeper this time, as Lady Crowley's title outranked Brynne's, who found herself impressed that he'd adopted such gentlemanly airs when just five years ago he'd been teaching her how to jump out of wagons.

"Lady Crowley," he said smoothly. "The pleasure is all mine."

"You are Scottish," said Lady Crowley.

It was a statement, not a question.

A critique, not a compliment.

The corners of Brynne's mouth tucked in. Anti-Scottish sentiment was not new amidst the British nobility. It heralded all the way back to the Middle Ages, when Highlanders in particular were thought to be warriors and savages. She'd read about the First War of Scottish Independence in a dusty tome she'd found on the bottom shelf in the library. Bloody and brutal, it had spanned nearly three decades, only to be followed five years later by the *Second* War of Scottish Independence.

Entire centuries had passed by then, but the British were known for their long memories, and Scots were generally looked upon with a wary eye for the same reason Americans were. Rebellion–even rebellion that was hundreds of years old–was not easily forgotten, or forgiven. And while Lachlan was no more savage than Weston, and Scotland was as much a part of the United Kingdom as England, there remained a distinct line drawn between the two countries that extended far beyond a simple land boundary.

"Aye." Lachlan's dimple flashed as his lips curved in an easy grin. "Born and bred in Glenavon."

Lady Crowley sniffed. "I am certain I have never heard of it, Mr. Campbell."

"I wouldna expect ye tae. And not that it matters all that much tae me, but it's Lord Campbell."

Brynne was reminded of the day she and Lachlan had first met. Her horrible governesses, Miss Hardgrave, had attempted to delegitimize his nobility in a similar manner in an attempt to make him seem small and less important. It was an old ploy, and a sad one, and she was glad to see that he was not giving it any more credence now than he had then.

"Lord Campbell's father is the Marquess of Kintore," she provided.

"Is he?" Lady Crowley said with obvious skepticism.

"Aye, that he is," Lachlan said cheerfully. "Inherited the title when some dobber fell off a ladder. Made for quite the fanfare in our little village. Which ye really should visit, Lady Crowley, if ye ever find yerself in Northern Scotland." His gaze slipped to Brynne. Held. Darkened. "The wild heather is beautiful this time of year."

As a rosy blush unraveled across her cheeks, Brynne ducked her head to the side. She'd been the recipient of flattery before. So much of it over the past four Seasons that the words had become empty and hollow. But whereas the compliments of other gentlemen made her feel as if she were simply another box to be checked in the hopes of making a good match, Lachlan's filled her with a warm, soft glow.

"Should I ever find myself with absolutely nowhere else to go, Lord Campbell, I may indeed consider Glenavon," said Lady Crowley, her dry tone carrying just enough humor to lessen the sting of her artfully placed barb. "Are you residing there currently?"

Lachlan shook his head. "I've rented a townhouse in Mayfair, and will be in London for the rest of the Season."

"That's splendid!" Brynne blurted. When both Lachlan and Lady Crowley stared, her blush deepened and she mumbled, "I mean...that is to say..."

Were she a girl again and Weston a boy, she would have poked him with her elbow and he would have rolled his eyes as they would have skipped off to their next adventure. But here, swathed in heavy silk and surrounded by curious onlookers, the last thing she was able to do was what she wanted.

Prim, proper, and poised, she recited silently.

The three hallmarks of a well-behaved lady.

Which she was trying very hard to be.

For her father.

For her brother.

For the memory of her mother.

For Lady Crowley.

For her peers.

For everyone, really…except for herself.

And it was silly. Absurd, even. But in that moment, there was a part of her that was half-tempted to take Lachlan by the hand and race out those terrace doors and never return. They'd go to Paris, or Rome, or even set sail across the ocean and see what America's finest cities had to show them. She'd bring nothing but her canvas and paints. Lachlan nothing but that devilish brogue of his. They would make their money from her art, and live in a rundown but charming flat above a baker's shop, and wake to the sweet smell of bread every morning.

There'd be absolutely nothing prim, proper, or poised about such a life.

She'd never be able to show her face in Polite Society ever again.

But oh, how *wonderful* it sounded.

Then again, dreams always did.

Which were all that her imaginings were, she told herself firmly. Nothing more than ridiculous fantasies, no doubt caused by a lack of oxygen to her brain courtesy of the corset squeezing the air from her lungs.

"I am sure what Lady Brynne *meant* to say," Lady Crowley interceded smoothly, "is that her brother, Lord Hawkridge, shall no doubt look forward to calling upon a former schoolmate. He is here, somewhere, if you'd like to speak with *him*."

Her enunciation…and the meaning behind it…could not have been clearer.

The half-Scottish second-born son of a laird, even a laird-turned-marquess, was *not* to be considered an eligible suitor for the Duke of Caldwell's only granddaughter. Neither he nor Brynne's father were in attendance, or even in London for that matter, but their expectations were all but written in ink on the inside of her wrist all the same. She was to marry a man of equal or (preferably) superior rank, which Lachlan decidedly wasn't. Which meant that any time spent speaking with him was time being taken away from her future husband. Never mind that she'd already met, and danced, with every other male occupant in the ballroom under the age of sixty at least thrice over the course of her previous Seasons.

In addition to maintaining Brynne's spotless reputation, Lady Crowley had one job to do. Make a *magnificent* match. The kind that would set the *ton* back on its heels for years to come. And given her vaguely repugnant expression, Lady Crowley did not envision Lord Lachlan Campbell as a magnificent match. Or even an almost-magnificent match. Or even an if-you-closed-one-eye-and-squinted-sideways-magnificent match.

And if he wasn't a match, then he was an impediment.

An impediment that needed to be removed from Brynne's path.

Immediately.

"Good *evening* to you, Lord Campbell," said Lady Crowley when he didn't move. "Lady Brynne, let's move along."

But neither of them stirred so much as a muscle.

Instead, they stared at each other, and the quiet, smoldering intensity of Lachlan's amber gaze was unlike anything she'd ever experienced before. Which was probably why Brynne abruptly uttered three words she'd never spoken before.

"Dance with me," she said breathlessly.

"*What?*" Lady Crowley squawked.

"It would be me pleasure." Lachlan bowed again, then offered his arm.

She took it, and even though multiple layers of fabric separated his forearm from her hand, she would have sworn she felt heat pulsing off his skin as they made their way to the middle of the floor. Either that, or she was coming down with a fever. Regardless, there was a flame there. Between them. Where once there'd been the tiniest hint of a spark. And where there was a flame, fire was never far behind.

"Yer patroness should like me head served up on a silver platter," Lachlan murmured.

"Nothing as fancy as that, I should think," Brynne replied, her blood all but humming when he cupped her shoulder and nudged her in a quarter of an inch closer than what was deemed seemly. Not that anyone surrounding them would be able to tell the difference. But *she* did. Lachlan as well, if the glint in his eyes was any indication.

Goodness, but he stole her breath. In a way that had nothing to do with the rigorous physical exertion required of the Viennese waltz and everything to do with the way he was holding her. The way he was looking at her. As if he were an archaeologist who'd just discovered a priceless treasure that he never wanted to let go.

"Where have you been?" she asked as they moved in perfect unison, their steps guided by the full orchestra in the viewing balcony playing the music of John Strauss II, a prolific Austrian composer well-deserving of the sobriquet "The Waltz King".

"Where have *ye* been?" he countered. "I returned tae Hawkridge Manor the following year, but ye werena there."

"Did you hope that I would be?" she said, a playful smile teasing her lips. She doubted, very much, that Lachlan had thought of her these past few years as often as she'd thought of him. After he left, she had expected her infatuation with him to gradually dissipate. But if anything, it had grown stronger. Unwittingly, he'd become the standard by which she compared every other suitor that crossed her path.

Did they make her laugh as Lachlan had? Did they challenge her as Lachlan had? Did they encourage her dreams as Lachlan had?

To a man, the answer was always no.

But now Lachlan himself was standing in front of her, and the answer was...

"Yes," he said simply, and her smile faded as she recognized the truth in his gaze…and the implication of what it meant.

"I…I would have been there, if I could." She wet her lips. "I was at school."

"Aye, that's what Weston said. Did ye enjoy it?"

"Not as much as I'd anticipated."

They released each other, completed a turn, and then rejoined their hands. This waltz was quick; its tempo nearly twice the speed of the other dances. Ordinarily maintaining a conversation would be difficult, if not impossible. But there was so much that Brynne wanted to say. So much that she wanted to hear. And even though she'd not spared a glance to the perimeter of the room, she knew that the instant the music ended Lady Crowley would come marching across the marble floor to collect her. Which meant this was the only opportunity she had to speak with Lachlan alone.

She didn't want to waste a second.

"This is yer third Season?" he asked.

"The beginning of my fourth."

His brows rose. "And ye havena found a husband yet?"

"Don't say it like *that*."

"Like what?"

"Like it's a bad thing I did not acquiesce to the first proposal I received."

"Have there been many of them?"

"Many of what?"

"Proposals," he said, his mouth twisting around the word as if he'd bitten into something sour.

Brynne tried not to sigh. A friend had asked her the same question just the other day, and it never failed to embarrass her when she admitted the answer, even though she had done nothing to be embarrassed *for*. It wasn't as if she had invited the proposals upon herself. If anything, she'd done all she could to discourage them. But no matter what she did, they kept coming, as predictable as rain on a

Tuesday.

"Sixty-seven," she said with great reluctance.

Lachlan's eyes widened. "*Sixty-seven?* Bluidy hell. Why havena ye accepted one?"

"Because I've been waiting."

"For what? The blessing of the pope?"

You, she replied silently. *I've been waiting for you.*

She hadn't. Not really. Not consciously, at any rate. For how could a tulip bulb possibly know it was waiting for the sun until it burst through the soil and felt the light on its petals for the first time?

They spun apart again.

Came together.

"For someone who wants to marry *me* and not my dowry, or to curry favor with my father or grandfather," she said matter-of-factly.

While Lachlan's mouth stretched in a grin, his eyes remained somber and serious. "Poor Bry," he said quietly. "What's a wealthy, beautiful heiress with the world at her feet tae do?"

"Find a husband who will not place me on the nearest shelf to collect dust with all of his other trophies."

The music swelled into the final crescendo, and then faded into silence as everyone ended the waltz with a bow or a curtsy, before breaking apart to either find their next partner or seek refreshments from the silver trays piled high with food and drink that were being circulated around the room by footmen dressed in matching black livery.

Brynne glanced over her shoulder to see that Lady Crowley was already approaching with all the unflinching determination of the Royal Navy bearing down on Cape Trafalgar at the height of the Napoleonic Wars. She looked back at Lachlan, and bit her lip in apology.

"Thank you for dancing with me. It was…it was good to see you again. Truly."

He'd not yet released her hand, and used it to tug her even closer. "Why does that sound like a farewell?" he asked, his breath fanning across her ear and causing a shivery ribbon of awareness to ripple down her spine.

"Because it is," she said regretfully. "We may see each other from afar, but I fear my patroness will do everything in her power to prevent us from being this near again."

Amusement flickered in his gaze. "The pretty English princess canna lower herself tae associate with the common Scottish folk, is that it?"

A dull flush painted the nape of her neck a deep crimson. "If Lady Crowley knew you–"

"If yer patroness knew me, she'd be running, not walking, over here tae rescue ye." He rubbed his thumb across her knuckles in a subtle caress that made her knees wobble. "It's all right, little songbird. I understand how the game is played. Perhaps if I had a proper title, and an estate tae go with it–"

"Those things don't matter to me," she interrupted.

He canted his head. Gave her a slow, measured stare. "Dinna they?"

Did they?

Given that she did not aspire towards superficiality, Brynne wanted her reply to be a firm, unequivocal "no". But as she looked deep within herself, she found the answer was far more complicated than that.

In a perfect world, a woman would be free to follow her heart with no consequences or repercussions. But this wasn't a perfect world, particularly for women. In *this* world, where appearance was everything and a person's title was the most important thing about them, women's heads were too often at odds with their hearts.

Brynne liked to believe that there was a time and a place, somewhere in existence, where she *could* take Lachlan by the hand and they *did* race out those terrace doors. But this ballroom, this music box that she kept spinning around and around in, was neither the time nor the place, and a lump formed in her throat as she backed away from him.

"I am sorry, Lord Campbell." She searched his gaze, willing him to understand that there were some things–most things–beyond her control. And she was far past the days where she might sneak outside to meet him in the moonlight and count the stars until dawn.

"We're not children anymore, are we, Bry?" He shook his head before she could respond. "It's all right."

The staccato *click* of Lady Crowley's walking cane was nearly upon them. Distress creased Brynne's brow. Every strike of polished ivory against marble tile was one less second she had to spend with Lachlan, but there was still so much left unsaid! In four Seasons, this was the first genuine connection she'd felt. Normally, once a waltz had reached its conclusion, she couldn't escape fast enough. But this time was different. This time, she wanted to stay. For a moment. For a minute. For an eternity. And she hated that she couldn't. More than that, she hated that the decision wasn't her own. It was being made for her. By Lady Crowley. By a father who wasn't even here. By a grandfather who would never–ever–permit his granddaughter to marry the second-born son of a Scottish Highlander.

"It's all right, little songbird," Lachlan repeated tenderly as he read her expression. The panic in it, and the despair. "It's going tae be all right. No need tae fret. As I said, I understand the game."

The game.

The *game.*

It was a game, wasn't it? All this pomp and pretense. An entire Season devoted to finding a husband, when it was really all planned from behind closed doors. Who could marry whom. Who needed to be avoided at all cost. Who might cause a scandal so large it would rock the entire *ton* to its foundation.

Why, Brynne had only to look to last year for what would happen if she strayed off the path that had been set for her from birth. Lady Henrietta Hartley, eldest daughter of the Duke of St. Albans and adored by all, had done the unspeakable. She'd fallen in love. With a *baronet*. And then–to make matters infinitely worse–she'd run off to Gretna Green and *married* him.

The last anyone had heard, the newlyweds were living somewhere outside of Leeds. Penniless, ostracized from High Society, and disowned by her father, Henrietta could never return to the life she'd known. Once a diamond of the first water with the world at her feet, now she was nothing more than another example of what happened to a young lady when she followed her heart instead of obeying her head.

"I may never be allowed to see you again," she told Lachlan, sweeping a troubled glance at him from beneath her lashes.

"Aye, ye will," he said, an arrogant smirk capturing his mouth as Lady Crowley, all icy indignation and thinly veiled fury, finally reached them.

"Lord Campbell," she said between clenched teeth, "you are wanted on the other side of the room."

"Somehow I expected I would be." He levelled his grin at Lady Crowley, who sniffed and deliberately looked the other way. As his focus shifted to Brynne, his eyes softened, and the tiny hairs at the nape of her neck lifted in awareness when she glimpsed the possessive gleam in the depths of his gaze.

"I'm sorry" she mouth again.

Helplessly.

Hopelessly.

"Not tae worry." He bent over her hand, and when he spoke, his low, rumbling brogue was for her ears only. "I said I know the game…I never said I had any intention of following the rules."

CHAPTER EIGHT

Present Day
Hawkridge Manor

S HE SAW LACHLAN twice more that Season, Brynne reflected as she gazed blindly out the window. Once at a private dinner party for a mutual acquaintance, and again by sheer happenstance in Hyde Park. At least, at the time, she'd assumed it was coincidence that their paths happened to cross. Now she knew that it had most likely been an intentional act, as her husband never did anything by accident.

He was not a man to leave things to fate or chance.

Every last detail was planned.

Including their marriage.

As a chill seeped through the glass and settled in her bones, she turned from the window just as the door to the parlor creaked open. Tension ratcheted through her, a drawing rein pulled too tight, only to ease when the housekeeper entered the room.

"Mrs. Grimsby," she said on a relieved exhalation of breath. "I thought…I thought you might be someone else."

"And who might that be?" Attending to a mountain of pillows piled high at the end of a divan, the housekeeper gave them a sturdy *thwack* with the side of her palm to settle the newly stuffed feathers into place. "The person responsible for your Episode yesterday?"

Crossing the sideboard where a fresh tea service always sat at the ready, Brynne poured herself a cup with remarkably steady hands given her strained nerves and opted to stand, rather than sit, behind an ornate sofa trimmed in rosewood.

"I do not care to discuss it." *Or him*, she added silently.

Perhaps, if Mrs. Grimsby wasn't the closest thing to a mother Brynne had ever had, the servant would have left it at that. But she was, and she didn't.

"Large Scottish husbands do not disappear simply because you wish it of them, dear."

Tea sloshed over the rim of Brynne's cup as her arm jerked in surprise. "You...you know?"

"Here, eat a piece of bread with jam and rest your feet. You're pale, and those circles under your eyes indicate that you didn't sleep well. Not that I can blame you." Fussing over Brynne like a mother hen, Mrs. Grimsby refilled her tea, pressed a plate into her hands, and spread a blanket across her lap. "There we are, dear." She sat opposite in a chair set on brass castor wheels, and as her kind brown eyes filled with understanding, Brynne's inexplicably filled with tears.

"I apologize," she gasped, setting aside her tea to dab at the corners of her eyes with a linen handkerchief procured from a hidden pocket stitched into the skirt of her gown. "I...I do not know what has come over me."

Generally speaking, she prided herself on controlling her emotions. It was a hallmark of every Weston; their uncanny ability to disguise what they were really feeling behind a cold smile and empty eyes.

Her brother had perfected the art following his return from Eton, and had been a veritable walking, talking glacier before Evie Thorn-croft melted him into a puddle. It had taken Brynne a little longer to learn how to effectively shield her innermost thoughts (as a woman, she was charged with the unique task of always being approachable while holding everyone at arm's length), but with a little practice she'd managed to erect a wall around herself and her feelings. A wall that had grown immeasurably taller after the complete and utter collapse of her marriage. Which was why she was dismayed to find that it was failing her at the moment she needed it the most.

"I cannot claim to be an expert on such matters," Mrs. Grimsby began, her humble, soothing tone a steady balm on the raw, exposed nerves that pricked and burned just beneath the surface of Brynne's composed countenance. "Mr. Grimsby and I have been blessed with a quiet, uneventful life. An impatient word spoken here and there, true, but for the most part, we have loved each other day in and day out since he stumbled his way through a proposal when we were both hardly more than children."

Brynne managed a wisp of a smile. "That sounds very nice."

"It is," the housekeeper nodded. "It is indeed. But I can imagine that a secret elopement, and whatever drove you to return to a place you've never been terribly fond of, and then the reappearance of the man who, if memory serves, you asked me to have shot on sight, would be enough to drive anyone to a few tears, if not worse."

"How long have you known?" She crumpled her handkerchief into a ball, but didn't return it to her pocket as she sensed she may have need of it shortly. "That Lachlan...that Lord Campbell and I...that we..."

"Are wed?" Mrs. Grimsby said gently.

She nodded past the lump in her throat.

"Long enough, dear. Do not forget your toast."

Obediently, she took a bite, then dusted the resulting crumbs off her lap. It really should have come as no great shock that Mrs. Grimsby knew about her marriage to Lachlan. Servants were often privy to information that was not widely circulated. Especially a housekeeper, who had the eyes and ears of every maid and footman in the manor.

"He wasn't supposed to come here." Bitterness chased away her tears as she made herself sit up straight, Miss Hardgrave's lessons (*"young ladies do not slouch, young ladies do not speak out of turn, young ladies do not fraternize with boys of ill repute"*) as much a part of her as the color of her hair. "When we...when we ended things between us, I made it clear that I never wanted to see him again."

"What did Lord Campbell have to say to that?" Mrs. Grimsby asked.

"He was not inclined to agree." *To put it mildly.* "But I did not give him a choice."

"I see." Lapsing into thoughtful silence, the housekeeper made an act of removing a small silver figurine off the table beside her and rubbing it to a shine with her apron. She replaced it carefully, then regarded Brynne with a calm, measured smile. "If Lord Campbell has come all this way, I can only presume that he should like to make amends for whatever transgressions he committed."

"I am not interested in any sort of reconciliation, and I have already asked him to leave."

"And here I just had him settled in the East Wing."

Brynne stared blankly at Mrs. Grimsby. "You did what?"

"He is your husband, dear. Estranged or not."

"He is a rogue!" What remained of her toast fell to the floor as she surged to her feet. "And a liar besides. I want *nothing* to do with him, and you've–you've put out the welcome banners? Mrs. Grimsby, how could you?"

The housekeeper clucked her tongue. "I had a room prepared for a family member, my lady. The same as I've done a hundred times before."

"Lachlan Campbell is *not* my family." As anger boiled and betrayal slapped, Brynne's natural defenses shored themselves up, encasing her behind a towering partition of ice. "You are excused, Mrs. Grimsby."

"My lady–" the housekeeper began, her brows knitting.

"Out," she whispered, jabbing a finger at the door.

"Very well." Stiffly, Mrs. Grimsby stood. But she did not immediately quit the parlor. "I shall say this once, Lady Brynne, and not again. I probably should not say it all, but I've known you since you were a girl. I've rocked you in my arms when you had bad dreams. I've stood guard over you when you were terribly ill with fever. I've mended your cuts and tended your bruises, and long have I considered you to be one of my daughters, even though there is no blood between us and I am your social inferior. Which is why I hope you heed my words when I say that in my experience, it is rare that a person has done something so grievous that it cannot be undone with time and forgiveness."

Guilt filled Brynne. Every word the housekeeper spoke was true, and she felt terrible for her harsh tone. It was a basic human instinct to cause hurt when you were hurt. To alleviate your pain by invoking pain in others. But it wasn't right, and it wasn't fair, and she owed Mrs. Grimsby more than the curt dismissal she'd given her.

"I apologize," she said. "I...I have not been myself. Not since Lord Campbell arrived. I wish forgiveness was as easy as that. Truly, I do. It would make everything that much more simple." As a smile, sweet and fleeting, stole across her lips, she hugged her arms to her chest. "Lachlan and I...we did love each other. Once. But now...now it's better for everyone that we stay apart."

Mrs. Grimsby raised a brow. "I never said anything about forgiveness being *easy*, dear. And love is many things, but simple is not one of them. It is, however, the third most important thing worth fighting for."

"And the other two?" Brynne asked.

Mrs. Grimsby may have never attended a ball in London or met the queen at Kensington Palace or sat in a box at the Royal Theater, but she was an indispensable source of wisdom nevertheless. Her common sense view of the world had often served as a guide for Brynne over the years. Certainly, the housekeeper had given her better advice than any nanny or governess, and while she hadn't the same experience with the *ton* as Lady Crowley had, her guidance was just as invaluable.

"The second most important thing is your children. Should you be a mother someday, you will defend that innocent babe whether they are small enough to fit in the crook of your arm..." Mrs. Grimsby gazed at Brynne with great affection. "Or old enough to run off with a striking Scot. Heavens, dear, and may my Mr. Grimsby forgive me saying this, but your Lord Campbell is a sight to behold, isn't he?"

"He isn't *my* Lord Campbell," Brynne said automatically. Then the side of her mouth quirked in a reluctant half-smile. "But yes, yes he is a sight to behold." Lowering her arms, she adjusted a pleat on her skirt that had folded over when she'd sat down on the sofa. "What of the last thing worth fighting for?"

"Yourself." Mrs. Grimsby clasped her hands together. "You must always fight for yourself, first and foremost. Now finish your tea before it goes cold. I'll have a maid bring in a platter of fruit to get some color into your cheeks, and then a walk to get some fresh air into your lungs, I should think."

It was, Brynne noted wryly, nearly the same advice she'd given to Sterling.

"Mrs. Grimsby," she called out as the housekeeper finally turned to leave.

"Yes, dear?"

"Thank you."

AFTER SPENDING A restless night in the same room he'd occupied during his first visit to Hawkridge Manor, Lachlan rose with a newfound sense of determination and purpose.

It was painfully apparent that Brynne did not want him here. She couldn't have made her disdain for him any clearer. A blind man could see it. But then had he really expected anything less, given how things had ended between them?

In tears and torment, rage and wrath. With both saying things they didn't mean, and holding on to stubborn pride when they should have held on to each other.

He had regrets.

A bloody ocean's worth of them.

But that was why he was here.

Not to start over. There was too much history to begin anew. But they could go back to their foundation. Build it stronger. Hardier. So that the next time the winds howled and the rain spat, they would be able to withstand the storm.

Brynne thought they were over. She believed they were a thing of the past. Something to be locked away and forgotten, like bloody pantaloons or powdered wigs. Except their love wasn't a damned fashion statement gone hideously wrong. It was long, and it was lasting, and even now–after all that had happened–he felt the spark of it. And he knew that, deep down, Brynne did as well. Or else he would have been greeted with apathy instead of anger. Because the opposite of love wasn't fury.

It was indifference.

"Aye, and we've none of that, do we?" Asking the rhetorical question of his mare, Aislyn, a chestnut of sturdy build and mind that he'd raised from a wee filly after she was rejected by her dam–he cinched off her girth and drew the reins over her head before swinging himself up and into the saddle.

He wasn't nearly so fine an equestrian as his brother, Robert, but he enjoyed a daily ride, and Aislyn enjoyed stretching her legs. Holding her to a trot until they were clear of the manor, he set his heels into her barrel once they had nothing but open field in front of them, and crouched low over her neck as they tore off through the tall, rippling sea of grass.

Overhead, the sky was a clear, seamless blue, and the air was crisp with the scent of autumn. The trees were heavy with leaves yet, but some had already begun shifting colors and it wouldn't be long before the branches clacked and the snow fell.

By then, he hoped to be sitting in front of a roaring fire at Campbell Castle with Brynne by his side, wearing a blanket of fur...and nothing else. He remembered, keenly, their first winter in the drafty old keep of wood and stone. How they'd laughed and played in the snow like children during the day, then warmed each other in front of the hearth by night. Four months of newly wedded bliss in the frozen Highlands...when they were too lost in each other to even notice the cold. Then spring came, and the weather wasn't the only thing to change.

If he could go back...if he could do it over again...but living in the past was a fool's errand, and the straightest path forward was always the one untraveled. He'd taken his first steps by coming here. Every day that he remained, he'd take a few more. And eventually, with persistence and truth and a little luck thrown in for good measure, that path would carry him and Brynne home again.

He was sure of it.

He had to be.

"Easy," he murmured in Aislyn's flattened ear as the mare's breaths began to labor and her stride shortened. "Easy now, lass. Ye dinna want tae overdo it."

He stood in the stirrups, bracing himself against the wind and the pull of Aislyn's forehead as he firmly guided the mare back down through her paces. A gallop to a canter, a canter to a trot, a trot to a walk. Loosening the reins, he gave her her head, and she guided them to a nearby stream where crystal clear water rushed over smooth rocks covered in moss.

Dismounting, he slapped Aislyn's sweaty shoulder and then slipped off her bridle so that she could quench her thirst and then nibble at the tender grass shooting up along the bank in clumps of vibrant green. Pulling off his jacket, he threw it on the ground and then sat on top of it, arms looping around his bent legs as he gazed thoughtfully at the bubbling brook.

Further up, shielded from the meadow and the road beyond it by a heavy thicket of wild elderberry, the stream widened into a pool. He had discovered the spot while exploring during his second summer at Hawkridge Manor, and he and Weston had spent many an afternoon drowning worms there.

It was also where he'd caught his first English trout. A pitiful specimen, hardly the length of his hand. But he had still been immeasurably proud of it.

It was where he'd encouraged Weston, far too serious by half, even as a young man, to shake off the responsibilities of an earldom.

And it was where he'd kissed a pretty blonde lass who would one day be his wife.

CHAPTER NINE

Four Years Ago
Hawkridge Manor

"CAN I TAKE it off now?" Her voice breathy with nervous anticipation, Brynne tugged at the cloth Lachlan had tied around her eyes.

"Almost," he said as he continued to guide her closer to the stream and the blanket he'd set out beside it. The sun was heavy at their backs and a warm evening breeze tickled the air, carrying the faintest sounds of raised voices and laughter from the garden party underway at the main house where two dozen guests, Lachlan among them, had been invited to spend a month at Hawkridge Manor.

The Westons' annual house party was as renowned as the Westons themselves. First held by Brynne's grandfather, the Duke of Caldwell, and then–briefly–by her father, the Marquess of Dorchester, they had since been delegated to her brother, the Earl of Hawkridge, which was who Lachlan undoubtedly had to thank for his unexpected invitation.

The letter had found him all the way at Campbell Castle, where he had resided for the past two years. Dividing his time between caring for his younger siblings and trying like hell to resurrect his great-great-grandfather's distillery, he'd skipped the past London Season with no set plan to attend another. Dull and dreary, the barrage of balls and social calls had been as appealing as nails on a chalkboard. The only bright spot was Brynne. Dancing with her, talking to her, just gazing at her...it was like holding sunshine in the palm of his hand. He could have basked in her light for the rest of the evening and every day beyond it, but Lady Crowley had cast a long, ominous shadow.

Wise to the wily ways of foxes and rogues, she'd guarded her precious hen with all of the weapons at her disposal.

Guilt being principle among them.

He'd never forget the words she'd spoken to him when he came to call the next day. As if she was anticipating his arrival, she, not a servant, had greeted him at the door. And kept her foot wedged in the frame the entire time so that even if he wanted to, he couldn't have entered. As if he were some sort of bloody vampire.

"Lord Campbell," she'd begun coolly, her blue eyes unblinking. "I had a feeling you would come. I am afraid Lady Brynne is not available."

"Should I return later, then?" He had tried to look past her into the foyer, but she'd blocked his view.

"No, I do not believe that would be wise."

He'd rubbed his jaw. "Ye dinna like me, do ye, Lady Crowley? Is it the red hair?"

"My personal opinion of you is irrelevant, Lord Campbell. It is what the *ton* thinks that matters."

"And what does the *ton* think?"

"That Lady Brynne is destined for a most favorable match. A match that she will not make if you are hovering about." Here the dowager countess had paused, as if weighing her words with great caution. What she wanted to say, and what she preferred to keep to herself. "Lady Brynne is...inordinately fond of you, Lord Campbell. That much is obvious. Were things different...if she were not the granddaughter of a duke and you were not...whatever it is that you are–"

"The spare son of a Scottish laird who inherited a marquessate by ladder tragedy?" he'd interjected cheerfully.

Lady Crowley's mouth had puckered. "Precisely. Lady Brynne's family has high expectations for her and her future husband. As you will never be suitable for that role, Lord Campbell, I wouldn't want to give Lady Brynne the wrong impression by parading you in front of her."

"Like chocolate in a window," he'd said with a sage nod. "Hard tae resist even though ye know it'll go straight to yer waistline."

The dowager countess hadn't bothered to deign such a comment with a response. "I hope I have made myself clear, Lord Campbell."

"Aye, ye have." Still, he had hesitated as a question nagged at the corner of his mind. "But what if she doesna?"

"Does not what?" Lady Crowley had snapped, her patience visibly wearing thin.

"Find someone tae marry that ye deem favorable."

"Oh, she will."

"Ye sound certain."

"Because I am. Lady Brynne will do what is expected of her. Now do what is expected of *you*, Lord Campbell, and find someone better suited to your particular…rank. Good day."

He'd left.

He could have stayed. Could have forced his way through the door. Could have demanded to see Brynne. He was even fairly certain he could have convinced her to run away with him.

But instead he'd left.

Not for himself.

Not for Lady Crowley.

But for Brynne.

Because the dowager countess was right. He would never be suitable for her. *Especially* if she knew the truth of his situation. And she deserved everything she'd worked so bloody hard for while being locked in that gilded cage all those years. Which was a duke. Maybe a marquess, or even a wealthy earl. But not a damned Scotsman who would never inherit a formal title of his own, or a proper estate to go along with it. A Scotsman who was saddled with a crumbling castle, and a distillery that had yet to turn a profit, and two brothers to feed. Make that three and a sister, counting the newborn twins, which he was sure would arrive in a pretty basket on his doorstep any day now.

They always did.

Thus he had left, and he had *stayed* away, for the better part of two years.

Until the invitation arrived.

Maybe a better man would have ignored it, or sent his apologies for not being unable to attend. But he wasn't a damned saint. And you couldn't dangle a rabbit in front of a wolf and not expect it to give chase.

He'd given Brynne two years to find a "suitable match".

Twenty-four months.

One hundred four weeks.

And when he had walked into Hawkridge Manor and their eyes had met from across the drawing room, it was as if not a single day had passed.

"All right," he said, untying the simple knot he had used to cover her eyes and shoving it into his pocket. "Ye can look."

He looked at her as she looked at the stream. Felt a rumble of pleasure in his chest when her gaze widened and her lips parted as she saw the checkered blanket he'd laid out and the wicker basket he'd paid a footman to sneak into the kitchens and fill with fresh melon, cheese, cold slices of beef...and a surprise, just from him.

"You...you've planned a picnic for us?" she asked, glancing at him over her shoulder. At her display of stunned wonder, it was all he could do not to pluck her up in his arms and kiss her until the sun fell below the horizon and the stairs painted the sky in diamonds.

"Aye," he said gruffly. Taking her by the hand, he led her to the blanket and gestured for her to sit, then poured them both a glass of the champagne he had nabbed from the grand white tent set up on the east lawn where the other guests were enjoying music, and drink, and caviar chilled in tiny porcelain bowls.

It wouldn't be long before Brynne, acting as her brother's hostess, was missed.

An hour at most.

But he intended to make use of every minute.

"Tae old friendships and new adventures," he murmured, lightly clinking their crystal flutes together.

"To old friendships and new adventures," she repeated solemnly. Then she took a sip of the champagne, and the lines of tension in her face–tension, it seemed, that only he was capable of seeing–eased and the stiff, formal lady of the manor who'd greeted him upon his arrival gave way to the bright-eyed, curious, happy lass who had stolen his heart on a bench underneath an old oak tree…and never returned it.

"Why go to all this trouble?" she asked. "There is food and champagne aplenty in the tent. A lovely string quartet, as well. Not to mention that I *really* shouldn't have snuck off. If someone notices my absence…" With a bemused shake of her head she trailed off, as if she weren't quite sure how she'd gotten here.

"Wasna trouble tae me." He lifted his shoulder. "I stole everything from yer brother."

"Lord Campbell," she chided with a sideways glance.

"*Lady* Brynne," he mocked with a half-grin.

She gave him a censorious frown over the rim of her glass. Then the corners of her mouth twitched. "You're still very much that young boy, aren't you? Disobeying rules. Pushing boundaries. Flirting with trouble any chance you get."

"I'm flirting with more than trouble," he mumbled into his champagne before he tilted his head back and downed the entire flute.

Her fair brows knitted. "What was that?"

"Nothing," he said easily. "Melon?"

"Yes, please."

They ate in companionable silence–Lachlan was hungrier than he'd thought–and when there was only a spattering of crumbs and a sliver of cheese remaining, he tossed the remnants of the basket into the water for the trout save a short, rectangular stick wrapped in a piece of brown paper.

"Ye want tae know why I did this?" he asked as he lowered himself onto the blanket directly beside her. Another inch, and his muscular thigh would be pressed firmly against her hip. Despite not having a chair at her back, she sat straight as an arrow, her skirts, a frothy seafoam green that brought out the shards of emerald in her eyes, arranged in a prim half-circle that covered her legs all the way to her evening slippers.

"I do," she said, flicking a demure peek at him from beneath her lashes.

He began to unwrap the paper, careful not to break what was inside. "I wanted tae do something just for ye."

She gave a short, bewildered laugh. "In case you hadn't noticed, we just left an entire house party that was for me."

"That tent, the music, the bluidy caviar–which is disgusting, by the way." His face contorted in a grimace. "Who in their right mind decided tae yank a poor sturgeon out of the river, take its eggs, and serve them up in a fancy bowl?"

"I believe it was Russian fisherman, and caviar is considered a rare delicacy."

"Delicacy me arse," he snorted. "Might as well pour saltwater in a cup and call it a day."

"It is an acquired taste," she admitted. Then she lowered her voice. "I don't like it very much."

"No one does. But ye serve at yer parties because that's what ye think ye're supposed tae do, and everyone gobbles it up with a smile on their face because everyone else is doing it. And nobody stops tae think 'bluidy hell, we're eating the raw eggs of a fish'."

"And that's why you planned a picnic?" she asked with a polite, albeit puzzled smile. "So that I wouldn't have to eat caviar? That's...that's thoughtful of you, Lachlan."

"Aye. Wait. No." Hell, he was already bungling it, wasn't he? At three and twenty, he had his fair share of experience with women. Had even kept a mistress for a time, a bonny village lass by the name of Allison Adair. Suffice it to say, he'd earned himself a reputation as quite the charmer. And he couldn't remember when he'd ever lacked for the right words to say. But maybe that was because the words hadn't carried any true weight or repercussions, and if he said the wrong thing, well, there was always another village lass to warm his bed on a cold night.

But there was only one Lady Brynne Weston.

He placed his hand on top of hers, his fingers–callused and tanned from hard work in the sun–enveloping her porcelain skin. "I brought ye here because this is where I knew ye would be happy. In the calm, and the quiet, where ye dinna have tae wear that mask on yer face. Where ye dinna have tae pretend. Where I can watch that pretty pink blush spread across yer cheeks when I tell ye how gorgeous ye are. Aye," he said huskily as her color deepened. "Just like that."

"Lachlan–" she began, but he wasn't finished.

"I see ye, Brynne. Every piece of ye. And I wanted tae bring ye out of the shadows of that bluidy mausoleum and intae the sunlight so that ye could shine."

He hadn't planned to kiss her.

But neither had he planned to fall in love when he was a lad of sixteen.

With Brynne, there was never a plan.

From the first second her saw her out that carriage window, it was all heart, and hope, and feeling. So when he brushed his mouth across hers in a silken caress, it felt as natural as breathing.

Because it was always Brynne for him.

"Was that all right?" he asked, intently searching her gaze as he pulled back to gauge her reaction. He'd never do anything to hurt her. And his stomach plummeted when she gave a small, hesitant shake of her head.

"No," she whispered as her hand splayed across the center of his chest, the tips of her fingers scalding his flesh with all the heat of a raging fire. "I want more."

His breath caught, then quickened. When arousal hit him like a punch to the gut, he ordered himself to remain in control. Brynne was no lusty barmaid who'd be content with a roll in the hay. She was a lady. Delicate. Pure. *Innocent.* And as the flames of passion crackled and hissed, his entire body trembled with the force it took not to press her onto her back and sate the wild hunger howling for release inside of him.

Instead, he gently wound his arm around her narrow ribcage, supporting her slight weight as he once again lowered his chin to kiss her and this time...this time, she kissed him back.

A tad clumsily, as far as kisses went.

It was obvious she'd never done this before.

But the novice press of her plump mouth against his was more enticing than anything–or anyone–he'd ever had the pleasure of experiencing.

Kissing Brynne was a softly falling mist on a spring day.

It was the first star twinkling in the sky at sunset.

It was a cozy hearth in the middle of winter.

It was coming home.

As they sank into each other, he followed the glass buttons running the length of her spine, all the way up from the small of her back to the nape of her neck where a tawny curl wrapped around his wrist.

He ran his tongue along the seam of her lips; strolled leisurely within to taste her sweet nectar when her mouth parted on a surprised gasp. She stiffened, then relaxed on a mewling sigh that went straight to his loins as he traced the sensitive outer shell of her ear with the rough pad of his thumb before sliding his fingers into her elegant coiffure.

Hair pins dropped to the blanket and her curls tumbled down over his hands in a spill of yellow satin as their kiss continued to deepen. To carry them someplace so high into the clouds he wondered if he'd ever see the ground again. But nothing could fly forever and, with great reluctance, he finally ended their embrace. It was either that or continue kissing her into the night. But as tempting a notion as that was, he'd need to return her to the manor sooner rather than later.

"Here, let me help ye," he said gruffly, scooping up whatever pins he could find hiding amidst the folds of the blanket and dropping them into her palm.

Biting her bottom lip, she averted her gaze as she fixed her coiffure, then adjusted her sleeves and bodice. Save for the rosy flush in her cheeks and the slightly dazed gleam in her eyes, no one would ever guess she'd stolen away from the party to be ravished by a Scot beside the stream.

Which was, Lachlan knew, how it needed to be.

At least for now.

Shyly, she peered up at him, and the uncertainty he saw in her eyes tugged straight at his heart. "That was my...that is to say, I've never...um..."

"Been kissed?" he asked bluntly.

Adorably, her blush intensified until her entire face was the shade of an apple ripe for the plucking. "Yes. I take it...I take it you have?"

"Dozens of times," he said, and crowed with laughter when those hazel eyes tempered with green flashed. "Are ye jealous, little songbird?"

"No," she snapped. Rising to her feet, she stepped off the blanket. "And you shouldn't laugh at my expense."

He stood as well, and put his hands on her shoulders. "I wasna laughing at ye, Bry. Not in the way ye mean. Yer innocence isna something tae be embarrassed about, and neither is me experience. I'll freely admit ye are not the first woman I've kissed, and I've done a great deal more than that."

Her nose wrinkled. "I really don't want to hear about your conquests."

"I've no plans tae share them, as intimacy is a private thing." When she would have looked away, he caught her chin on the crook of his finger and lifted it so that their gazes met. "As I said, ye are not the first. But I'd like ye tae be the last."

He could see that the importance of his words didn't strike her immediately. But when they did, the color drained from her countenance and she simply stared, unblinking, while he questioned if he was about to go down in history as the world's largest arse.

He gritted his teeth. "Say something."

"I...you...we..."

He gave her a harmless shake. "Bluidy hell. Ye're going tae kill me. Say something that's more than a syllable."

"Lachlan–"

"That's a start."

"I–"

Just then, a loud spill of raucous laughter sounded from the east lawn, and Brynne froze.

"I shouldn't be here," she said, her gaze darting as if she half-expected Lady Crowley to come springing out of the bushes. Given the dowager countess' dedication to her young charge, it wasn't a completely unfounded fear.

"I'll walk ye back," Lachlan offered, scooping up the blanket and tucking it under his arm along with the basket.

"No, I...thank you." Her smile was fleeting, and already beginning to freeze along the edges. "But it would probably be best if I went back alone. I'll say I went for a brief walk in the stables."

"Aye." Ignoring the twinge of hurt that came from the woman he loved needing to use an alibi to conceal the time she'd spent with him, Lachlan brandished his grin like a shield. "The stables. As tried and true a way tae cover up a scandalous tryst that there's ever been."

Her eyes still slightly wider than they should have been, Brynne nodded slowly, then started towards the trail that would take her back to the estate. But before she disappeared into the trees, she paused and partially turned, affording him a glimpse of her profile as a beam of dwindling sunlight filtered through the leaves to place a golden crown upon her head. "I want to be your last, Lachlan."

Then she was gone, and he was left to wonder if he'd fallen for a fairy from the woods and wilds or a real, flesh-and-blood woman.

A bit of both, he decided as he waited to follow in her footsteps, not wanting to arouse suspicion by having them both return at the same time. Spying a champagne flute that had rolled off the blanket, he went to retrieve the glass...and stopped short when something crunched beneath his heel.

It was the gift he'd brought for Brynne; he must have dropped it when he'd leaned in to kiss her. Wrapped such as it was in a piece of plain brown butcher paper, the small package had blended perfectly with the autumn grass.

There'd be no giving it now, he reflected wryly as he picked up the paper and the gift it contained. The weight of his foot had turned the barley stick to sugar dust.

Inexpensive and easily replaceable, it was no great loss.

Which didn't explain the abrupt sense of foreboding that overcame him as he folded the paper up and returned it to his pocket...or the unease that slithered between his shoulder blades as he set off for the manor.

CHAPTER TEN

Present Day
Hawkridge Manor

WITH SOME BEMUSEMENT, Lachlan shook his head to clear it of old memories and went to gather his horse.

His grandmother, a crafty old crone who'd lived to the ripe old age of ninety, had been of the Old Lore. She'd believed in selkies and sprites and kelpies as clearly as she'd believed in anything, and he'd learned all about the Ghostly Piper of Clanyard Bay, and the dragon that killed the Five Maidens of Dundee (a bloody tale that had kept him up for weeks after its telling), and the haunted ships that sailed along the sea of Solway.

He had also learned–but never fully believed–that fate pulled strings mere mortals could not see, and when a person felt a chill in a warm room, or a prickle on the nape of their neck, or (in his case) a quiver of unexplainable disquiet, it was a harbinger of things yet to come.

Which was bollocks, of course.

He made his own way, his own decisions, and fate had no say in what had passed or what was yet to come.

Breaking that barley stick hadn't sent him and Brynne on their path to ruin. They'd skipped along miserably enough all on their own.

And now it was up to them, not some higher mystical power, to fight their way back through the brambles and the brush.

A groom was waiting to take Aislyn when he returned to the stables, and he handed the mare off after feeding her the carrot he'd kept hidden in the inside of his jacket.

"See that she's given a good rub down," he instructed. "With a liniment for her legs. Menthol and calendula, if ye have it."

"We do, my lord," said the groom before he led Aislyn, happily crunching on her treat, around the back of the barn to the washing stall.

Going to a nearby trough, Lachlan removed his jacket, rolled up his shirt sleeves, and splashed cool water on his face and arms. It was hotter out than he'd anticipated, and with the temperature creeping upwards of seventy, he found himself in need of a good rub down as well.

In more ways than one.

As if his thoughts–wicked as they were–had the power to summon, Brynne appeared, walking out of the barn and into the light with her left hand slanted across her brow and her right holding the reins of a gray gelding.

To his fascination (and appreciation), she wore breeches that clung to her shapely thighs and derriere in such a way that they could have only been custom made for her tall, willowy frame. Her torso was concealed beneath a tweed coat with a high collar and stock tie, and her hair was gathered in a twist beneath a narrow hat that tilted jauntily to the side.

If Lachlan wasn't already in love, he was fairly certain he would have fallen right there. As it stood, he barely managed to keep his tongue from falling out of his mouth as he pushed away from the trough and sauntered across the freshly raked courtyard.

"Would ye look at that," he drawled, allowing his gaze to travel across every possible inch of her delectably exposed body. "As I live and breathe, Lady Brynne Campbell is wearing trousers."

Ducking her head, she glared at him beneath her horse's neck. "It's Lady Brynne *Weston*," she hissed with a quick, furtive glance behind her. "What are you doing here, Lachlan? Why are you forever turning up where you're not wanted?"

"That's the bad penny in me, I suppose." He pushed his fingers through his hair, combing the thick, unruly mane off his temple as he continued to drink in the sight of his wife in men's clothing. If this was a new fashion trend, it was one he adamantly supported, unlike the bloody crinoline.

A hooped petticoat made of whalebone or wood, a man needed a damned saw to hack through it…and then there were the half-dozen layers of undergarments to contend with. Brynne's current attire was much more practical. A few buttons, and he could have her stripped to her drawers in a matter of seconds.

If she was even wearing drawers.

Bloody hell.

Did she have *anything* on underneath those arse-hugging breeches?

When his tongue threatened to roll onto the ground, he swiped a hand across his mouth and shifted his balance in an attempt to alleviate the sudden snugness in the front of his own breeches. "I just came back from a ride. But I'd be happy tae have another go. Ye should have a companion."

She gave a small sniff. "As it so happens, I already do."

Lachlan's eyes thinned as a man, vaguely familiar with dark hair, gray eyes, and the chiseled features of an aristocrat, came out of the barn holding the reins of a large bay horse.

Make that stumbled out of the barn, he corrected when Brynne's riding companion staggered over to where she was standing and leaned heavily against his mount's shoulder.

"It's too early for physical exercise," he complained, and when Lachlan heard his voice–a deep, cultured baritone–he instantly connected his face with a name.

"Yer Grace," he greeted Sterling Nottingham, Duke of Hanover. "Good tae see ye again."

Squinting at him even though the sun had since gone behind a cloud, Sterling grinned and extended his hand. While Brynne looked on with thinly veiled displeasure, the two men engaged in a hearty shake and obligatory manly back slapping.

"Lachlan Campbell!" Sterling exclaimed once they'd broken apart. "Devil finally dragged you back to civilized country, I see. How long has it been? The last time I saw you–"

"Was here." He flicked a glance at Brynne, whose expressionless countenance was impossible to read. "For a house party."

"That's right. Now I remember." The duke scratched under his hat, a black beaver top, and gave the brim an absent tug. "Just missed another, mate. Rollicking good fun."

"Says the guest who spent the majority of the past four weeks sleeping in the parlor," Brynne put in with an arched brow. "We should begin our ride, Your Grace, if we're to return before luncheon."

"But there was something I wanted to ask Campbell. What was it…what was it…" Sterling muttered, tapping his chin with the end of his riding crop. His eyes lit up. "Now I remember! Whisky."

"Whisky," Lachlan repeated blandly even as a muscle ticked in his jaw.

Beside him, Brynne sucked in a breath.

"Indeed," said Sterling, completely oblivious to the cloud of tension that had descended onto the courtyard. "From Glenavon Distillery. You gave a bottle of it to the Earl of Hawkridge, and I'm after one for myself. Name your price."

Lachlan clearly remembered gifting Weston the bottle. A congratulatory gift for making it through Eton, and a token of the friendship they'd developed both there and during their summers spent together here, at Hawkridge Manor.

"There's no price tae name," he said, his apologetic shrug belying none of the strain that simmered right beneath the surface of his amiable façade. "I'm afraid there's none left of that vintage. The original distillery was started by me great-great-grandfather, Robert Campbell, and abandoned soon after. Only a few barrels survived, and what wasna drunk by the immediate family has since been given away."

Sterling frowned. "That's a deuced shame."

"Aye." He hesitated, gave another glance at Brynne, who was refusing to meet his eyes. He squared his shoulders. This was his dream, his lifelong aspiration, and he wasn't going to let himself feel guilty for pursuing it. Not anymore. "But if ye wouldna mind the wait, I should have a new batch come spring. It's already barreled, and while it willna taste exactly the same, I seeded and grew the barley in the same field my great-great-grandfather used."

Now Brynne looked at him. With a startled gasp, her eyes widened, and she even took a step towards him before she caught herself. "You did it, Lachlan. You really did it."

"Aye," he said, hating that there was bitterness to be had in the accomplishment. "I did."

"But that's–that's *splendid*. You must be inordinately proud." She clasped her hands together. "Congratulations. That's wonderful."

He could have let it pass.

Probably should have, given the company they were in.

But his Scot's temper was riding high, and he wasn't of the mind to rein it in.

"Congratulations, is it?" he sneered. "That's not what ye said before."

Sterling cleared his throat. "*Ahem–*"

"It was different before."

"Was it?" His head canted. "How so?"

"This is not the place for such a conversation," she said tersely.

He barked out a laugh. "Somehow it's never the place, is it? Nor the time. If ye dinna want tae admit that ye were wrong, Lady Brynne, simply say as much and be done with it."

Sterling started to edge backwards. "I'm just going to–"

"I was wrong? *I* was wrong?" She jabbed her finger at him. "I always wanted you to succeed! Always!"

Lachlan snorted. "Then ye have a damned funny way of showing it."

"Did you hear that?" Sterling asked. "A nap is calling my name." Tossing his horse's reins at Lachlan, the duke bolted out of the courtyard with such speed that little plumes of dust rose in his wake.

"Now look what you've done!" Brynne cried.

"Aye, it's forever me fault, isna it?" When the bay gelding shifted nervously at his tone, Lachlan laid a reassuring hand on the horse's withers, but his gaze remained hard as he glared at his wife. "How much better yer life would have been if I hadna dared ask ye tae marry me."

She flinched as if he'd physically struck her. "I have *never* said that."

"Some words dinna need tae be spoken aloud."

"If you've come all this way to berate me–"

"I bluidy well didna come here tae hear ye offer me congratulations after ye hoped the distillery would fail!"

"Is that what you think? That I wanted you to *fail?*"

The genuine shock in her voice gave him pause. "What else was I supposed tae think, when ye asked me tae choose between the distillery or ye?"

"*And,*" she said fiercely, her wee hands knotting into fists. "I was a new bride, with a new home, in a new country, who wanted her new husband to choose her *and* his dream. It was never one or the other, Lachlan. Not until you made it that way."

Something inside of him twisted unpleasantly tight.

Not because he didn't find truth in her admission...

But because he did.

In his eagerness to make her his bride, he'd blurred the lines between what she needed and what he desired. Shy, uncertain, and–aye– even vulnerable, she had needed solid ground beneath her feet. A stone foundation from which they could start building their life together. A life that her tutors, and governesses, and that fancy school she'd despised, had never prepared her for.

From infancy, Brynne had been raised to rule over a lavish estate with every modern convenience at her disposal and an army of servants to do her bidding. Instead, she'd found herself dropped into the middle of a castle with holes in the roof and straw in the mattresses.

He'd taken her from the lambs and tossed her in with the wolves. And even though she'd gone willingly, wolves were wolves. With sharp teeth and ragged fur and a savage nature. But instead of coddling her, of helping her adjust to her new surroundings and her new pack, he had taken to spending all of his days trying to get the distillery up and running again.

For them.

He had done it for *them*.

So that he had a means by which to provide her the opulence she was both accustomed to and deserved.

But he could see now, without the hurt and the bewildered anger that had blinded him then, that he hadn't managed his time as wisely as he should have.

That he had, in the end, forced an untenable ultimatum.

And they'd both chosen wrongly.

"Bry." Leaving the bay gelding where it stood, Lachlan approached his wife, arms spread apart and palms raised. He slowed when she shook her head. Stopped when he saw the sheen in her eyes. "Bry, I–"

"Congratulations," she repeated softly. Then tossing the reins over her horse's head and swinging herself into the saddle in one smooth motion, she gave a kick and galloped out of the courtyard.

As STERLING WATCHED Brynne tear off down the drive from the reclusive safety of the parlor, he whistled low under his breath and muttered, "Poor bloke. Better him than me."

It was clear that there was history between Brynne and Lachlan.

Even clearer that he did *not* want to be mixed up in...whatever it was.

He had enough of his own troubles to deal with, thank you very much. He didn't need to be sticking his nose into matters that didn't concern him. Especially when a volatile Scot and his best mate's sister were involved.

After a quick glance into the hallway to ensure there were no servants lingering about, he went to a cabinet in the corner of the room and removed the bottle of gin he'd stashed there before Brynne made good on her promise to lock away Weston's best liquor.

Ordinarily, he wouldn't touch the stuff. But he needed *something* to take the edge off his nerves. And since he'd been denied access to the Earl of Hawkridge's exclusive collection of port and whisky, then cheap gin smuggled in from the local village it was.

"Bloody hell," he gasped, his eyes tearing after he took a swig and the alcohol burned its way down his throat. "How do people drink this shite?"

"Did they make the tea too hot again?" a feminine voice asked. "I hate it when they do that."

"*Bollocks!*" Sterling cursed again when he nearly jumped out of his boots and almost lost his grip on the bottle in the process. What a misery *that* could have been. Catching the gin before it could fall, he cradled it against his chest like it was a newborn babe as he crossed the room to scowl at the young woman sitting in the middle of a large sofa. Its high back had hidden her from his view when he'd entered the parlor, leaving him to believe that he was completely alone. But it was apparent from the open book on her lap that the girl had been here the entire time.

"This," he said, thrusting the bottle out for her inspection, "is definitely not tea."

"No, I don't suppose it is." Carefully marking her page with a piece of blue hair ribbon, she closed the book. "Isn't it a tad early in the day to be drinking spirits?"

Sterling scowled. First she'd nearly given him an attack of the heart, and now she was judging him?

Just who did this impertinent chit think herself to be?

Gray eyes narrowing, he took a closer look while she smiled at him in an expectant manner, as if she were waiting for him to say something, but he was damned if he knew what it was.

She was pleasing enough to the eye, but there was nothing about her heart-shaped face or plain brown hair that would make her stand out in a crowd of prettier, more exotic beauties. Which probably explained why she was hiding in the parlor with her nose in a book. In Sterling's experience, wallflowers–which this woman definitely qualified as–were like furniture that no one used.

There was nothing *wrong* with the furniture, per se.

But there was a reason it was shuffled to the rear of the room to collect dust while brighter, flashier pieces were displayed out front for everyone to admire.

Tilting the gin to his mouth, he indulged in another sip and immediately regretted his decision. God, but it really was bottom of the barrel, wasn't it? Which, coincidentally enough, was exactly where he found himself. Shuddering, he set the bottle aside on a table and crossed his arms.

"Have we met?" he asked.

Her smile faded. "Yes, Your Grace. In this very room, in fact."

"Are you sure?" he said, frowning.

"You asked me to bring you a cup of coffee."

"Ah, you're a servant, then." Which explained that hideous potato sack of a dress she was wearing. The color of a sock that had gotten lost underneath the bed for the better part of a week, it was doing her complexion no favors. Or her curves, for that matter. If she even had any. The tan gown was so ill-fitting and had so many bows stitched onto it that she could have been flat as a board or hiding an elephant underneath her skirts. It was anyone's guess. "Shouldn't you be doing"–he gestured around the room–"servanty things?"

"I am not a *servant*." Her brows, a tad lighter than the mousy brown of her hair, drew in over her nose.

It was, Sterling noticed with detached interest, a very comely nose. As far as noses went, that is. Straight and delicately shaped, it was centered right above a mouth that was heavier on the top than the bottom and curved in the shape of a cupid's bow.

"Who are you then?" he asked, his frown deepening as he dragged his gaze up from her lips.

Her fingers curled around the book on her lap. "You really don't remember?"

Sterling racked his brain. Truth be told, the last few weeks were all a bit of a fog. Too much drinking, too much guilt, and not enough sleep were not a recipe conducive to a clear head and sharp memory.

"No," he admitted. "But you shouldn't take it personally."

"You...you called me a sweetheart," she said in a hushed, fluttery voice, as if she were admitting to some deep, shameful sin.

His mouth quirked. "That *does* sound like me."

"Rosemary. Miss Rosemary Stanhope." She searched his gaze. "Does that ring a bell?"

"Ah..."

Rosemary's sigh was resigned, as if people being unable to recall her name was a regular occurrence. "Evelyn and Joanna Thorncroft's cousin."

"Yes!" He snapped his fingers. "That's it. You're the cousin."

While this Miss Rosemary Stanhope only stirred the vaguest of recollections, he knew who Evie was without any prompting. He'd even tried to seduce the stunning American into being his mistress. Or his wife. Whichever she preferred. Admittedly, it hadn't been his best effort–he was foxed to the gills at the time–and she'd gently turned him down. The last he had overheard, she was engaged to Weston, the lucky sod.

Hard to believe Rosemary and Evie were related. And cousins at that. Then again, potatoes did grow in the same soil as roses.

Nothing wrong with potatoes, he thought generously as he picked up his gin and took another swig. Very sensible, productive vegetable. But no matter how hard a potato tried, it could never be a rose.

"What are you still doing here?" he asked. "I was under the impression that I was the only lingering houseguest."

"I'll be leaving soon, once my grandmother is fit for travel. She hasn't felt well these past few weeks. A flare up of her gout."

Sterling grimaced.

Bloody hell, but he didn't want to get old.

He especially didn't want to get old in a jail cell serving a life sentence for a crime he hadn't committed. But he wasn't thinking about that. Which was why he was drinking himself into oblivion every day and night, as it seemed to be the only thing that drowned out those vicious little whispers and worries in the back of his mind. Except when he lifted the bottle to take another drink, he was disappointed to find he'd already finished it off.

"Bollocks," he muttered.

Rosemary slid to the edge of her seat. "What is wrong?"

He meant to cast her a dismissive glance. Instead, he found himself staring, momentarily transfixed, as he canted his neck to the left and then the right. "Your eyes...rather unusual color, aren't they? I didn't notice before, but when the light from the window hits them just so..." Trailing off, he gave a bemused shake of his head.

"You remarked on them before. My eyes." She nibbled at her bottom lip. "You *really* don't remember?"

"It's the gin," he said a tad sheepishly as he held the bottle aloft. "Makes the mind foggy."

"Couldn't you just…not drink it?" she ventured.

"I suppose, but then I'd remember."

"Remember what?"

"Everything," he said darkly.

With that, Sterling quit the room.

CHAPTER ELEVEN

B RYNNE DIDN'T KNOW for how long she rode. When she finally made her way back to the stables, the sun was barely a glimmer in the sky and Lachlan was nowhere to be seen.

He did not make an appearance at dinner, or the next morning at breakfast.

By luncheon, she was tempted to think he'd left Hawkridge Manor altogether. Until she went to the gazebo, paint box in hand, and discovered him lounging over the railing, looking roguishly appealing in a white linen shirt and waistcoat, sans cravat, exposing the golden line of his throat and a hint of the auburn hair that dusted his muscular chest.

Ignoring the hitch of her own breath, she planted her heel in the grass and turned right back around. But before she'd gone more than two steps he called to her, and even though she hated herself for it, she was as helpless to resist the allure of that velvet brogue now as she'd been when they first met.

"Ye are as pretty as a daisy this morning. As bonny a lass as I've ever seen."

Ignoring his flattery, she placed her art supplies on a bench. "What do you want?"

"Tae have a civil discussion without ye running off tae England or galloping away on a horse." He sat down on the top step of the gazebo and patted the open space beside him. When her mouth flattened, he rolled his eyes. "We've shared a home and a bed. Surely we can sit next tae each other on a stair. I willna bite." His dimple flashed as he grinned. "Not tae hard, that is."

Wicked Scot, she thought with an uncomfortable surge of familiar affection.

"I'll be fine over here," she said primly, sweeping her skirts to the side as she sat next to her painting box which contained everything from turmeric powder to mix the deep hue of a sunset to brushes specifically carved to fit her hands and tipped with horsehair from her beloved pony, Peach, who had passed five years ago but whose spirit she felt whenever she worked on a canvas.

Peach had been a present from Weston.

The powders and pigments she used to mix her paints she'd bought herself.

And the set of brushes...the set of brushes was an engagement gift from Lachlan.

Or maybe they were a wedding present.

Things had happened with such unprecedented quickness, there'd hardly been a line distinguishing her from a fiancée to a bride. And then, just as fast, an estranged wife.

She'd worn so many crowns in such a short period time.

Was it any wonder that none had fit as she hoped they would?

"You should know that I've already sent word to my solicitor," she began. "I'll be traveling to London to meet with him in person at the end of the week."

Leaning forward, Lachlan balanced his chin on the heel of his hand. "And what is it ye're paying him for?"

"To find a rapid and relatively painless way to dissolve our marriage."

"We canna get a divorce," he said, almost smugly. "I've already had *my* solicitor look intae it, and we meet none of the standards."

"No, but we can apply to the courts for judicial separation."

As his smirk swiftly changed to a scowl, he sprang to his feet and began to pace while Brynne looked on, using every facial muscle she possessed to keep her expression from revealing the tumultuous waves of emotion that were crashing inside of her.

She knew, of course, that they'd have to eventually have this conversation.

She just hadn't expected it to be this soon…or in person. Where she could *see* the impact it had on him and feel the weight of it on her own shoulders. Pushing her down below the water where the past and the present were impossibly entwined. Down where she couldn't see the light. Down where she couldn't draw a full breath.

"What the devil does that mean?" he demanded. "Judicial separation. Sounds like a bluidy disease."

"Essentially, it is what we have been doing. But–but we'd be making it permanent." When her heart rate started to accelerate and her throat tightened, she reminded herself to breathe in through her nose and out through her mouth. When that didn't work–when it only made it worse–she staggered to her feet and turned blindly towards the house. "I…I need to lie down."

Lachlan's countenance darkened. "The hell ye do. We're going tae have this out, Bry. Right bluidy here and right bluidy now. No more excuses. No more running. We've both things we need tae say, and we're going tae say them."

"You–you don't understand," she gasped as spots danced in front of her eyes and the earth tilted beneath her feet. "I…I…"

"*Brynne!*" Lachlan's shout of alarm echoed in her ears as if from a great distance.

With a graceful spin, she started to slide bonelessly to the ground and would have collapsed in a heap of satin and crinoline if her husband hadn't been there to catch her, his strong arms sliding around her ribcage to support her against the hard, flat plane of his chest.

"Easy, little songbird," he murmured in her ear. "I've got ye."

He guided her into the gazebo and placed her in the shade, then flagged down a maid and, within minutes, a glass of cool lemonade was pressed into her trembling hands.

A few moments in the blessed quiet, a few sips of tart lemonade, and her vision began to clear, the awful pounding began to subside, the slippery taste of copper in the back of her mouth began to recede. As her internal balance was reasserted and the world righted itself, she saw that Lachlan was kneeling beside her, his hand on her knee and a line of worry etched between those thick warrior brows.

"Thank you," she said, managing a grateful, albeit weak smile.

"What happened? Are ye ill?" For an instant–just an instant–his gaze slipped to her belly and his face paled. "Are ye...?"

"No. No. I haven't...since we separated...that is to say..."

"I'm glad tae hear it. The idea of someone else touching ye...I wouldna be able tae bear it." His grip on her leg intensified, fingers curling possessively around her thigh. "Ye're *me* wife, Bry. No other man has a right tae ye but me, and I'd meet any who tried with pistols at dawn."

For some husbands–for most–such a statement would have been hyperbole. She found it hard to imagine any of her brother's friends being bothered enough by their wife's indiscretions to put down their cigar, let alone put their lives as risk. But then Lachlan had as much in common with those foppish dandies as a wild wolf did with a lazy house cat.

It was one of the reasons she'd fallen in love with him. Which also made it the cruelest of all ironies, for it was also one of the reasons she'd left.

"Have you...?" She wet her lips. Averted her gaze as a lump the size of a small boulder formed in her throat. A lump that had nothing to do with anxious mannerisms and everything to do with acknowledging the door she had left open behind her when she'd fled

Campbell Castle. A door that she'd given up any right in knowing what was on the other side of it. Still, she had to ask. "With a mistress, or–or a paramour?"

"Nay," he said solemnly.

"You–you haven't?" She hadn't thought about it very much. Hadn't *allowed* herself to think about it. But there was no part of her that had expected Lachlan to remain celibate these past eighteen months.

Hoped, yes. She'd hoped. In the way that little girls hoped to be princesses and little boys hoped to battle dragons. But he was a passionate man with a healthy appetite for carnal delights...and she hadn't expected him to forsake pleasures of the flesh to remain faithful to the woman who had left him.

As she recalled–in detail–some of those delights, her cheeks pinkened. "Not even with–"

"Nay," he interceded. "I'd never do that tae ye, Bry. Then or now. When I took my vows, I meant them. Every word. I know what ye think ye saw that day–"

"It's not what I *think* I saw. It's what I saw."

"I wish I'd known that Allison was saying things in yer ear leading up tae that moment, or that she was far more conniving than I'd ever thought her capable of being. But that doesna change the fact that when I went tae sleep that night, I was the only one in the bed. I wanted *ye* there with me. I never once asked for Allison. Never encouraged her. Never wanted tae wake up beside her as I did." Placing his hand on Brynne's other knee, he crouched between her legs, her handsome Scot, and met her gaze unflinchingly. "She was a part of my past, it's true. I willna deny it. I never have. But *ye*, Bry. Ye have always been my future."

Brynne had heard all this before. But she had never been able to listen past the roaring in her ears.

No, that wasn't right.

She hadn't *wanted* to listen.

Because in listening, she'd have to admit that finding her husband in bed with another woman wasn't *why* she had left.

It'd just given her the excuse she'd already been searching for.

"I am sorry," she whispered. Of its own accord, her arm reached out, and Lachlan closed his eyes as he pressed his rough cheek into her smooth palm. "I saw...I saw what I wanted to see, and used it as a reason to break what was already breaking. But you did not deserve to be blamed for something you never did. And for that, I apologize."

It was the most honest she had been in a long time.

With Lachlan...and more importantly, with herself.

"I love ye, Bry." His eyes opened, and the light in them was fierce. "I love ye, and I want us tae be together. Tae hell with the solicitors and the courts and the bluidy Judas scepter."

"Judicial separation."

"Aye, that." He grabbed a fistful of her skirts, knuckles pressing into the tender inside of her thighs. "Dinna ye remember how it was between us?"

Yes, she remembered.

She remembered it all.

CHAPTER TWELVE

Two Years Ago
Hawkridge Manor
The Weston's Annual House party

"LORD CAMPBELL." STRUGGLING to keep her quiet thrill of delight at seeing Lachlan contained, Brynne swept the voluminous skirts of her gown out to the side in an elegant curtsy as he approached.

The house party commenced tomorrow, which meant tonight was the grand ball when everyone turned out in their best and were given one last opportunity to rub elbows and make connections and lend an ear to all of the relevant gossip currently making the rounds before they descended upon London for the Season.

For the last three weeks Brynne had rested on pins and needles as she waited like some sort of forlorn lover for Lachlan to appear. With every day that passed and he did not arrive, her disappointment grew, creating a cloud of melancholy that followed after her wherever she went, like mists rolling out across the moor.

She'd not seen him for nearly a year, and even then only in passing. Another chance meeting in the park, but she had been in the company of a suitor whose name she no longer remembered and Lachlan had been escorting a bright-eyed woman with glossy black hair whose brogue had mimicked his own.

How jealous Brynne was!

Lachlan, too, if the murderous glare he'd cast upon Lord-Only-Talked-About-Trout-Fishing was any indication.

They'd exchanged a few words. Hardly more than a sentence. And then he was gone, taking the woman–Miss Allison Adair, a name Brynne was *not* soon to forget–along with him.

She'd been furious.

Sad, as well.

Lachlan hadn't made her any promises after their kiss by the stream. Nor had she asked him to. Because they both knew, without needing to put it into words, that they couldn't be together. That their worlds were simply too different. But that hadn't lessened the hurt of seeing him with someone else. Of realizing that he would soon go on to marry, and raise a family, and their encounters–however brief and spread out they were now–might eventually stop altogether.

Then the first letter arrived. And the second. And the third. For the remainder of the Season, she and Lachlan had corresponded on a weekly basis, pouring out all the thoughts and musings and dreams onto parchment that Society prevented them from sharing in public.

She told Lachlan that she was gathering the courage to ask her father if she could spend the next six months training at the *École des Beaux-Arts* in Paris, one of the finest art academies in the entire world.

He'd shared with her that he was attempting to rebuild his great-great-grandfather's distillery, and had even gone so far as to line up a meeting with an important investor, which was why he'd come to London...and why he'd been spending so much of his time in Scotland.

Even after he returned to Glenavon–investor's money in hand–the letters kept coming. When all was said and done, Brynne had all but worn a trench in the middle of the drive from running out every day to greet the post rider.

And now he was here.

Six feet of tall, rugged Scot standing close enough for her to reach out and touch.

When her fingers tingled, she discreetly reached behind her back and gave herself a hard pinch.

"Lady Geiringer." Politely referring to the brunette standing to her left side with whom she'd been idly conversing before she caught sight of Lachlan, she set about making proper introductions. It was either fall back upon her manners, or fall forward into Lachlan's arms. And as tempting as that was, she couldn't even begin to *imagine* the scene and the scandal it would cause. "This is...an old family friend, Lord Lachlan Campbell of Glenavon. Lord Campbell, may I introduce you to Lady Geiringer. We attended Cheltenham Ladies' College together."

Lachlan, magnificent in a black tailcoat that outlined the broad set of his shoulders and a satin vest in emerald green that brought out the gold in his eyes, slanted her an amused glance. "I was under the impression that all of yer schoolmates were self-absorbed harpies more concerned with finding a wealthy husband than learning anything of substance."

"That was exceptionally rude," Brynne chided gently as Lady Geiringer gave a huff and walked away. Although she couldn't deny his statement held merit. For while they maintained the appearance of civility, it wasn't so long ago that Brynne had sat in the library at Cheltenham Ladies' College, hiding her red face in the pages of a book, while Lady Geiringer and her gaggle of...well, harpies *was* as good a word as any...snickered and sneered and pointed from the doorway.

"Social misfit" was the term they'd used to describe the awkward, shyly withdrawn daughter of the Marquess of Dorchester. Among other, less kind monikers. Brynne had *tried* to fit in. But while Weston had met some of his best mates while away at academy, including

Lachlan, she found herself floundering in a pool of more worldly, more experienced girls who hadn't spent the better part of their young lives sequestered away in the country.

It was all water under the bridge at this point. If nothing else, her time at Cheltenham Ladies' College had taught her the value of appearance. How apt High Society was to turn an icy shoulder if you didn't meet their expectations...and what it felt like to be left out in the cold while everyone else celebrated in the warmth.

As that terrible sinking sensation in the pit of her stomach as her peers laughed at her behind her back wasn't a feeling she cared to replicate ever again, Brynne had taken great pains to mold herself into someone who was never left out of anything.

Instead of being awkward and shy, she was renowned for her elegance and charm. Instead of being an easy target for mockery and malice, she was considered to be one of the *ton's* premiere hostesses. Women wanted to be her. Men wanted to marry her. And if she constantly worried about falling off the tightrope of perfunctory perfection that she'd made for herself, it was a small price to pay for the adoration and acceptance heaped upon her.

The two things her father's money could not purchase...and he was incapable of giving freely.

"She is not going to talk to me for the rest of the evening," Brynne predicted as she watched Lady Geiringer weave her way through the crowd, disgruntled steam all but pouring out of her ears.

"Aye." Candlelight gleamed in Lachlan's hair as he leaned closer, turning the barely tamed mane from auburn to a burnished copper that her hands itched to sink into. "But it worked, didna it?"

"What...what were you hoping to achieve?" She gasped as he angled his body to shield her from prying eyes while he ran the tip of his finger up the length of her arm, lingering on the inside of her elbow where her pulse fluttered with the speed of a butterfly's wing. "And where have you been? I expected you weeks ago."

"There was a setback with the distillery. And I sent Lady Geiringer along so that I could have ye all tae meself. I'm a greedy man, Lady Brynne, and I dinna like tae share yer attention." He slowly trailed his knuckles along the rounded edge of her shoulder, and her entire body quivered when his gloveless hand met the exposed skin above the lace-trimmed bodice of her gown. "How is it ye are more beautiful every time I see ye?" he said huskily.

"I...I..." How was it, she wondered dazedly, that some of England's most renowned rogues had tried–and failed–to seduce her with flattery and flirtation, yet all it took was a single touch from Lachlan and her knees turned to jelly?

"Dance with me," he said, his mouth a hairsbreadth from her ear.

"I've promised my next dance to Lord–"

Under the guise of sharing an intimate secret, he nipped her earlobe with his teeth, then soothed the bite with his tongue. "Dance with me."

"All right," she said helplessly, and his eyes held a glint of possessive triumph as he led her to the middle of the ballroom floor where painted wooden tiles had been set up in a large rectangle to accommodate the couples spinning past in a myriad of colorful silks and satin.

Brynne and Lachlan hadn't waltzed together for four years; not since Grotonborough House. But despite all of that time gone by–or perhaps because of it–they moved together in perfect unison, anticipating each other's movements as if they were of the same mind.

When the pointed heel of her shoe caught on the hem of her dress, he was there to steady her before she ever had the chance to stumble. When he would have inadvertently backed into the Earl of Chadwick, she guided him out of the way with the slightest pressure of her fingertips on his bicep.

Either by accident or design–she wasn't sure which–they gradually moved to the center of the room, and beneath a grand chandelier sparkling with the light of a hundred crystals, they spun and twirled through the complicated steps of the Viennese waltz as if they'd wings beneath their feet.

After the dance was over, the entire room, from the main floor to the marble steps to the outdoor terrace, broke into spontaneous applause, and it took Brynne a moment to realize what the object of their praise was.

"They're clapping for you," she said softly.

"No, little bird," he replied as he bowed in front of her and then took her hand to kiss the back of it. "They're clapping for *us*."

So they were, and that knowledge brought a pleased bloom of pink to her already flushed cheeks. "Would you care for something to drink?" she asked. At his nod, she nabbed two flutes of champagne off the tray of a servant and then led Lachlan to a quiet corner filled with empty chairs where they would be able to speak in relative privacy while remaining in full view of the other guests.

As she stared into the frothy gold bubbles rising up from the bottom of her glass, it was impossible not to recall the last time they'd shared champagne...and what had followed its consumption.

Her one and only kiss.

Sweet, magical, momentous.

Everything that a girl could ever hope for.

With a man that a woman could only dream about.

"Ten years," said Lachlan.

Lifting her gaze to his, she blinked in confusion. "What?"

"Ten years ago ye made me a promise, Lady Brynne Weston." His eyes glittered, two comets racing across a sky cloaked in ebony. "We Scots take our oaths very seriously, and I've come tae collect me prize."

She didn't have to ask to what promise he was referring to; she still remembered as if it had happened yesterday.

"In ten years, if ye havena married some wealthy bounder, we'll meet back here, at this very spot. And we'll marry each other."

She raised the flute to her lips and took a lingering sip as she attempted to gauge the level of his sobriety over the rim. He certainly *looked* serious. But surely he was jesting. Having a bit of fun to lighten the mood. "Very amusing, Lord Campbell. Have you any strawberry drops handy?"

While the edges of his mouth softened, his gaze remained solemn. "I thought lime fruit was yer favorite."

"So it is." She waited for a crack to appear in all that somberness. When none did, she finished off her champagne and, although she rarely drank more than a glass at a time, and then strictly on special occasions, desperately wished she had an entire bottle handy. Maybe then she'd be prepared for the discussion it appeared they were about to have.

A discussion that she feared was only going to end in one way.

With hurt feelings...and bruised hearts.

"Lachlan, I...I know what I agreed to. But I was a girl. Hardly more than a child." She gave a laugh that he did not return. "Surely you cannot mean to hold me to an agreement I made when I was fourteen. Besides, it hasn't been a full ten years. Not yet."

"Have ye plans tae marry in the next few months?" he asked.

"No, but–"

"Then it's close enough."

Arrogant Scot she thought with no small amount of affection.

"Why *havena* ye married?" He arched a russet brow. "I've not spent much time in London, it's true. But I've been there enough tae know that ye're as prized a diamond as ever there was. Yet ye have turned down countless proposals. Tae dukes, and earls, and viscounts. Even tae a prince, if the rumors are tae be believed."

"They are," she said reluctantly. "But he wasn't *really* a prince. Just in line for the throne."

"Just in line for the throne." Lachlan's second brow rose to join the first as an incredulous smile played across his lips. "Do ye even hear yerself, little bird? Ye could have had a bluidy *prince*. But ye turned him down. Why?"

"He...he was too old. Nearly five years my senior."

"Nearly one foot in the grave, then." He grasped her wrist. Rubbed his thumb across the bluish green veins that ran like ribbons beneath her skin. "Why, Bry? Why havena ye taken a husband in all these years? Ye have had every opportunity."

"Maybe I am still waiting."

"For what?"

Turning her head to the side, she pinned her gaze on the outdoor terrace where a small collection of gentlemen had gathered to smoke cigars, her brother among them. The embers glowed in the darkness, small circles of orange fire. "How is Miss Adair? You've not mentioned her in your letters."

"Are ye asking me if I am involved with another woman?"

Her eyes cut back to his. "And if I am?"

"Then I'd tell ye that while Allison and I remain friends, we ended our affair months ago. Shortly after I saw ye in the park, in fact."

"Why?"

"Ye already know the answer."

"If I knew the answer, I wouldn't be asking the question."

His mouth curved. "Aye and ye would make a fine interrogator, Lady Brynne Weston."

She tugged her wrist free. "I am not trying to interrogate you."

"I found pleasure in Allison's company, 'tis true. I willna deny it, or apologize for it, as we were two consenting adults who knew what the other was after. For me, it was a means by which tae pass the time while I waited."

"What were you waiting for?"

"Ye, Bry." As he met her gaze, his eyes shone as brightly as the cigars. "I was always waiting for ye. Just like ye have always been waiting for me, or else ye would have married that prince."

She was unable to deny it.

Not without lying.

And that…that she couldn't do. Not to Lachlan, who often seemed to know her better than she knew herself.

"When he asked me to marry him…" When she hesitated, her heart gave a wild *thump* against her ribs, as if it were a feral thing trying to break down the walls of its cage. "When he asked me to marry him, the first thing I thought of was you."

"I canna promise ye the world, Bry. Or a fancy estate high on a hill." He turned into her. Gently took her hands in his. Squeezed her fingers. "But I can promise that I'll never put ye on a shelf. I'll never take ye for granted. And I'll love ye every single day for the rest of our lives on earth and in heaven. Marry me, little bird. Marry me, and give us what we've both been waiting for all these years."

Brynne had long last track of the number of proposals she'd received. It was not a statement bred of arrogance, but rather resigned truth. Ever since her debut, she had found herself inundated with them, some more memorable than others.

The Duke of Tremblay had filled the entire parlor with roses. Their overwhelming scent—and the sight of the duke, a man twenty years her senior, down on bended knee—had sent her running for the nearest chamber pot.

Once she had chased a baby tiger—a *tiger*—through the halls after the Earl of Sutton had presented it to her with a ring tied round the animal's neck and it had promptly bitten him on the arm.

She'd felt more sympathy for the tiger.

The Marquess of Rutherford had paraded a troupe of somersaulting acrobats in front of her.

The Duke of Sommersby had lit the sky with fireworks and then attempted to get her into a gas balloon to view them from above. It was most fortunate that she had declined his offer, as a flying spark had caught on the silk canopy and promptly burned the balloon to the ground before takeoff.

Now Lachlan was asking her to marry him. Without flowers, or animals, or flying deathtraps. Without even a ring. Yet the simplicity of his proposal was more heartfelt, and more genuine, than any she had ever received.

"Lachlan, I–"

"*There* you are!" As if on some terribly ill-timed cue, Lady Theresa Hillbrook–as renowned for her outlandish taste in fashion as she was for her shrill voice–toddled towards them, the train of her orange gown adorned with bright pink bows billowing in her wake. "I've been looking *everywhere*." Breathless and beaming, she blinked curiously at Lachlan. "Who might this fine gentleman be? Goodness but you're tall, aren't you? And so broad-shouldered. It's a wonder you fit through the door."

Having instinctively snatched her hands from Lachlan's grasp at the first sound of Theresa's war cry, Brynne stepped discreetly to the side in order to put the appropriate amount of distance between them. She could all but *feel* his displeasure, but what else was she to do? Announce to the entire ballroom that he'd just proposed and she had…what? Not yet accepted, but also not declined.

Sequestering her upheaval of emotions behind a pleasantly empty smile, she proceeded with introductions. "Lady Theresa, may I present Lord Campbell. An old–"

"Family friend. Aye, so ye keep saying," he cut in, and were glares possible of doing such things, Brynne feared she would have found herself turned to stone on the spot. He had never looked at her like that before, and it was a struggle not to wither beneath his obvious contempt of what he conceived as cowardice.

Easy for him, she thought with a nudge of resentment. What did he have to lose if they were to become engaged? Nothing. Absolutely nothing. While she ran the very real risk of angering her entire family, from her grandfather all the way to her brother. Not to mention the fallout that would occur with the *ton*. One of their own breaking ranks to marry a Scot who had never made any effort to shield his disdain of High Society?

They'd tear her to shreds.

But did any of that really matter, if she loved him and he loved her?

Marrying Lachlan would take her away from everything she'd ever known, but it would also provide her with things she'd never had.

How was one to even *begin* to calculate such an equation?

"Lord Campbell, Lord Campbell…" Retrieving a fan from between her ample bosom, Theresa snapped it open and waved it in front of her face while ogling Lachlan over the top of it. "Of the Mayfair Campbells?"

"Lord Campbell and his family herald from Northern Scotland," Brynne explained when it became clear from his stony silence that Lachlan wasn't going to bother to answer. "The village of Glenavon."

"Oh," she trilled. "How *exotic*. But where is your kilt?"

"Should I drop me trousers and let ye have a peek?" he said with a dangerous sort of pleasantness that sailed straight over Theresa's head.

"I am sure that won't be necessary," Brynne interceded hastily even as Theresa made a noise caught somewhere between a purr and the sound of a cat hacking up a hairball. "Besides, Lord Campbell was just expressing his farewells. Weren't you, my lord?"

"Aye," he said coolly. "That I was. I'll be making a stop at the town square tomorrow at noon, and then I'm back tae the faraway land of the Scots. Did ye hear, Lady Theresa, that in a few years' time we might even have the telegraph in Edinburgh? That is, if we ever get steam engines tae pull the lines and the poles we'd need for such a modern invention."

"You haven't trains or the telegraph?" she said in dismay.

"Nay," he said solemnly. "Just lots of sheep."

Brynne's eyes threatened to disappear into the back of her skull. "He has trains and telegraphs." She pointed her finger at Lachlan. "You have trains and telegraphs. The steam engine was *invented* by a Scottish engineer. Without it, Europe wouldn't have had an industrial revolution!"

His smile was razor-sharp. "Aye, but how will the English continue tae think so highly of themselves if they've no one tae step on?"

With that, he walked away, leaving Brynne staring after him with a mixture of exasperation and amusement. Lachlan may have grown up, but so much of the boy he'd been still remained. The boy who had taken on bullies and dared the wrath of an overbearing governess and showed a young girl the stars. The boy who had made no apologies for where he came from or where he intended to go.

"Scotland is a proud country, Lady Theresa." While Brynne knew that the other woman had meant no harm with her careless ignorance of Lachlan's homeland, that didn't mean it hadn't stung. Especially since Brynne was certain that hadn't been the first time Lachlan had encountered such a sentiment. "They've many agricultural and scientific advancements far beyond our own. It's much more than just kilts and claymores."

Theresa snapped her fan closed and tucked it under her arm. "Is he married?"

"Lord Campbell? No, he does not have a wife." Brynne's eyes narrowed in suspicion and a spark of jealousy. Which was absurd. Lachlan would no sooner marry Lady Theresa than he would spread his wings and attempt to take flight. But a dog with a bone was naturally protective. Particularly when that bone was six feet of delectable, roguishly handsome Highlander. "Why do you ask?"

"No reason," Theresa shrugged. "My parents would never allow it, of course. Such a misfortune that the gentlemen who are easiest to look at almost always have something wrong with them."

"There is nothing *wrong* with Lord Campbell."

"I didn't mean to imply that there was. Just that, being who is he, Lord Campbell isn't exactly marriageable material, is he?" She clucked her tongue sadly. "A blessed shame, given how he fills out those trousers. I really would like to see him in a kilt."

"James Watt," Brynne said succinctly.

Theresa peered across the room. "Who is that? Is he titled?"

"James Watt was the man who improved upon the first steam engine. He was a Scottish inventor, instrument maker, and chemist. His design adaption enabled the steam engine to produce power at maximum capacity. Without it, our entire railway system would be all but nonexistent."

"How fascinating," Theresa said in the absent tone of someone who didn't find it fascinating at all. "Oh, there's Lady Wellesley! I must speak with her about her new modiste. Parisian, you understand. Won't you excuse me?"

"With pleasure," Brynne muttered under her breath.

As brooding in the corner of the ballroom wasn't behavior fitting of a hostess, she went outside, using a door that circumvented the terrace and instead brought her out to the side lawn where she went through a grove of silver birch trees before reaching a path made from thin slabs of hand cut granite set on white pebbles.

When she and Weston were children, they'd often come here, to what they called the Stone Garden. So-named for the statue of their mother that resided in the center, it was a maze of stepping stones and boxwoods and hedges that towered far above her head.

The manor loomed in her wake, a beacon in the night that was visible for miles around. But in the stone garden, shadows prowled and darkness reigned. What did it say about her, Brynne wondered, that she felt more comfortable out here, alone, than surrounded by three dozen of her closest friends?

In the dim and the dark, she didn't have to wear a smile as if it were a glittering necklace. Something to be shown off and admired, even as the stones remained hard to the touch. She didn't have to pretend to be someone she wasn't. Unfortunately, the problem with that was she'd spent all of her life being molded by other people into what *they* wanted her to be that she didn't have a clear picture in her head of who she was.

Was she a future duchess, set to preside over the *ton* as an example for aspiring debutantes of what could happen if you minded your manners, followed all of the rules, and never challenged the status quo? Her perfect reputation maintained, but her heart left barren.

Was she a runaway bride who eloped to Scotland, leaving everything and everyone behind, because she'd made a vow a decade earlier over barley sticks and strawberry drops? Her name besmirched, but her heart content.

Or was she someone else entirely? Someone she'd yet to have the opportunity to meet.

An owl cried out as she stepped nimbly from one granite slab to the next, its eerie call causing the hairs at the nape of her neck to lift. Raising her skirts past her knees to keep the fabric from tearing on a rose bush's sharp thorns, she went straight to the middle of the labyrinth where a bench sat in a swath of moonlight beside the marble statue of her mother.

People who had known the late Marchioness of Dorchester often remarked that Brynne, with her blonde hair and hazel eyes, was her living image. An observation that helped and hurt all at the same time, for it was something that she would have liked to have seen for herself. Instead, she was forced to rely upon this statue, and the painting above the mantel in the library, and the recollections of others.

They said that children needed their mother the most, and that was unequivocally true. But to Brynne's way of thinking, a mother was not something you outgrew as you got older, like a shoe or a dress. No, a mother was meant to be there far past childhood. To mentor, and nurture, and lend a listening ear in times of trouble.

They also said you couldn't miss what you never had, but she believed that to be falsehood as well. For as she sat on the bench and gazed up at the face of the woman who had brought her into the world before leaving it far too soon, Brynne felt the ache of loss as keenly as if she'd known her mother for her entire life. And she wished, desperately, that she had the ability to heed her counsel.

The crack of a stick, the scrape of a boot heel on stone, and Brynne knew she was no longer alone. Letting her skirts fall to her ankles, she rose from the bench and fixed her gaze on a large shadow moving straight towards her with a lithe, prowling grace.

"I knew you'd come."

CHAPTER THIRTEEN

IF BRYNNE HAD been beautiful in the ballroom, she was stunning in the night. With moonlight in her hair and mist pooling at her feet, she really did resemble a fairy princess. And while he was more dragon than prince, Lachlan still intended to make her his bride.

He wanted her–*had* wanted her, all these years past–with a fierceness that occasionally set him back onto his heels. The breadth of it, and the enormity, was unlike anything he'd ever experienced before. Which was fitting, as Brynne was unlike anyone he'd ever met before.

While their interactions had been painfully brief and stuttered, the impact of them was no less than if he would have spent every day in her company. Of this, he was certain.

Killed off long ago for their pelts and threat to livestock, wolves hadn't roamed the Highlands for centuries. But when they did, it was rumored that the wild creatures–savage to both man and beast–mated for life. Some met their partner early, others later. But when a male chose his female, they said there was nothing that could separate them aside from eternal slumber. Even then, the one left behind never took another mate for as long as it lived. Such was the strength of their allegiance. Their dedication. Their devotion.

Brynne was Lachlan's she-wolf.

And he'd loved her since he was sixteen.

That was not to say he hadn't let his head be turned by a pretty face or two in the nearly ten years between then and now. He was a Scot, not a saint. But no matter who he'd used to sate his physical urges, his thoughts had never strayed far from a girl with golden hair and an angel's face.

Finally, the day had arrived to claim the prize he'd waited almost a decade for. A prize he'd done his best to earn by sinking countless hours, money, and resources into a business venture that he hoped would give Brynne the life and the material possessions she was accustomed to. That she deserved. For the loneliness she'd endured. For the way she'd been dressed up and pranced about as if she were a show pony on display. For the pain she was hiding behind a vacant smile that no one ever seemed to notice except for him.

"I knew you'd come," she said simply as she rose from the bench in a waterfall of pale blue satin. Her hair was swept off her temple in a crown of curls adorned with sapphire combs. A loose tendril had escaped and dangled on her shoulder, drawing attention to the creamy sea of flesh revealed above the daringly low cut of her bodice. The gown fit her long-limbed frame to perfection, with nary a stitch that needed to be taken or given. While other women at the ball sought to bring attention to themselves with ornate bows and oversized bustles, this dress, while somewhat plain in design, allowed Brynne's natural beauty to take center stage. And oh, how she glowed.

His abdominal muscles clenching as desire rippled across his skin like the cool waft of a breeze on a hot summer day, he stopped and looked at the statue of a woman standing upon a marble pedestal who bore a striking resemblance to the one standing beside it.

"Yer mother?" he asked.

"Yes. My father had this built in her honor." Brynne's fingertips glided across the edge of the pedestal. "I like to come here when I've something important to think about. It's foolish, but there's a part of me that believes she can hear me when I sit next to her statue."

"Not foolish," he said. "There's a cliff not far from Campbell Castle where the waves wash shells upon the shore. I go there tae gather the shells for the wee ones, and every time I set foot on that beach, I swear I feel the warmth of me mum's smile on the back of me neck. She passed after birthing me, as yers did."

Brynne's lips parted. "You never told me that. I'm sorry, Lachlan. I…I assumed she was alive. I should have asked."

He rolled her sympathy away with a shrug. "It's not a pleasant thing tae have in common."

"No, it's not. But I am still sorry. Will you…will you sit with me?" She gestured at the bench. "We can speak freely here."

"Aye." Wood creaked as he settled his rangy frame, then canted his head. "Are ye going tae join me?"

"Yes. I…I am." But she remained standing, the whites of her knuckles gleaming bone white as she laced her fingers together. "But I want to say something first."

Although his throat tightened and his palms dampened with sweat, he masked his apprehension with a brusque nod. "Go ahead, then."

"You were right."

His teeth flashed in a grin. "Always something I like tae here. About what, exactly?"

"The marriage proposals. I turned them down…I turned them down because they weren't you. Oh, at the time, I gave myself an endless litany of reasonable excuses. Too old, too young. Too this, too that. But the truth is that their only fault was they were not Lachlan Campbell."

Was it possible for a heart to grow?

If so, his had just expanded two sizes.

"Come here," he said gruffly, and this time she sat beside him, her voluminous skirt nearly taking up the entire bench. He reached for her hand and when she gave it, all it took was a slight tug to have her nestled into the crook of his arm. "I'll make ye so happy, Bry. I swear it. Anything ye want, and I'll find a way tae make it yers."

"I...I have not agreed to marry you, Lachlan."

He stiffened, and she lifted her head, hazel eyes wide and wary.

"I wish to," she said before he could speak. "I want to. But there's so much we haven't discussed. So many questions that I still have."

"Like?" he said, his brows gathering as he struggled to temper his annoyance. Having waited this long, he was loath to waste another second. But he also recognized that while his personality had always directed him to leap before he looked (the distillery being case in point), Brynne's descent was much more cautious and careful.

"Like where would we be married?" she asked.

"Aye, and that's easy enough tae answer. Gretna Green."

She nodded slowly, as if that had been the answer she'd been expecting. "Where would we live?"

"Campbell Castle, tae start. The lands hold the distillery, and with neither me father nor eldest brother taking an interest in the grounds or the keep itself, I've become the unofficial laird." His mouth twisted. "More or less."

It would have been an excellent time to add that in addition to the castle and the thousand acres surrounding it, he'd also taken over the care of Callum and Blaine, with the twins likely to join any day. But if Brynne was already wavering at having him as she thought he was, what would she do if she learned the full truth of what she was marrying into?

Run, he answered grimly. If she'd any sense in that pretty head–which she did, his Bry was as sharp as a whip–then she'd run for London and the *ton* as fast as those delightful calves could carry her.

His plan was to introduce her to the reality of it in pieces. He already had three nannies waiting in the wings to swoop in and care for his brothers when he returned. There wasn't the money to pay for them to stay longer than a month, but surely Brynne would be used to the children by then and her kind, caring heart would be able to look past their grubby cheeks and feral antics to the sweet cherubs underneath all of the grime and mischievousness.

Then there was the castle itself, which a stern wind had a good chance of knocking over. But he'd taken care of that as well. In so much as he'd started renovations on the master suite...and only the master suite. Given that he had no plans for them to leave their bedchamber for the first half-year of their marriage, Brynne would hardly have cause to notice the holes in the roof or the walls being supported with wood and prayers.

It'd be fine, he told himself. First, he just had to get her willingly to Scotland. After that, everything would fall into place.

Or the castle would simply fall down.

Either way, they'd have each other.

He lifted her hand. Kissed the back of it where her skin was smooth and slightly chilled. "Do ye trust me, Brynne Weston?"

A short hesitation, and then...

"Yes. Yes, I trust you Lachlan. But–"

"Then what else is there tae discuss? I've already arranged travel. A carriage that will take us straight across the border, and lodging in Gretna Green. Ye *are* of the age tae marry here, in England, if ye'd like. Ye dinna need anyone's permission."

"No," she said hastily. "If we are to do this, I–I would rather elope."

Lachlan nodded. It didn't make a damned bit of difference to him where they were married, as long as he was able to call her his wife when it was all said and done. A cathedral in London or a blacksmith shop in Scotland. What did it matter? The location wasn't important; the woman was.

"Then there's only one thing left tae do." He settled his hands around her waist. God, but she was a tiny little thing. Delicate and fragile in some places, hard and determined in others. He was very much looking forward to exploring every luscious curve, every slim line. Her body was a banquet of hidden delights that he wanted to feast upon. But for now, for this night, he'd settle for a slight taste of the heaven that was to come.

"What—what's that?" she said, her voice caught somewhere between a gasp and a whimper when he trailed his fingers up her ribcage and stopped just shy of her breasts. Lifted by the heavy boning of her corset, they were but begging to be caressed. The flesh firm and plump. The nipples, already budding, barely concealed beneath a thin layer of satin.

"Practice our wedding kiss," he rasped before he bent his head and captured the sweet silk of her lips with his own.

Almost immediately, the kiss burned hotter than the one before it.

That kiss was gentle, innocent, gradual. And while there had been fire—there had *always* been fire—it had smoldered low and steady, like coals left behind to keep the hearth warm until morning.

But this kiss...this kiss *roared*. And crackled, and set off a wave of such intense heat that they were both singed by the flames.

A humming sound vibrated in Brynne's throat as she opened her mouth and his tongue slid inside. She tasted of champagne and something a tad more decadent. Chocolate, perhaps. Or a rich, velvety cake.

He angled his head, kissed her jaw, then lightly took her earlobe and suckled as her fingers threaded into his hair and pulled. On a growl, he traced a fiery path down the slender column of her neck, following the edge of her collarbone out to her shoulder where he pulled at the top of her bodice with his teeth.

More flames, more heat, as her gorgeous breasts, dusky nipples bathed in moonlight, spilled into his waiting hands.

Her eyes, closed until now, fluttered open and filled with shock, then flooded with desire as he lavished his complete, undivided attention upon the sensitive ivory globes. First with his fingers...and then with his mouth as her head lolled back and a mewling cry of pleasure escaped from her lips.

Fascinated by a freckle on the underside of her breast, he nuzzled the tiny imperfection. She raked her nails across his shoulders, digging them into muscle and sinew as he drew her nipple between his teeth and rolled his tongue around it. Another whimper, the tiniest, instinctive lift of her hips, and it was all Lachlan could do not to lift his face to the sky and howl at the moon.

He would have taken her then and there. He wanted to.

Bloody hell, did he want to.

His entire body was filled with need.

His cock was throbbing with it.

But he wasn't about to let Brynne's first experience with lovemaking occur on a bench in the dark with her skirts rucked up around her waist.

Reluctantly, he raised his head and kissed her, one last time. A kiss to tide him over until tomorrow, where there was ample room in the carriage to see if she had freckles hiding anywhere else.

He helped her lift and straighten her bodice. Secured a button that had come loose between her shoulder blades. Held a sapphire comb in his hand as she repaired her coiffure.

"Thank you," she murmured, adorably shy when he returned it to her. "Do I look all right?"

His eyes glinted. "If ye're asking if ye look like ye were just thoroughly ravished, the answer is aye. But I'm the only one tae know, and ye can blame that pink in yer cheeks on a second glass of champagne. Would ye like me tae escort ye back?"

"I know the way, thank you. And…it would probably be best if I went alone."

Although he nodded in agreement, he was ready for the day when he was able to walk into a room with Brynne next to him, to hell with anyone who didn't think an English rose belonged on the arm of a Scottish briar.

"I'll see ye tomorrow, then. At noon in the village square."

"Lachlan…" When her gaze dropped to the ground, his blood ran cold.

"Bry–"

"I'm not saying no," she interrupted. "Or that I refuse your proposal, or that I don't want to marry you. It's just…once I do this, once I leave, there won't be an easy way back for me. I need time to think it over."

For Lachlan, there was no question. No doubt. His heart, his soul, his life–they belonged to Brynne. He'd walk through hell to stand by her side, and the pain of knowing that she wasn't certain if she was ready to stand by his was sharp and swift, like the slice of blade.

How much more did he have to give? What else could he say to convince her? That he was enough. That *they* were enough. That she didn't need the trappings of a society that would rather see her caged than open her wings and fly.

"Tomorrow," he said flatly. "Noon."

"Lachlan–"

But he was already walking away.

NO SOONER HAD Brynne returned to the ballroom than she found herself besieged by Lady Crowley, almost as if the dowager countess had been lying in wait.

At the age of three and twenty, she no longer required a formal chaperone at events such as these, but the dowager countess remained both a friend and a wise confidante. Which was why, the instant Lady Crowley's sharp blue gaze met hers, Brynne knew what she was going to say before she said it.

"I noticed a specific guest was in attendance tonight," the dowager countess said archly. "I was of the mind that we'd seen the last of Lord Campbell."

"What gave you that impression?" Stepping out of the way of a servant carrying a tray overflowing with an assortment of empty plates and glasses, she linked her hands together behind her back and adopted an expression of bland indifference. This was not a conversation she wanted to have. Not when her nerve endings continued to hum from Lachlan's passionate kisses and her heart felt as if it were being torn in half. Unfortunately, Lady Crowley was not easily dissuaded, or set aside.

"A vain hope, I suppose." The dowager countess was quiet for a moment. "I may be old, but I am not blind. I see the...*appeal* of such a suitor. But he is not for you, Lady Brynne. He never was, and he never will be."

As Lady Crowley's thoughts echoed her own doubts, Brynne found it difficult to disagree. Guilt gnawed at her, as if she were betraying Lachlan in some way by not jumping into his arms and running away with him into the sunset. But if she did that without giving herself time to come to a decision on her own, then she'd be betraying herself.

Still, she wasn't about to let anyone denigrate the man she loved.

Not even Lady Crowley.

"He understands me better than anyone else ever has," she said, lifting her chin.

"He will never inherit a meaningful title, or an estate. Should you marry him, you would be required to rely upon *earned* wealth." Wrinkling her nose as if a particularly bad odor had just wafted in from the kitchens, Lady Crowley leaned heavily on the silver-tipped cane she'd taken to using after a fall down a slick step last winter. "Not to mention that your father would surely disapprove of such a match."

"Given what little interest he has shown in my pursuits thus far, I sincerely doubt he would be bothered to notice." Here, Brynne's voice cooled. Only a fraction, but in addition to her sight, the dowager countess possessed excellent hearing.

"The Marquess of Dorchester has provided you and your brother with everything you could have ever asked for."

Except for love, Brynne added silently. *Affection. Acknowledgement.*

Weston had responded to their father's lack of attention by putting up an icy shield. As a man, her brother had the luxury of choosing to isolate himself without suffering repercussions. He could be hard without being thought of as mean. He could be arrogant without being considered overbearing. He could be callous without being accused of being cruel.

But as a woman, especially a woman in High Society whose reputation was constantly being scrutinized, Brynne's choices were far more limited. Her actions were much more harshly judged. Which was why she'd taken to wearing a smile on the surface, and shivering with cold where no one could see.

Except for Lachlan.

"Our father has been exceedingly generous," she acknowledged. "But I am not a girl anymore, in need of governesses and pretty dresses."

Lady Crowley's mouth thinned. "No, you are a woman rapidly approaching spinsterhood in need of a good husband."

"Lord Campbell is a good man," she said defensively.

"That may be true. But is he—will he—be a good *husband*? That is the question you need to ask yourself. Why, your children wouldn't even be *titled*." By the horrified inflection in the dowager countess' tone, she might as well have said Lachlan and Brynne's future offspring would be thrown to the wolves upon birth. "Where would you live? To the best of my knowledge, Lord Campbell does not have a permanent residence in London. Or even England, for that matter. How would you maintain your social standing?"

As Brynne felt her breathing begin to accelerate, she closed her eyes and counted to three. "Perhaps I wouldn't. Perhaps I'd leave Society altogether. To be a wife to a man that loves me, and a mother to children who, while not titled, shall be adored beyond measure every day of their lives." Her eyes opened. "Surely there are worse things than that."

"If you marry Lord Campbell then all of your training and tutelage will have been wasted," Lady Crowley said flatly. "Along with all of the sacrifices that your father has made. You must–"

"*He* has made?" Brynne had never–not once–interrupted Lady Crowley before, but she refused to let such a bold–and verifiably false–statement stand. "My father has had as much to do with my upbringing as Queen Victoria."

"Your father has been through more hardship than you know."

She threw out her arms in a rare display of uncontrolled emotion. "Because he won't *tell* me! I barely see him, let alone speak with him about personal matters."

"It is not a parent's job to burden their child with their personal heartache."

"I know that my parents were separated sooner than they could have ever anticipated, but I am not under any illusion that it was a love match."

"I was not referring to the late marchioness," Lady Crowley said evenly.

That took Brynne aback. "You're...you're not? But–"

"There was someone else, after your mother. A young woman your father loved dearly."

Brynne was stunned. Her father, the epitome of frigid reserve, in *love*? It was all but impossible to fathom.

"Who was she? What happened? Where is she now?"

"That is not my story to share." Lady Crowley tapped her cane on the floor. "I wouldn't even say this much, but I feel it is my duty to impart whatever knowledge I can to prevent you from repeating past family mistakes. Your mother and father were an excellent match. One of the best the *ton* has ever had the fortune to witness. Because your father had the good sense to follow his *head* instead of his heart. Had the marchioness lived, I am certain they would hold the most

SEDUCED BY THE SCOT

celebrated positions in High Society to this day.

"By the contrary, the woman whom the marquess fancied himself in love with after your mother died was wrong from the start. Had he married her, they'd have risked alienation that would have also affected you, and your brother."

"If he loved her, why *didn't* he marry her?"

"I've no doubt he would have, if given the opportunity. Thankfully, she had the common sense to return to where she'd come from, and aside from a small scandal, no permanent damage was sustained."

"No permanent damage," Brynne said quietly.

Except that the Marquess of Dorchester was all but a ghost, preferring to spend his time in his remote hunting cabin or traveling across Europe or setting sail for weeks at a time. Anything other than remaining in England where he'd be forced to interact with his children.

Was this woman–the one who he had loved and then lost–the reason for his absence? Surely the two were somehow connected. At the very least, it helped shed some light on his prevailing bitterness that she could always sense, even as a child, but could never quite pinpoint the cause of.

"Lachlan would never leave me." She squared her shoulders. "It wouldn't be the same."

"I should hope not, or else what would you do? Trapped in a foreign country, isolated from your family and friends. Shunned by those who once admired you. Pitied by those who expected such great things from you." Lady Crowley gave her an appraising look, then clucked her tongue. "But at least you will have followed your heart. I shall pray that will be a comfort, when nothing else is."

When the dowager countess made a slow, stiff departure, Brynne remained behind to oversee the final waltz. There was nothing she wanted more than to seek her bed, but duty and obligation demanded she stay until the last guest had quit the ballroom.

Fortunately, it wasn't a responsibility she had to undertake alone.

"Everything all right?" asked Weston as he joined her, the cigar smoke clinging to his clothes indicating he'd come straight from the terrace. "You look...unsettled."

"Tired," she said, mustering a wan smile. "Only tired."

"It has been a long night. A long month, at that. I'll be glad to watch the carriages leave in the morning." He loosened his cravat. "I saw that Lord Campbell decided to finally make an appearance."

"And I saw you dancing with Lady Martha Smethwick," she said in a deft attempt to change to subject, as she didn't want to discuss Lachlan any further tonight. She *couldn't*. Not until she had a chance to sit by herself, and wrap her head around everything she'd learned...and all that she'd been offered. After all, it wasn't every day that a girl received a wedding proposal ten years in the making *and* was subtly threatened not to accept it.

Fortunately, her maneuver worked.

"What do you think of her?" Weston asked. "Lady Martha."

Taller than his sister by six inches, the Earl of Hawkridge had the lean build of a blueblood thoroughbred. His dark hair and gray eyes were the opposite of Brynne's fair coloring (he took after their father), but the twins shared the same straight nose and stubborn chin.

"I think she would be a fine wife for the Earl of Hawkridge."

"But?" He gave her a tiny bump with his elbow. "Go on, I can hear it in your voice."

"But what about a wife for Weston? Do you love her?"

He started to chuckle. Stopped when she didn't join him. "Oh. You're serious."

"I do not understand why that is not a requirement when deciding with whom to spend the rest of your life with," she said with an agitated stomp of her heel.

"Because...it isn't important?" he ventured.

"Not important. Not *important*. So much is said of titles, and wealth, and estates. But no one ever says anything about love, or commitment, or–or *passion*. Aren't those things the *most* important?"

Weston regarded her suspiciously. "Have you nipped into the brandy?"

On a sigh, she dropped her head back to gaze at a chandelier. The candles, over three hundred of them, had all but sputtered out. Those that didn't extinguish on their own would be doused by a servant, and the entire thing would be taken down on the morrow for a good cleaning, along with the rest of the manor once all of their houseguests had departed.

"Be a dear and get the stragglers to bed, West. I'm going upstairs."

"Glass of water and a cold compress for when you wake up."

She rolled her eyes at him. "I am not foxed."

"Then what are you?"

In love, she replied helplessly. *I'm in love, and I don't have the faintest idea what to do about it.*

CHAPTER FOURTEEN

A NIGHT OF sleep did not bring the definitive answers that Brynne sought. After she and Weston finished seeing off the last of the carriages, she considered confiding in her brother. It was a rare problem that they did not share. A benefit of being born at the same time…and often only having each other to rely on.

But it was *because* of that close bond she knew that Weston's opinion wouldn't be all that different from Lady Crowley's. And while she had the courage to defy her former chaperone, she doubted if she'd be able to do the same with her twin.

"Are you leaving for London today or tomorrow?" he asked, neatly slicing a knife through the middle of his sandwich. They sat across from each other in the solarium at a table that felt infinitely larger now that it was just the two of them sharing it.

"Tomorrow," she replied, absently spearing a pickled beet with her fork even though her appetite left much to be desired. "Or perhaps the day after. There are some things I need to tend to yet."

He dabbed at his mouth with a linen napkin. "What sort of things?"

Even though she understood it was nothing more than idle conversation, her back still stiffened. "This and that," she said, being purposefully vague. "Not to mention, I've yet to begin packing up my art supplies, and that's a trunk unto itself. I'll most likely join you at the end of the week."

If I join you at all, she thought silently. Her grip on the fork tightening, she stabbed another beet with unnecessary force and it split in half, causing the metal edge of her utensil to clang loudly on the plate.

Weston sat back in his chair and crossed his arms. "If you're planning what I think you are, you'd best reconsider now, because I won't stand for it."

Her face paled. "You–you won't stand for what?"

"Bringing that hellhound into town with us."

Brynne breathed a sigh of relief.

"That hellhound" was her dog, Drufus. An impulsive purchase from a nearby farm (she already had two bassets, Ellie and Emma, who, at ten years of age, spent most of their days napping in the sun), he'd quickly grown from an adorable puppy into an enormous, rambunctious mutt with paws the size of saucers and all the grace of a bull in a china shop.

For the past two Seasons, she'd attempted to bring him to their manor in Grosvenor Square and the results had been…less than ideal. While Ellie and Emma were content to sleep on a divan in the music room, Drufus had gamboled around the entire house. Chewed shoes, knocked over tables, and dug holes in the garden that a dinosaur bone could fit in had all promptly led to his premature return to Hawkridge Manor.

Happy to chase the swans in the pond, accompany Mr. Grimsby on his daily rounds, and guard the horses in their fields during the day before sleeping in the barn at night, Drufus was far more suited for the country than the city.

While she would miss his presence and jester-like personality, Brynne had already decided weeks ago to keep him at the estate. It was where he was the most content. And anymore, he belonged as much to Mr. Grimsby as he did to her. The aging groundskeeper would never say as much, but he absolutely adored the hound and, on more than one occasion, she'd caught him slipping Drufus chicken livers that he'd specifically asked the cook to set aside.

"No," she said, smiling. "I am not going to set Drufus loose on the *ton* this year."

"Thank God," Weston said with feeling.

It occurred to her then, as it should have before, that if she went to Scotland, none of her three pets would be able to accompany her. Ellie and Emma were too old for such a disruption, and if Drufus were to get loose in the hills and valleys of the Highlands, then she'd never see him again.

Her position in Society, her family's goodwill, and now her dogs...what else would she be giving up if she threw caution–and the weight of the *ton's* expectations–to the wind and eloped to Gretna Green?

Oh, a tiny voice whispered. *But what will you gain?*

Ellie, Emma, and Drufus were happy at Hawkridge Manor.

But she wasn't.

She never had been.

Yet if she didn't leave now, would she ever have the daring to do it later?

People were loath to abandon what made them comfortable. And she *was* comfortable in this life, with enough awareness to understand that her perceived difficulties were someone else's paradise. But that was not an excuse to keep her feet where she'd been planted.

She thought of an exchange she'd had with the gardener once, when she was young. It was the summer before she met Lachlan. Weston was away touring schools, her father was heaven knew where, and she was–again–all alone.

After sneaking out early from a lesson, she'd gone to the pond to feed the swans stale breadcrumbs where she discovered the gardener, Mr. Treadwell, tending to a long row of heirloom roses.

He was weeding, and as she sat on her haunches to watch (a very unladylike position, but what Miss Hardgrave didn't know wouldn't get a ruler struck across Brynne's backside), she'd noticed that he had missed one.

"There," she'd said, pointing at a spindly white flower that clearly did not belong amidst the cultured roses. "Should I pull it?"

"That's not a weed, Lady Brynne," Mr. Treadwell had said in his deep, somber voice. He'd scratched beneath his plain cap, and smiled kindly at her.

"Then what is it?" she'd asked, frowning.

"That's a wildflower. A daisy. See the yellow center?" At her nod, he'd gone on to say, "It must have blown in on the wind when it was a small seed and germinated there."

"But why don't you remove it?"

"Can I tell you a secret?"

A secret was a very important thing indeed, and she'd nodded seriously. "Yes."

Mr. Treadwell had cupped his hands around his mouth. "Because the daisy doesn't know it isn't a rose. And as long as we don't tell it, it will continue to grow where it was planted."

She'd considered that for a moment. "But it's in the shadow of that rosebush. Wouldn't it be happier in a wide open field? By the stone wall, or the meadow across the way. There's plenty of room there."

"Maybe," he'd said. "But if we were to try to move it, there's a high likelihood it wouldn't survive the journey. Best to leave it where it is, Lady Brynne. It's safer here than it would be anywhere else."

But as she'd looked more closely at the daisy, and noticed how its leaves were already beginning to wilt, Brynne had wondered if it wasn't more humane to give it a chance to blossom in the sun than to let it slowly perish in the shade.

"Weston," she said abruptly.

"Yes?" he asked, pausing with his fork halfway to his mouth.

She pushed her chair back. "I need to blossom."

"In the middle of breakfast?"

"I don't want to marry Lady Martha Smethwick."

Her brother's dark brow furrowed in bemusement. "I should hope not. Brynne, are you sure you're feeling well? You still seem...out of sorts. Should I call for Mrs. Grimsby? Or a doctor?"

"No doctors," she said as she stood up. "But I will need Mrs. Grimsby. I'm going away, and there are some things I'd like to go over with her before I do." She took a deep breath. "Weston, I need to tell you something."

"I already know," he said briskly. "And I think it's brilliant."

She stared at him in astonishment. "You–you *do?*"

"Yes. I saw your latest painting of the seascape where we went on holiday last year. You're talented, Brynne. Very talented. And the *École des Beaux-Arts* is the best in the world. How long is the program?"

"Six...six months." He thought she was talking about art school, she realized. The one in Paris that she'd asked her father if she could attend and had yet to receive a response.

"You'll miss the Season, then. But there will be others. When do you leave?"

"Today." She wet her lips. Half of her wanted to tell Weston the truth. To confess everything. But the other half of her, the colder, more logical half, recognized this as an opportunity to avoid hurting the two men she loved the most. If Weston knew her *real* plans, he'd try to stop her. And if he did that, she'd never make it to Lachlan by noon. But this way...this way she could have her proverbial cake and eat it, too, as the Duke of Norfolk had once commonly written in a published letter to Lord Thomas Cromwell.

When guilt threatened, she tamped it down.

She wasn't lying.

Not outright, anyway.

And this would grant her the time she needed to acclimate her brother to the idea of his sister eloping with one of his oldest friends.

Really, she was doing him a kindness.

"So soon?" he asked.

"I'll write you when I get there." Impulsively, she went around the table to wrap her arms around his shoulders and kiss his freshly shaven cheek. "I love you, Weston."

He twisted in his chair to observe her with a critical eye. "Are you *positive* that you're all right? Nothing has happened that I should be made aware of? Someone didn't say anything untoward at the ball last night, did they?"

With her mind finally made up, Brynne's smile rivaled the sun. "I am fine," she assured him. "Better than fine, I think I might actually be happy."

"Now I know you're feeling off," he said wryly. "Our family is many things. *Happy* isn't one of them."

"That, brother dear, remains to be seen."

SHE WASN'T COMING.

As Lachlan prowled back and forth beside the brougham he'd rented to ferry them across the border to Gretna Green, his ungloved hands clenched and unclenched, giving cause for the other pedestrians in the village square to give him a wide berth.

He looked at the clock tower, and when he saw the time–five minutes past noon–his heart sank all the way down to his boots.

No, Brynne wasn't coming.

And he was a bloody fool for ever thinking that she would.

"Let's go," he growled at the driver, a thin man with a head as smooth as a billiard ball that he kept diligently covered with a black cap.

"Yes, my lord." The driver hesitated. "Do you still wish to continue on to Gretna Green?"

Lachlan's mouth twisted. "That depends. Am I tae marry meself?"

"Straight to Carlisle, then."

"Aye," he said bitterly. "Carlisle."

Courtesy of an influx of new rail over the past decade, Lachlan could board a train in Carlisle, a growing city ten miles shy of the Scottish border, and be in Glasgow within five hours. From there, he'd board the Highland Railway, and after a stop to change trains in Perth, would arrive in Inverness, the closest major town to Glenavon, by day's end.

Excluding the time it would take the carriage to reach Carlisle, a journey home that had taken two weeks when he was a boy had since been reduced to a mere twelve hours by rail. Begetting the question of what advancements in transportation the next decade might bring.

The world was changing. Old ways constantly being shuffled out to make way for new. But whether ships one day sailed the skies or trains hurtled down the tracks at the unthinkable speed of fifty miles per hour, one thing would always remain the same: he'd love Brynne Weston until the day that he died.

Stepping up into the carriage, he was about to slam the door shut when he heard her voice calling his name.

At first, he thought it was a cruel trick his ears were playing on him. A manifestation of his greatest desire to help fill the hole her absence had carved out of his chest.

"Bluidy hell," he groaned, striking the back of his head against the wood paneling above the velvet-upholstered bench seat. Then he lifted his arm, and slapped the palm of his hand on the underside of the roof to signal his readiness to depart. But the pair of horses, a bay mare and a brown gelding, didn't move.

"It appears there is a lady trying to get your attention," the driver called. "Should I go around her?"

Lachlan erupted from the brougham with such force that the entire carriage rocked on its wheels. His heart lodged somewhere in his throat, he scanned the village square with the panicked, hopeful desperation of sailor spying a lifeboat as he churned water.

And there she was.

Walking, no, *running* towards him across a flat section of grass, her skirts flapping in the wind, her hat partially dislodged, and her blonde hair blowing in the breeze all the while clinging to a cumbersome leather carpet bag.

Passersby stopped and stared as he ran to her, picked her up by the waist, and spun her around. The carpet bag fell to the ground with a heavy *thud*, but neither Brynne nor Lachlan bothered to retrieve it. They were too busy gazing into each other's eyes and laughing, like two people gone mad.

And maybe they *were* mad to be eloping together based on a vow they'd made as children. Or maybe it was everyone else, everyone who went about their daily lives without doing everything in their power to grab on to this sort of delirious, once-in-a-lifetime-love, that were the mad ones.

"Ye came." He resisted–barely–planting a kiss upon her mouth the likes of which would have sent the elderly spinster observing them from the doorway of the teashop into a dead faint. Instead, he swung her around once more, and then reluctantly returned her feet to the ground.

"I apologize for being late," she said breathlessly, brushing a tendril of hair out of her eyes. "I had trouble finding the dress I wanted to wear for our wedding, and then Drufus made off with one of my shoes. My maid found it in a flowerbed, and–"

"Ye came," he repeated. "Nothing else matters."

"Is that our carriage?" she asked, glancing over his shoulder.

"Aye. I know it's probably not as large as ye are used tae, but as long as the horses hold up, we'll be in Gretna Green tomorrow eve."

She ducked her chin, then peered at him from beneath her lashes as a demure smile played across her lips. "I would think a smaller carriage would lend itself to a more intimate seating arrangement, Lord Campbell. Don't you agree?"

"Aye," he managed to growl as lust gripped him by the bollocks and gave a tantalizing squeeze. "I do."

"Then what are we waiting for?" She flitted past him and, after lifting her carpet bag, he quickly followed suit.

"Gretna Green," he told the driver, who tipped his cap.

"With clear skies and smooth roads, we should make excellent time, my lord."

Lachlan barely heard him. He was too busy admiring the plump curve of Brynne's backside as she climbed into the brougham and settled against the far window, the narrower skirts of her emerald green traveling habit taking up far less room than her gown from the night before.

Every fiber of his being wanted to pounce on her the instant they set off. To be this close, with nary a hawkish chaperone in sight...suffice it to say, it took a *considerable* amount of self-control to remain on his side of the carriage.

"Ye packed lightly," he remarked, having noted the inconsequential weight of her luggage before he'd pushed it beneath the seat.

She nodded. "Enough for a few days. I thought it would be easier to have my belongings sent to me once we reach Campbell Castle. My maid is packing a trunk as we speak." As she shifted to face him, her eyes shone with curiosity. "Can you tell me more about it? The castle, that is. You've shared bits and pieces over the years, but I would enjoy having a clearer picture of where we are going to live. I'm sure it's absolutely breathtaking."

Aye, he thought silently. *If ye dinna mind bats in the stairwell and fresh rain falling from the ceiling.*

"It does have its own unique charm," he allowed. "Given her age– nearly four hundred years–there's always work tae be done and improvements tae be made. But she's a sturdy old lady, whose walls have withstood many a battle with a flood thrown in here and there for good measure."

"And your father doesn't live there anymore?"

"When he inherited Kintore Manor, there was a lot of work tae be done. He stayed here for most of it, and then moved a few years after I left Eton. Fancies himself a real gentleman now." Lachlan grinned as he recalled the last time he'd gone to visit his sire. Robert Campbell had been wearing an actual cravat, with a tailcoat to finish it off. He'd even carried a silver-tipped cane, which he had used to whack his son good-naturedly across the shins when Lachlan doubled over in laughter. "He wouldna lower himself tae be caught in a crumbling castle."

"Crumbling?" said Brynne, her head tilting.

"A matter of speaking," he said hastily. "What...what did yer brother have tae say when ye told him we were eloping? I willna lie, I expected tae see him hot on yer heels and tae be rocked back onto mine if he caught ye." He grinned. "Not that I'd blame him, seeing as I'm running off with his one and only sister."

"He...didn't have much to say about it."

"Really?" Lachlan said skeptically. "I find that hard tae believe."

Brynne looked down at her hands that she'd folded neatly across her lap. She wore ivory kid gloves that extended past her delicate wrists and ended in a scalloped lace edge. "Maybe because I...I didn't tell him."

His eyes narrowed. "And why wouldna ye do that?"

"Just as you said. I knew Weston would try to stop me, and...and I didn't want him to. This was *my* decision to make, Lachlan. Not his. Not anyone's but mine."

It was a plausible explanation, and yet...

"Then ye mean tae tell him by post after we're married."

"I...of course. I'll send a letter straightaway explaining everything."

The hesitation was slight, he'd given her that.

Less than half a second.

But the lack of sound it made was the equivalent of a cannon sailing through the air right before it blasted through a wall.

"Are ye ashamed tae marry me, Bry?" he said stiffly. "If ye are, then say it now, and I'll have the driver return ye tae Hawkridge Manor before we go another step."

Lachlan acknowledged that he wasn't nearly as wealthy or highly titled as the sort of gentleman that Brynne and her family were accustomed to rubbing shoulders with. Her grandfather was a bloody *duke*, for Christ sakes. While Lachlan only had a "Lord" in front of his name because some bloke had fallen off a ladder and snapped his neck. The social distance between himself and his bride-to-be could span a large country. But while he was able to stomach others looking at him in silent judgment as they questioned how the hell he'd managed such a fine catch as Brynne Weston, he'd be damned if he gazed upon his wife and saw the same question in her eyes.

Money didn't make a man.

Drive and determination did.

He had plans. Grand plans. And he wanted Brynne by his side as he executed them. But he was not without his pride, and he'd not have her there out of pity or hiding in his shadow because she was afraid of what others would think of her if she stood at his side.

"That's not it at all," she protested as the color drained from her cheeks. "I am not ashamed of you, Lachlan. What a horrible thing to accuse."

"Then what reason—what *real* reason—do ye have for not telling yer brother?" he said roughly. "Yer father, I can understand. For all that the man's given ye his attention, ye dinna owe him a second of yers. But there's no one ye are closer tae than Weston, and lying tae him—"

"I didn't lie," she cut in defensively. "I...I merely did not dissuade him of the assumption he made that I was going to Paris to attend art school. Not because I want to hide our marriage, but because I want to *celebrate* it. And I won't be able to do that if Weston is storming the blacksmith shop while we're trying to say our vows. I'll write to him once we're settled at Campbell Castle. I will." She reached across the space dividing them and placed her hand on his thigh. "I love you, Lachlan."

He sucked in a sharp breath.

"What is it?" she asked uncertainly.

"That's the first time that ye have said that ye love me." Enveloping her small hand with his larger one, he shifted closer and rested his chin upon the top of her head. Her hair was soft and smelled subtly sweet, like honeysuckle warmed in the afternoon sun. "We're going tae have a wonderful life together, Bry. We'll chase down all those dreams ye told me about when we stared at the stars, and we'll raise a beautiful family. There will be hard times, aye. There's no use pretending that there willna." He moved his fingers down her back. "But they'll always be outweighed by the good."

"I'm sure they will be, Lachlan." On a quiet sigh, she slid her arm across his lap and closed her eyes. "As long as we're together. That is most important."

This time, he pretended not to hear the hesitation in her voice.

CHAPTER FIFTEEN

THEY ARRIVED AT the tiny parish of Gretna Green as the sun was setting. After changing horses in Kendal, they'd traveled through the night and all the next day, leading Brynne's legs to fill with pins and needles as she descended from the brougham.

"Oh," she gasped, and Lachlan was there to catch her before she stumbled.

"The train will make for an easier trip," he said, looping an arm around her waist. "At least we can walk around and stretch our legs when the mood strikes us."

As part of the reason her muscles were so cramped was due to the fact that she'd spent the majority of her time practically sitting on Lachlan's lap, she didn't know if the train would be much different. But if aching legs were the price for having a handsome rogue's arms wrapped around her, she'd pay it gladly.

He hadn't tried to kiss her again.

She'd somewhat hoped that he would.

But there was intimacy to be found in the quiet moments as well. In the holding, and the rhythmic stroke of a hand, and the subtle beat of a contented heart.

"I haven't traveled this far since Weston and I spent a week on the coast in Scarborough. I forgot what to expect. But this…" Her eyes widening, she stopped short. "This isn't what I expected at all."

Admittedly, Brynne hadn't known very much about Gretna Green before embarking. It was a destination associated with scandal and discussed in hushed tones, with rarely a positive word to be shared amidst Polite Society. She'd assumed it would be like…well, it would be like the time her driver had taken a wrong turn and they had ended up in the East End of London.

But instead of narrow alleys and broken windows, there were cobblestone streets and cheerful blue shutters and a wide main thoroughfare lined with quaint houses and shops. At the far end of the street, on the top of a short knoll, sat a building all by itself. Long and white, with large windows beneath and dormers above, it had a black door flanked on either side with green shrubbery and a wooden sign neatly printed with "Enter Here".

Her stomach pitched; a rapid rise and fall of excitement and anxiety and an intangible feeling that defied description. She took a half-step towards the building, as if drawn to it by some magnetic force of destiny calling her name but, with a husky chuckle, Lachlan pulled her back.

"Aye, and that's where we'll be married in the morning. But for tonight, we've food and rooms waiting for us at The Queen's Head."

"Rooms?" she asked, questioning the plurality as he effortlessly hoisted their luggage—her small carpet bag and his slightly bigger valise—over his shoulder and proceeded to the inn while she walked beside him, her head on a swivel as she attempted to take in all of the sights and the sounds of her surroundings without letting any detail, no matter how seemingly inconsequential, escape her notice.

She wasn't a girl who had dreamed about her wedding day at St. Paul's Cathedral, which was where both her grandparents and parents were married. She hadn't envisioned hundreds of guests lining the pews, or the half-dozen attendants it would take to carry the heavy train of her gown, or the smell of incense burning.

That day had always remained blank. A canvas yet to be painted.

And now that she knew what colors to add, she did not want to miss a single one.

"As we're not yet husband and wife, I thought ye would be more comfortable in a room of yer own," Lachlan explained as they entered through the pub and were greeted by the innkeeper. Money was exchanged, the luggage was handed off, and then they were free to find a table.

Her appetite barely that of a rabbit's, Brynne managed a bowl of broth and a slice of the most delicious bread she'd ever eaten. Still warm from the oven, crispy on the outside, and soft as a pillow within, it tempted her into a second piece, and then–feeling slightly self-conscious–a third.

"What is this called?" she asked, swallowing a moan as she sank her teeth into a fresh slice.

"Fife bannock. A Scottish staple," he replied, his gaze pinned to her mouth with such blazing intensity that she stopped eating.

"Do I have a crumb on my face?"

"Aye." But instead of handing her a napkin, he reached for her hand.

She gasped when he took her thumb between his lips and slowly swirled his tongue around it, his eyes–molten shards of garnet–never leaving hers.

"*Lachlan!*" Her voice was a whimper. A pleading. Although whether she was asking him to stop or to continue, even she wasn't certain. Shrinking low in her seat, she darted a glance to the left, then the right. The dining room, such as it was, was dimly lit with a combination of wax candles and lanterns, but it wasn't completely dark. And their table, while positioned in a corner, was hardly hidden from view. "There are people all around."

Releasing her thumb with a *pop* of suction, he guided her hand and pressed her thumb, still damp from being inside of his mouth, against her chin.

"There," he said huskily. "I got it. And I wouldna worry about anyone disapproving of us. In case ye havena noticed, this is a place for lovers. No one is looking further than the lad or lass sitting right across from them."

Another surreptitious glance around the room confirmed that he was speaking the truth. Of all the inn's occupants, only one–the barkeep–was without a partner. But an entire lifetime of propriety was a difficult thing to disregard.

As was the humming in her blood or the slippery wetness between her thighs.

She pushed her chair back. "We should go upstairs."

"Poor wee lamb," he said, the corner of his mouth lifting in a rueful smile as he joined her in standing. "Ye must be exhausted, and we've another day of travel in front of us after the ceremony. Let's get ye tae bed."

By no means would Brynne describe herself as brazen. She was well aware of her sexual inexperience. Her innocence. Her naivety with all things having to do with the bedroom. That wasn't to say that she was not aware of how the act was done in its most rudimentary form. She'd read books, and Hawkridge Manor had plenty of foals every spring which did not exactly appear out of thin air. Yet watching something as a bystander, and being an active participant, were two entirely different things.

If she were being completely honest, she'd have to admit that she was somewhat intimidated by the idea of sharing her body–her *entire* body–with Lachlan.

But she was also intrigued.

And having thoroughly enjoyed everything he'd done to her thus far, she could only assume that committing the deed itself would produce just as much (if not more) pleasure than all their kisses combined.

"Yes, I am ready to go to bed," she said demurely. Then she swallowed, and before she lost her nerve, blurted out, "Except I've no intention of sleeping."

He went very, very still. But for the sudden throb of his pulse at the base of his neck, he might have been frozen.

"Lachlan?" She bit the inside of her cheek. "Do you...do you understand what I mean, or–"

"Aye, I understand," he said hoarsely. "If this room was empty, I'd already have ye stretched across this table and ye would soon know just how much I understand."

"*Oh,*" she squeaked as her entire face erupted with heat. "I–I see."

"Are ye sure?" He searched her gaze. "We can wait until tomorrow, after we're married. Or even until we're at the castle and ye have had a few days tae unwind yerself. There's no hurry, Bry. Not when we've the rest of our lives tae enjoy each other."

A flicker of nervousness–followed closely by anticipation–coursed down her spine. "Do *you* want to wait?"

His answer to that was a short, incredulous snort. "What I dinna want tae do is push ye before ye're ready."

"It's not pushing if I'm pulling." Darting another glance around the room to ensure no one was paying them any mind–they weren't–she lowered her voice and murmured, "Could you...could you do that thing with your mouth on my thumb again? I quite liked that."

"Oh, love." Lachlan's grin, wide and wicked, could have rivaled Lucifer's own. "If ye liked that, ye're going tae *love* what else I can do with my tongue."

A SINGLE CANDLE lit the bedroom in a hazy orange glow, casting shadows far and wide. Brynne was grateful for them, as they helped to disguise the pink blush rapidly overtaking every inch of her skin as Lachlan closed the door and quietly locked it behind him.

The ceiling was low, accentuating his massive height and the breadth of his shoulders. Goodness, but he was *large*. Far larger than she. In the vast halls of Hawkridge Manor, the difference wasn't as obvious. But here, in this little room with its single bed and dresser, she couldn't help but wonder how they were possibly going to fit together. For an instant, her gaze centered on his loins, and then jerked guiltily back to his countenance as her blush deepened.

"What...what do we do first?" Her fingers curled inward, nails pressing into palms that were already slicked with perspiration.

The wooden floorboards creaked beneath Lachlan's weight as he crossed to her; a small sound compared to the pounding of her heart. He clasped her hands, raised them to his mouth, and placed a kiss on every single knuckle before staring into her eyes.

"First, we make ye comfortable. This isna something tae be rushed, or endured. It's meant tae be enjoyed, every bit of it, from the first moment tae the last. I willna lie and say there willna be an awkward moment or two, as surely there is with any new thing. But it doesna have tae be as serious as ye would have some people believe. Nor nearly as fast. Lovemaking is intended tae be a celebration. A feast for the senses, and the souls, for all involved." While he spoke, he began to undress her. Slowly. Gradually. A tied string here. A button there. As if it were the most natural thing in the world when no one else had ever taken off her clothes except for herself and her lady's maid.

Her dress was the first garment to fall. It pooled at her feet, was followed by her petticoat, a swath of fabric that tied at the waist to give shape to her skirt, and then her boned corset. Her drawers were next and, finally, her chemise, leaving her clothed in nothing but air and shadows and the weight of Lachlan's gaze.

"Ye have a beauty that outshines the moon on its fullest night." Lowering his head, he pressed his mouth to her shoulder, his breath warm against her ivory flesh. "A thousand stars would bow before ye, and it's a blessed man that I am tae be able tae claim ye as my own."

A poet, she thought dazedly as he kissed a path across her collarbone and up her neck. She hadn't known he was a poet. With his words as much as his hands.

She trembled when he traced the shell of her ear. Quivered when his hands skimmed down her back to cup her buttocks, and who knew there so many nerve endings in *that* particular part of her anatomy?

He kissed her lightly. A teasing brush of his lips across hers. A little nip. A husky sigh. Then he stepped away and began to undress himself, his countenance somber save for the faintest tilt of his mouth.

With half the amount of clothing to remove, he was naked within a matter of seconds, and her breath caught as she studied the rugged planes and valleys of his chest and abdomen, his sculptured muscles carved from a land that made men out of boys and warriors out of men.

"You're so...big," she ventured, and that was even *before* her gaze traveled below his waist.

"Thank ye," he said solemnly, as if she were the queen with a scepter in her hand and she'd just placed it upon his shoulder to award a knighthood or other valor of honor. "Surely the greatest compliment I've ever received from the lips of the bonny lass whose opinion matters the most."

Her brows jutted in bemusement...until she happened to glance lower, and then with a sharp gasp she met his twinkling eyes. "You're...you're..."

As comfortable with his nudity as she was self-conscious of hers, he rested his hands on the edges of his hips. "Big is as fine a word as any, and the perfect way tae stroke a man's ego if ye were after such a thing."

Big?

He was *enormous*.

And if she'd questioned whether they were going to fit before, she was convinced they wouldn't now.

"Lachlan," she said hesitantly, "I–I don't think this is going to work."

"Aye, and I'm sure that's what they said about the Great Pyramids when they started laying the first row of stone."

"We are not the Great Pyramids."

He grinned. Glanced down. "Speak for yerself."

If his intention was to make her laugh and thus loosen the coil of tension wrapping her body in thin, invisible string, he succeeded. Her fingers relaxed. Her shoulders eased. The knot in the middle of her temple unraveled.

His toes bumped into hers as he cupped her jaw with one hand while the other plucked the pins from her hair and scattered them across the floor. Undone, her pale tresses tumbled all the way to the small of her back where he gathered a fistful of curls and gazed at them with the reverence of a pirate king admiring his chest of golden treasure.

"Blessed," he repeated, letting the tendrils slide through his fingers before he brought his mouth to hers and slid his tongue between her lips in a kiss that was neither light nor teasing.

She tasted his hunger. His need. His raw, aching desire to possess. To take. To conquer. All tempered with an exquisite level of self-control that far exceeded her own.

As lust smoldered and flames licked, she wound her arms around his neck, nipples tingling where they rubbed against the soft mat of curls spread across the top of his chest. She tentatively probed his mouth with her own tongue, and when he growled and hitched her against his body in a taut embrace that brought her belly in direct contact with the hardest, hottest part of him, her exploration grew bolder.

They went to the bed, the back of her knees pressing against the wooden foot rail before Lachlan picked her up and placed her on the mattress, her head cocooned on a pillow stuffed with goose down, her arms never loosening from those broad shoulders.

He knelt over her, bracing his weight in his thighs. Cords of muscle rippled and stretched beneath her fingertips as he kissed the sensitive space right beneath the curve of her jaw, and then the base of her neck, and then her breasts, suckling the tender buds one at a time while those large, callused hands spanned her ribcage before beginning a perilous descent that had her arching off the bed, first in surprise...and then pleasure.

When he touched her *there*, gliding a single fingertip along the velvety wet seam of her most intimate place where even she hadn't dared venture for fear of committing some ungodly sin, it was as if a new color had been added to the rainbow. A shimmer of light that she never knew existed before Lachlan opened her eyes and allowed her to see it.

It was stunning.

Glorious, even.

Then his finger slid inside of her...and the rainbow fractured into a hundred different colors, each brighter than the last.

For a long while, Lachlan just petted, and stroked, and kissed, all while whispering sweet nothings in her ear in a language that her ears didn't comprehend, but her heart did. Dividing his attention between her lips, and her breasts, and the curls between her legs, he seemed to be driving her *towards* something...a hill, or a peak, or even a mountain. She was too delirious to care which. Too drunk on desire to notice how high they were climbing.

"Aye, and ye're wet and wanting, are ye not, *ionmhainneach*?" he rasped, and when she nodded–because of course she nodded–he captured her wrist and gently guided her hand to the core of his body where he was nearly as damp as she, and hot, and pulsing besides.

Tentatively, and then with a growing confidence spurred on by his groans, she encircled his staff and ran her palm along its heavy length all the way to the base before reversing direction, instinctively pleasuring him as he had pleasured her.

His jaw clenched. Candlelight reflected off the sheen of sweat clinging to his temple. Without warning, he grabbed her arm, and when she looked at him in question, he made a tortured sound caught somewhere between a laugh and a moan. "I was soon tae spend meself like a green lad if ye didna stop." He tenderly brushed a curl off her cheek. "Are ye ready for me, Bry?"

Her eyes widened. "That wasn't…that wasn't it?"

There was that devilish grin again. Stealing across his mouth like a thief through the night. "Oh, *luaidh mo chèile*. We've barely begun."

She didn't understand what he meant…and then, all at once, she did.

He was right.

There was more.

So much more than she was ever capable of imagining. But then, how could you explain the infinite vastness of the ocean to someone who had never stepped foot upon the sand?

As sensation after sensation washed over her, she clung to him, her slender calves wrapping around his muscular buttocks to follow the undulation of his hips as he filled her, deeper and deeper. Until suddenly, they weren't climbing the mountain, they were standing on top of it.

A plunging thrust of his hips as he claimed her mouth in a possessive kiss that demanded she give all of herself to him, and both Lachlan and Brynne soared over the edge together.

CHAPTER SIXTEEN

NEVER, IN ALL his life, had Lachlan felt complete.

There was always something...*restless* stirring inside of him. Something that never permitted him to fully settle. To halt whatever he was doing, take a breath, and find satisfaction in what he'd already done.

But as he laid beside Brynne, his arm draped securely around her waist and her wee little feet tucked between his legs, he knew nothing but contentment. Nothing but a sense of fulfillment that came not from a job well done or money earned, but from filling a space inside of himself that he hadn't even known was wanting.

Or maybe he *had* known, and that's why Brynne was always the one for him.

As a boy teetering on that sharp, uneven edge of manhood, he'd found solace in her company. She was a safe harbor to share his innermost thoughts and feelings. Someone who accepted him as he was when no one at Eton, with a few rare exceptions, wanted to accept him at all.

As a young man with no bloody idea of how to navigate the shark-infested waters of High Society, she'd provided another port in the storm. Their one dance, on that one night, had carried him through an entire Season of dullness and drudgery.

As a man full grown and filled with ambition and grueling purpose, she'd given him a reason to continue his uphill battle in resurrecting the abandoned dreams of his great-great-grandfather. The kiss by the brook, his first taste of genuine magic and all the power it contained, had led him to persist when everyone else told him to quit. And while the distillery was a dream still outstanding, this–finally having his arms around the woman he loved–was not.

Every step he'd taken, every decision he'd made (both the good and the bad), every road he'd gone down...it brought him here. To this night. To Brynne. For that he was grateful, and humbled, and more determined than ever to see the rest of his hopes realized. For himself. For his soon-to-be wife. For the children they'd make together. Raise together. Love together.

When morning dawned, he watched his bride get dressed, his heart filled to the brim with pride and possibility as she patiently ran a comb through all that thick, luscious hair before using the pins he'd dropped the night before to fashion it into a loose chignon at the top of her head with tendrils to frame her face. His gaze lingered unabashedly on her shapely calves as she donned her stockings, and a delightful blush, warm and pink, spread across her chest when she caught him staring at her breasts as she slipped into her chemise.

"It isn't fair," she said, slanting him a reproving glance. "All the layers of clothing women are required to wear as opposed to men. You've been ready for nearly an hour, and I've yet to even put on my corset."

He gave a dismissive shrug. "Go without it."

"Go without a *corset*?" For all the incredulity in his tone, he might have suggested that she parade down the aisle naked.

"Aye. They're little more than devices of torture as it is, and I'd like tae meet the person who decided the female shape needed tae be changed from the way God designed it. Ye dinna alter perfection. Besides," he went on, a roguish glint shining in his eyes, "I'm just going tae be undressing ye later. Seems a waste of time tae wrap up a package that's soon to be opened."

"I suppose it would make for more comfortable travel on the train," she relented. Forgoing the corset–they really were accursed contraptions–she stepped into a pair of white drawers that tied at the waist, and then turned to the dress she'd carefully laid out on the back of a chair. "Would you…?"

It was the invitation Lachlan was waiting for. In an instant, he was off the bed and guiding the gown over her outstretched arms.

"This was my mother's," she said softly as he went behind her to assist with the round pearl buttons that ran between her shoulder blades. "Not what she wore to the cathedral, but after, at the reception. I found it several years ago while looking for an extra trunk to store my canvases."

Finishing with the top button, he pressed his mouth to the nape of her neck. "Ye make a beautiful bride, Brynne Weston. Yer mother would be beaming with happiness tae see ye in her dress."

With flowing lines, an empire waist, and capped sleeves, the gown was a token of a bygone era before bustles and bows and corsets and crinoline. It was the spring green of a tulip, and the swath of beige ribbon beneath Brynne's breasts matched the delicate lacing along the bodice.

There was only one thing missing.

He went to a satchel he'd brought along with his valise and withdrew a long piece of woven wool dyed in a checkered pattern of red, black, green, and traces of silver. "This is my family's tartan, and it's a proud husband I'd be tae see my wife wear it on our wedding day." He glanced down at the cloth. Once, his ancestors had worn these colors into battle. Now, they hung on a tapestry in the great hall and were largely ceremonial, their significance lost to the unwritten pages of history. But they remained an important piece his ancestry. Of where he'd come from, and who he was. He cleared his throat, and in the emotion of the moment his brogue thickened. "If ye dinna want tae–"

"I would be honored," she said, cutting him off as she laid her hand on top of his. "You need only tell me how to place it."

Lachlan was not embarrassed that his fingers shook as he folded the tartan in half, and then folded it again before laying the wool diagonally across Brynne's chest like a sash and securing it over her right hip with a sterling silver kilt pin that would hold the heavy fabric in place. Unlike the English, who were taught to shield their emotions behind a stiff upper lip, he'd been encouraged at an early age to show what he was feeling. Whether it be with his fists, his words...or his lips.

"The next time we do that," he murmured after he'd finished a kiss that left them both a bit breathless, "ye shall be my wife and I yer husband."

She straightened his collar. "I can hardly believe it's time."

In addition to a black jacket and waistcoat, neither of which would have appeared out of place in a London ballroom, Lachlan wore a kilt in the same colors as the tartan and a traditional Kilmarnock bonnet that sat at a rakish angle over his right eye. His socks itched, and his shoes pinched, but he'd have gladly cut off both legs at the knee if that was what it took to marry the bonny lass standing in front of him. "Aye, and we'd best go now, before a line forms. Are ye ready?"

It was the question he'd asked before he took her maidenhood.

To his relief, her answer was the same.

THE CEREMONY, ONCE they got to it, was short and strikingly poignant.

Brynne and Lachlan held hands in front of a vicar who, oddly enough, reminded her of Mr. Treadwell, the gardener. A fitting comparison, as it was Mr. Treadwell's words that had helped her commit to this path. A path that ended with an anvil in front of her, a Scot beside her, and a wooden bench filled with two witnesses behind her.

Sunlight trickled in through stained glass windows, catching on spiraling swirls of dust that rose from a leather tome that the vicar procured from the folds of his brown robes and dropped onto the pulpit which was really nothing more than a large slab of stone. He slid thin wire spectacles onto a long, hookish nose, cleared his throat in an official manner, and then peered straight at them, his first direct acknowledgement since they'd entered the blacksmith shop.

"And who might ye be?" he asked as he laid the tome open.

Lachlan squeezed Brynne's hand before he spoke. "Lord Lachlan Campbell, sir, and me bride-tae-be is Lady Brynne Weston."

"Weston...Campbell..." the vicar muttered, running a bony finger up and down the page in front of him. "My we've a busy day today, havena we? Everyone's looking tae wed before the snow sets in, I suppose. Old Vanna McDougal says it's tae be a fierce winter, and she's not been wrong yet. Except for the year 1837, and then she can hardly be blamed for that, as she was riddled with triplets and nursing twins besides. A prolific husband, Old Vanna had. May ye be blessed with the same, me lady. Let's see here." Squinting, the vicar slowly turned to the next page. "I've a Herron and a Greenwood. Ah, and Lord Beckwith is here tae try again. Had his lass whisked right out from under his nose last time. Angry father, ye understand." The vicar lifted his head. "Campbell, did ye say?"

"Aye," Lachlan replied, the corners of his mouth twitching.

Brynne bit back her own smile.

They were certainly a far cry from the pomp and circumstance of St. Paul's Cathedral in London, but there was warmth here. Charm as well. *And love*, she thought, stealing a glance at Lachlan. So much love that it was a wonder the little building with its dirt floor and stone walls was capable of containing it all.

And if there was also a whisper of something else, a sense of...unease, well, what bride wasn't nervous on her wedding day? She was making the right decision. She *had* made the right decision. For short of spinning around and racing out the door, she was marrying

Lachlan today.

If the vicar ever got around to it, that is.

"Ah!" he said at last, dipping an old-fashioned quill in ink and dashing a neat line through their names. "Here we are. Lord Campbell of Glenavon and Lady Weston of Yorkshire. Yer names have been in my register for some time, havena they?"

Brynne flicked a startled glance at Lachlan. She'd assumed their visit here was unplanned, as he'd only asked her to marry him three days ago. But it appeared that he had been confident as to what her reply would be. Or maybe he'd simply hedged his bets, and had wanted to be prepared regardless of whether they ended up here or not.

Clever, her Scot.

Very clever.

Arrogant as well, but wasn't that what she liked about him? His confidence. His unwavering *assurance* that things would happen as he wanted them to, for no other reason than he refused to accept the alternative. In that way, Lachlan was like the tide coming in, letting nothing–not sand, or rock or steep embankment–stand in his way. And when he went back out, he pulled whatever was closest along with him...no matter their own intentions to remain on the shore.

"Aye." He gave her hand another squeeze. "I've always known I was going tae marry this one. It was just a matter of timing."

"Never a good time or a bad time tae commit yerself to wedlock, in my humble opinion. Ye're not marrying a clock. But some seem tae think that if they marry in June instead of October, they'll have a better go if it." The vicar removed his spectacles, polished the lenses on the sleeve of his robe, and then slid them back into place. "I've yet tae find that tae be the case, but what do I know? Only been married tae me Mae for forty-seven years and performed more ceremonies than this old book can contain." He raised his arm, coughed into his elbow, then peered straight at Brynne over the rounded edge of his spectacles. "Did ye have yer own vows prepared, or should I read the standard? The fee is the same, either way."

"Oh." Flustered, she shook her head. "I didn't realize—"

"We've our own vows," Lachlan interrupted.

"But I don't—"

"Just repeat after me if ye can." He briefly rested his forehead on hers. "And if ye find the words tae difficult tae remember, then all ye need tae do is promise tae love me and tae remain loyal tae me. A man canna ask for more than that."

When he put it that way, it didn't seem too difficult.

"All right," she said, and he gave her a wink.

"That's me lass."

"Are ye ready?" the vicar asked. "I've a line nearly out the door, ye know."

"Aye." Lachlan's chest lifted as he took a breath, and then took her other hand. Fingers entwined, they faced each other, and everything else...the vicar, the pedestal, the witnesses...faded away, blurred into obscurity by the fiercely possessive glow in Lachlan's gaze. "This is a Celtic blessing that me father spoke when he married me mother. It's been used tae bind kings and queens, warriors and maidens, farmers and milkmaids. I use it now, tae bind ye tae me, in the hopes that nothing from within or without will ever tear us asunder.

"Brynne Weston, ye are the star of each night. Ye are the brightness of every morning. Ye are the story of each guest. Ye are the report of every land. No evil shall befall ye, on hill nor bank, in a field, valley, on a mountain, or in a glen. Ye are mine, and I am yers, from this moment forward until death comes tae part us asunder."

A single tear ran down her cheek.

Lachlan caught it on his thumb before it could fall, and pressed his thumb to his lips. "This is my solemn promise tae ye," he said quietly. "As a man, a husband, and a lover."

Then it was her turn, and her voice trembled with emotion as she repeated the vows that would bind them together for the rest of this life and the next. "Lachlan Campbell, you...you are the star of each night. You are the brightness of every morning. You are the story of...of..."

"Each guest," he provided helpfully.

She was crying in earnest now; her face as wet as if she'd stepped out into an early morning mist. But they were silent sobs born of joy, not sadness, and she smiled through them at the man that she loved as all of her misgivings and doubts were washed away by the cleansing rain of her tears. "You are the report of every land, and no evil shall ever befall you on hill nor bank, in a field or in a glen. You are mine, and I am yours, from this moment forward until death comes to part us asunder. This is my solemn promise to you as a woman, and a wife, and..."–sneaking a peek at the vicar, she discreetly lowered her voice– "a lover."

"Well done," the vicar said with an approving nod and what might have been a tear of his own, although it was hard to tell with the spectacles. "With the power invested in me by the Church of Scotland, I hereby pronounce ye as husband and wife. Ye may...yes, ye may do that."

He obligingly looked the other way as Lachlan yanked Brynne against him and gave her a kiss that would have surely burned St. Paul's Cathedral to the ground and earned them a lifetime of repentance besides.

Clinging to his shoulders as he lifted her off the floor in his exuberance, she laughingly wrenched her mouth free. "Lachlan, people are *staring*."

And so they were. The vicar, and the witnesses, and even the other couples waiting to be wed, peering in through the doors and the windows with varying expressions of shock and amusement and disgruntlement.

"Let them stare," he growled. "It's me wife they're looking at, after all. And I'm pleased tae show her off."

She slid down his body a few inches. Gasped when her thigh encountered something quite unmistakable in both its size and shape. "*Lachlan.*"

"Aye," he said with a grin that bordered on the sheepish. "Maybe we'd best take this someplace private."

Evidently spying his opportunity to move them along, the vicar seized upon it. "If ye'll sign here and here," he said, all but throwing his quill at Lachlan, "ye may be on yer way tae a more...*discreet* location tae celebrate yer matrimonial bliss."

They wrote their names; Lachlan's penmanship rough and hurried, Brynne's elegant and perfectly spaced. A fitting juxtaposition that went far beyond a signature.

"Lady Campbell," said Lachlan, gesturing towards the door with an exaggerated sweep of his arm.

"Lord Campbell," she replied, sinking into a curtsy before she preceded him out of the shop with all the feigned aplomb of Queen Victoria exiting the throne room at Buckingham Palace.

Her husband–how strange and delightful it was to describe him that way!–followed right on her heels, and like the children they'd been during that wild, reckless two weeks nearly ten years prior, they raced across the village square, giggling all the while.

This, she thought dazedly as he pulled her into an alley, pressed her up against the brick side of a milliner's store, and began to kiss his way down her neck. *This is what heaven must be like.*

And for a while, it was.

CHAPTER SEVENTEEN

"LACHLAN, THE CEILING is leaking again!" Sputtering like a wet cat caught in a rainstorm, Brynne staggered out of bed, dragging the coverlet with her. The fire in the hearth had turned to ash overnight, the temperamental Highland winds were howling, and water was lashing at the windows–and pouring out of the ceiling–in a freezing spray of wet.

Shivering from head to toe, she cast her peacefully slumbering husband (who, she'd discovered during five months of marriage, would sleep through an earthquake if there were such things this far north), and went to retrieve a bucket from the closet down the hall.

Were she at Hawkridge Manor, she could have sent a servant for such a task. Of course, were she at Hawkridge, there wouldn't have been water waking her up in the middle of the night when any sensible person was tucked cozily in their beds, dreaming of warmer days soon to come.

But oh no.

Not her.

She was stumbling blindly through the dark, her teeth chattering with such force that she feared they were going to rattle right out of her skull. Managing to find the closet, she opened the door...and released a hiss of frustration when she discovered that she wasn't the first to go looking for a bucket to stem the flow of rain on this stormy eve.

Not surprising, given that nearly every room in the castle had some sort of hole in it. Holes made from mice (and other creatures she dared not think about), holes from rot, holes from the menagerie of feral siblings that had somehow slipped Lachlan's mind whenever he'd spoken about his family.

Four.

Four children under the age of fifteen trapped together beneath one (very leaky) roof.

Even now, she could hear Eara and Tavish, the twins, calling out, their thin, squalling wails louder than the booms of thunder that threatened to raze the already crumbling stone walls to the ground.

When it became apparent by the increasing fervor of their cries that the nursemaid was not going to attend them, Brynne gave a resigned sigh and took on the duty herself as she'd done nearly every night, in some capacity, ever since Lachlan's one-year-old brother and sister were unceremoniously dumped on their doorstep by his stepmother, Lady Heather, with a vague promise to "return quite soon". To Brynne's consternation, there'd been no sign of Heather for the past seven weeks. To the best of her knowledge, Lachlan's stepmother was "recovering" from the labors of childbirth at the steam pools in Bath with no sign of returning anytime soon.

"There, there," she said soothingly as she entered the nursery and lifted first Eara and then Tavish out of their cribs. The nursemaid was a useless lump of covers in the corner; her loud snores indicating that she was even more of a sound sleeper than Lachlan. "Let's make you some milk, shall we?"

She carried the twins down the winding stairs to the kitchen where she placed them into a round basket by the fire–which, thankfully, was still smoldering–and warmed cow's milk over the glowing embers before transferring it into two porcelain bubby pots.

Shaped like a traditional teapot with a slightly longer spout, the pots had a top that fastened securely in place and a spout that was sealed closed with the exception of three holes just large enough for liquid to dribble through. Ideally, the twins would be nursing at their mother's breast, but short of that–and with no wet nurse to be found– these were the next best thing.

Latching on to the spouts with all the ferocity of two starving hyena cubs, Eara and Tavish immediately ceased their cries, and Brynne sighed with relief as she sat down beside them in a pool of dimly flickering light and hugged her knees to her chest.

She'd wanted to be a bride, she reminded herself as a not-unfamiliar longing for the life she'd left behind began to creep up the back of her throat. A bride and a wife to the man she was in love with. The man she loved still, even though he was upstairs peacefully slumbering away while she was sitting on a cold, damp floor feeding his siblings. Siblings he'd neglected to tell her about until *after* they were married.

Ironically, despite their attachment to the witching hour, Eara and Tavish were the best behaved of the bunch. At least they didn't release snakes to slither in the hall, like Callum. Or sneak frogs into her pockets, like Blaine. *Those* two–thirteen and eleven years of age, respectively–were in a perpetual state of mischievousness. And Brynne found herself the target of their playful antics more often than not.

Yesterday, while playing swords at the table, they'd accidentally cut down the chandelier. The *chandelier*. It was a small miracle the room hadn't gone up in flames. Which, considering the state of the castle, might have been an improvement.

Through it all, Lachlan just chuckled and dismissed the behavior of his brothers as "lads being lads" while Brynne did her best to create some semblance of order and docility from the chaos. It was, to put it mildly, an uphill battle.

She'd wanted to be a bride.

Instead, she was a bride, *and* a mother, *and* a lady's maid, *and* a scullery maid, *and* a cook, *and* a wet nurse, *and* an amphibian keeper. All the while, her paints, which she'd had delivered from Hawkridge Manor in secret courtesy of a trusted maid, remained in a trunk, with her dreams of travel packed away right beside them.

There could be no seeing the world when she was quite literally responsible for the lives of four children whose mothers were either deceased or divorced or soaking in pools in Bath and whose father was too busy chasing skirts in London to be bothered.

But the worst part–even worse than being awoken by a deluge of icy water or changing foul-smelling nappies or finding slimy worms in her shoes–was the loneliness.

In a rambling castle filled with the bellowing war cries of infants and adolescent boys alike, more snakes than she cared to count, a skeleton staff of servants, and a husband, Brynne was *lonely*. The type of wrenching isolation she hadn't felt since she watched Weston's carriage leave for Eton.

At least then she'd had Lachlan. Only for two weeks, it was true. A blink of an eye for some, but what felt like an entire lifetime to a lost, lonely girl yearning for love and attention. And now she was married to him. Now they really *did* have an entire lifetime to spend together. But then why did she feel more alone than she ever had before?

Oh, the first month had been wonderful! A hazy blur of lovemaking and laughter and nearly ten years of longing to fulfill. Then somewhere along the way, the honeymoon–such as it was–had ended, and her new husband had taken to spending sunrise to sunset at the sight of his great-great-grandfather's distillery and its surrounding fields as he struggled to coax seedlings from fallow soil. Which left Brynne at the castle, tending to any manner of things, none of which her army of tutors and governesses had ever prepared her for.

She did not begrudge Lachlan chasing after his dream. She simply did not want it to come at the expense of her own. And as she returned Eara and Tavish safely to their cribs, she was unable to completely silence the little voice that reminded her if she wasn't here, she might be in Paris, sitting shoulder to shoulder with some of the greatest artists to ever yield a brush.

Instead, she was stuck in a wet castle yielding bubby pots.

"There ye are," Lachlan mumbled, rolling across the mattress to wrap his arms around her as she climbed back into their bed, careful to avoid the large puddle forming at the foot of it.

"The storm woke the twins." Evading his grabbing hands even as her blood began to heat, she sat up on her elbow and frowned at him in the darkness. "I really think we ought to see about hiring a new nursemaid. This one cannot do her job properly if she's asleep all the time."

Lachlan grunted. "Tavish and Eara need tae start learning how tae sleep through the night."

Easy for him to say, as he wasn't the one constantly being awoken by their cries.

"What they *need* is their mother," she corrected. "Has there been any word from Lady Heather on when she might return for them? Or your father, for that matter? They're his children as much as they are hers. I know you only mean to do well by all of your brothers and Eara, but–"

"Canna we discuss this in the morning?" Dipping his head, he took her nipple into his mouth through the thin fabric of her nightdress as his fingers skimmed beneath her hemline and along the inside of her quivering thigh to where her curls were slick with moisture.

"Lachlan…" she groaned, exasperation at his evasiveness warring with the sizzling licks of desire rapidly turning her flesh to flame.

"Aye?" he grinned, lifting his head for the fraction of an instant before he began to kiss his way down her navel and across her hip. As his tongue parted her curls and sipped the nectar within, she abandoned herself to the inevitable thrall of their passion.

Brynne had never partaken in opium, but if she ever did, she imagined it would be like this. A heavy velvet curtain falling around her, drowning out the noise of her doubts, and worries, and frustrations until the only thing left was pure, unadulterated pleasure.

This was what kept her from sinking.

This was what kept her nails dug into a board floating aimlessly amidst the waves.

She wasn't drowning.

Not yet.

But neither was she swimming.

And if she did dare to let go of that board…would she return to a ship that was on the brink of disappearing, or retreat to the safety of the shore?

WHEN BRYNNE WOKE the next day, the rain had ceased and Lachlan was gone. She was pleasantly surprised by the first–it *was* spring in Scotland, when rain was as natural as breathing–but felt an ache of disappointment at the second…followed swiftly by a sharp twinge of guilt.

She didn't want to be selfish. Which she would be, if she required all of Lachlan's time to be lavished upon her. But surely she was allowed *some* of it. At least more than she'd been getting, which was an hour of blissful heat in the middle of the night…and a cold bed come morning.

She'd gone to the distillery. Seen the fields for herself. The vastness of them, and the difficulty of the task her husband had chosen to undertake. For that reason, she knew that his inattentiveness wasn't born of maliciousness, but rather distraction. Which, in some ways, made it worse. In ranking of importance, she was above food–there were times Lachlan hardly remembered to eat–and below barley seeds. But she hadn't come here to trade one type of loneliness for another. That wasn't the life promised to her. She and Lachlan were supposed to be *partners*. With no half of them greater or more important than the whole.

If she was going to be set aside on a shelf for the sake of convenience, she'd rather it be at Hawkridge Manor where at least the roof didn't leak and she could put her hands in her pockets without fear of encountering something furry or slimy.

Things needed to change. Things *were* going to change, she thought with a renewed sense of determination as she donned a practical cotton dress and sturdy leather shoes capable of withstanding the quagmire of mud that surrounded the castle. Because *she* was going to change them.

After she changed the twins' nappies, that is.

SOMETHING MORE THAN the weather had shifted over the past few weeks. Lachlan felt it as keenly as the wind in his hair and the loamy soil beneath his feet. While the air had gradually warmed and the trees had begun to bloom, a noticeable chill had overtaken the castle.

And it was emanating from Brynne.

Admittedly, the first five months of their marriage hadn't been nearly as easy nor carefree as he'd anticipated. With planting season upon him and the entire fate of the distillery hanging in the balance–if the barley and wheat didn't take, there'd be no grains to ferment to make whisky–he had practically been living in the small lodge on the other side of the hill. Trudging home at the end of a long day to eat, bathe, and collapse into bed beside a wife that was already sleeping.

Sometimes, he didn't even make it that far.

Then there was the state of Campbell Castle itself. When it was only him and his brothers, he'd known that the grand old lady was in need of repairs...but seeing the shock in Brynne's gaze as their carriage had rounded the turn and the full scope of the castle had come into view–leaning towers, cracked windows, entire sections of roof clumsily patched with cheap tin shingles–he'd been forced to open his eyes to the fact that a complete restoration was needed. Which he'd be able to afford…once the distillery turned a profit.

It was a vicious circle. The faster it spun, the further he and Brynne were pushed apart. Sometimes it seemed as if she was all the way back in London…or she was *wishing* that she was in London, which was even worse. Not that he blamed her. Why would she want to be here, in the mud and the muck, when she could be sailing about a ballroom without a care in the world?

In his desperate desire to have her, he hadn't fully stopped to consider what the devil he was going to do with her once he did. The truth…the hard, difficult, unavoidable truth…was that he should have waited. A year, two, even three, and he'd be able to provide her with the life she was accustomed to. The life she *deserved*. But he'd run when he should have walked, and there was nothing to be done about it now but to keeping moving.

Well, almost nothing.

"I sent a firmly worded letter tae me dear stepmother," he informed Brynne as they engaged in a rare walk together through the orchards that wrapped around the edge of the fields where he and a crew of lads from the village had finished planting another seven acres of barley just that morning. "She and me father will be here tae collect the hellions before the week is out, and take them tae Kintore Manor."

Rather like the state of the castle, he'd vastly underestimated the sheer wildness of his siblings. From Callum to baby Eara and every brother in between, they were no more housebroken than a litter of wolf pups. He'd believed he was doing them a service by letting them roam the grounds without rules or regulations to abide by, both of which he had despised when *he* was a boy, but it was clear they'd benefit from more structure than he was capable of providing them at Campbell Castle.

Brynne stopped short. "You're sending them away? All of them?"

Taking note of the faint hint of censure in her tone, Lachlan leaned against the gnarled trunk of an apple tree and lifted a brow. "I assumed ye would be pleased."

"While I do think children should be with their parents, I would have liked to be consulted." She crossed her arms. "This is something we should have decided together."

And here he thought he'd been doing her a favor. "They're me siblings."

"Yes, but *we* are a family. And while I will hardly miss finding snakes in my undergarments, this was a choice that I'd have liked to discuss with you before you made it for both of us."

"Ye're angry," he observed as she resumed walking, albeit with a noticeably stiffer gait.

"I am," she tossed over her shoulder.

"Why?" he asked, genuinely puzzled.

"Because if I wanted important decisions to be made without any-one bothering to ask for my opinion, I would have remained in England!"

Ah, there it was.

He'd been waiting–no, *expecting*–this to happen.

It was only a matter of time.

Or so that little voice in the back of his head had whispered when shadows crept and owls cried. That it wouldn't be long before his bride began to yearn for the luxuries she'd left behind. That he'd never be able to give her what she needed to stay.

A piece of him had been preparing himself for this moment since Gretna Green. It was why, without fully realizing what he was doing or why he was doing it, he'd been keeping her at arm's length. Because you couldn't be hurt from losing what you didn't have.

And he did not have Brynne.

Not all of her, at any rate.

Six months of marriage and a part of her remained tied to the *ton*.

A tether waiting to reel her in.

A net ready to cushion her fall.

This wasn't a *marriage* to her, he thought with a surge of resentment. It was a bloody experiment. If it failed, she'd fly back into her gilded cage with nary a feather ruffled while he bled out on the ground.

And he had the means to prove it.

"Have ye written tae yer brother yet?" he snarled as anger filled him. Tangled up with his own shame, it pulsed hot and heavy through his veins, driving up his temper from a place of fear and desperation as his nostrils flared and his jaw clenched.

"I…" She gave a bewildered shake of her head. "What does he have to do with this?"

"Just answer the question, Bry. Have ye told Weston that we're married or not?"

"No," she said after a long pause. "Not yet, but–"

"*Goddamnit*," he cursed, throwing his arms wide as he started to stalk away, only to whip around to confront her with glittering eyes and a bitter heart. "Was that yer plan all along, then? Tae have a laugh in Campbell Castle for a while, and then jaunt back tae Hawkridge when ye grew weary of playing the poor lady wife in a castle ye despise?"

Her hazel eyes widened. "What? How could you say such a thing? I didn't write to Weston because our wedding was too important to tell him about in a letter. And I don't *despise* Campbell Castle. I just…" Her hands lifted helplessly. "It isn't what I was expecting."

"Aye, I should have told ye there'd be no butlers tae wait on ye hand and foot." A part of Lachlan acknowledged that he was being a right brutish bastard. But that was the problem with shame. More than any other emotion, it twisted a person up inside. It made them defensive when they didn't even know what they were defending against. And it made them lash out when they'd be better served to retreat to their own corner until cooler heads prevailed. But there was no calm to be found here. Not when the woman he loved had all but admitted she was too embarrassed of him to tell anyone they were married.

Oh, not in so many words.

But silence, pauses, hesitations…they spoke volumes.

And it was past time he started listening.

"I can do without a butler," his wife snapped back, lifting her chin. "I am not helpless. If you hadn't noticed, while you've been gallivanting about your precious fields, I've been taking care of four children!"

"*Gallivanting?*" he repeated incredulously. "*Gallivanting?* I've worked meself intae the bluidy ground. For *ye!*"

It was all for her.

It was always for her.

And it cut–it sliced to the *bone*–that it wasn't enough.

That no matter what he did, she would always be Lady Brynne Weston, granddaughter of a duke…and he would be Lachlan Campbell, the second-born son of a man who'd inherited his title because some dobber fell off a ladder.

"Well ye dinna have tae bother yerself with the boys and the twins any longer," he said when her lips flattened and her gaze went to the tree beside him. "Me father will collect them tomorrow, and they'll go tae where they should have been tae begin with. Callum's soon for Eton, with Blaine not far behind. Lady Heather can manage the two little ones and the twins easy enough with a few nannies tae keep them from toddling off." His mouth hardened. "Then ye willna have tae concern yerself with them."

Brynne's eyes cut to his. "While I do believe their needs will be better met at Kintore Manor, sending them away *is* a decision that should have been made between the both of us."

He gave a snort. "Dinna pretend ye ever wanted them here."

"I won't lie and say I haven't been overwhelmed, but that is only because I don't know the faintest thing about being a mother to four children! If you had bothered to tell me how many there were, and that we hadn't the resources to afford a nanny or a governess–"

"Ye never would have come," he said flatly.

"That's...that's not true," she argued.

But all Lachlan heard was another hesitation.

"Then let's talk about what's *true*. The second ye saw the castle, ye wished ye had never married me. That's true, isna it? Aye, that's what I thought," he sneered when her cheeks pinkened.

"If you'd just *told* me the state of things–"

"And what was I tae say?" His shout was loud enough to startle a pair of nesting warblers. Chattering in disapproval, they swooped low overhead before disappearing further into the orchard. "Leave yer fancy manor tae live in a place that's a stiff breeze away from tumbling over?"

"At least I would have known to bring an extra bucket for rainy nights!" she cried. "How could you think so little of me? My love for you is not *conditional*, Lachlan. I would have followed you anywhere. To a castle in the Highlands, or a cottage by the sea. The destination was never important."

Would have.

Would have.

"Then why havena ye told yer brother, or anyone else for that matter, that we're married? I'm not a fool, Bry. I know that ye are ashamed of me. Ashamed of *us*." Just speaking those words aloud caused a reddish flush to spread across the front of his chest and up his neck. He felt as if he were being boiled from the inside out, like a salmon tossed into a pot.

"That's a despicable thing to say, and hurts you as much as it does me." She stabbed her finger at him. "This winter has been difficult, I won't deny it. And the spring hasn't started off any better. I don't like fishing tadpoles out of my bath, or waking to sheets soaked through with rain. I don't know anyone in their right mind who *would* find pleasure in such things. But they were bearable because of you.

Because of the vows we took and the love we were supposed to have for each other."

He wondered if Brynne was even aware that she was speaking in past tense.

"*Supposed* tae have?" Snatching her by the wrist, he yanked her against him. Their bodies collided and the sparks were immediate; a burst of fireworks shooting off across a dark and turbulent sky. But then, they'd never lacked for physical attraction. Perhaps he'd let the burn of it blind him to what he should have seen all along.

"I love ye with every fiber of me being," he said hoarsely while she stared at him in defiance. "With every breath I take. With everything that I am and hope tae ever be. It's not me love that is in doubt, Bry. So I'll ask ye this one last time, and then let it rest." His grip tightened. "Why have ye not told Weston that we're married? I dinna claim tae know everything, but I do know one thing, and it's that people dinna keep secrets out of pride."

She struggled for an instant and then subsided, her eyes flashing with brilliant shards of green as she tossed back her head to glare.

"Is this some—some sort of *test*?" she exclaimed furiously.

Another non-answer.

Another evasion.

His shoulders slumped as his anger abated, leaving him empty and achingly hollow.

"Aye," he said heavily as he let her arm slip through his fingers. "And ye just failed."

CHAPTER EIGHTEEN

ROBERT CAMPBELL WAS a large man with an even larger voice. From the instant he stepped onto the grounds of Campbell Castle, his gravelly baritone infiltrated every inch of the castle. And that was even before he entered the stone foyer.

Apprehensive to meet her new father-in-law, a man whom she'd already unconsciously judged and found wanting for both his affairs and abandonment of his kin, Brynne lingered behind the children as they threw themselves into Robert's enormous arms.

They were, she noted with some relief, happy to see him. Even the twins stopped their squalling to stare at him with big, wondrous eyes. After doling out candy from a paper sack, he settled Tavish on his left side, Eara on his right, and beckoned Brynne over with a laughing shout.

"Aye, let me have a look at me new daughter!" he roared, leading her to question if he wasn't a tad hard of hearing. Dressed in a kilt and leather vest with his red hair, several shades lighter than Lachlan's deep auburn and peppered heavily with gray, loose and flowing over his shoulders, he was the very picture of a Scottish warrior of old…and not at all what she had expected.

Certainly *her* father had never dangled his children off his hip or bribed them with sweet treats. When the Marquess of Dorchester had seen fit to visit–despite it being his home as well as theirs, it had always felt like a visit–he was cold and contained. Brusque, even. And he'd *never* shown them any sort of physical affection.

Brynne gasped aloud when Robert wrapped her in a hearty embrace that stole the breath from her lungs and lifted her onto her tiptoes. It was like being hugged by a giant! Giggling, Eara and Tavish pinched her cheeks and stroked her hair as Robert rocked all three of them back and forth.

"Pwetty," Tavish gurgled, closing his chubby fist around one of Brynne's curls, and Lachlan's father gave a shout of laughter.

"That's me boy!" He tossed his youngest son into the air and caught him in the crook of his elbow as Brynne gave a tiny squeak of alarm. "Already flirting with the ladies, are ye? A Campbell rite of passage, tae be sure."

Unsure of what to make of the Marquess of Kintore, Brynne darted a glance at Lachlan, but he was little help. Standing off by himself in the far corner of the foyer, her husband gave her as much acknowledgement as he had this morning after joining her for breakfast. Which was to say, none at all.

After their argument yesterday, he'd gone off to the distillery and had spent the night there while she'd laid awake staring at the ceiling, replaying his words over and over again in her mind as she struggled to make sense of his rage.

What had begun as her attempt to communicate that she merely wanted to be included in important decisions had quickly spiraled into something else. In all the time they'd known each other, she had never witnessed such anger. Such animosity. Such…such *fury*. The things he had said to her, coupled with the way he had said them, had revealed a side of his personality that she'd never witnessed before.

The Lachlan she knew–the Lachlan she had married–was sweet, and endearing, and charming. But the Lachlan in the orchards, the Lachlan who had unleashed a torrent of barbed accusations that she'd been helpless to protect herself against, was abrasive, and callous, and hostile.

She wanted to be as angry with him as he was with her.

But she couldn't.

Because he was right.

About her reluctance to tell Weston she was married. About her dismay at the condition of the castle. And while she wasn't *ashamed* of their marriage, she was self-conscious of it. Of what others would say once it became public knowledge. Of what they would think. Of what they would do.

She knew that she shouldn't have cared. And maybe she wouldn't have, if she hadn't learned at her governess' knee that the *ton's* opinion of her wasn't just one thing, it was *everything*.

Who was she, without the approval of her peers?

She'd prayed that the answer would reveal itself when she came to Campbell Castle. Or disappear entirely. Instead, all she had were more questions…and a husband who refused to look at her. Biting the inside of her cheek in an effort to quell the unease in the pit of her belly, she turned her focus to the other red-haired Scot in the foyer.

"I've light refreshments in the parlor if you'd care for some, along with fresh lemonade," she offered, bestowing upon Lachlan's father the same smile she'd used when she'd met Queen Victoria. By her estimation, making a good impression on one's father-in-law was just as beneficial as impressing England's reigning monarch.

"Och, and are not ye a sweet lass tae offer such a warm welcome?" Robert boomed. "Ye have married a fine lady, Lachlan. A far sight better than that witch yer brother stuck himself with."

"Ye didna think she was a witch when *ye* asked her tae marry ye," Lachlan said mildly.

"Aye." Robert gave an unapologetic grin. "That's the truth of it. A good thing she said no, as I wouldna have wed me Heather, and she wouldna have blessed an old man with these two bairns." This time, he tossed *both* Eara and Tavish high into the air and they let out matching squeals of delight while Brynne cringed and clapped a hand over her eyes.

"Where *is* me dear stepmother?" asked Lachlan.

"Decorating the nursery with as many toys and rocking horses that she can find." Robert waggled his bushy eyebrows at Callum, who'd been about to drop a tiny garter snake into Brynne's pocket as a farewell gift. Blushing, the boy put the creature into his own pocket instead. "She feels poorly for leaving the children here for this long. We both do." He sobered. "It wasna yer burden tae bear, Son, and the last thing ye need is a pack of cubs running underfoot when ye're trying tae begin a new life with yer bonny bride."

Brynne found such an admission touching, but Lachlan merely snorted.

"And what do yer mistresses have tae say about sharing yer attention with yer wife *and* four brats?" he said even as he gave Blaine's tangled black hair an affectionate tousle.

"They will not complain after I give them a shiny bobble," Robert said cheerfully. "What do ye think, Daughter? Would ye rather rubies or emeralds tae soothe yer injured feelings?"

Brynne blinked. "Ah…"

"Ye are shocking my bride's delicate sensibilities." At that, Lachlan finally crossed the room to stand beside her. He even slipped an arm around her waist, but either did not see or chose to ignore the cautious curve of her lips. "Ye forget, Father, that the English are not nearly as bluntly spoken."

"But she's no longer an English rose, is she?" Handing Eara and Tavish off the nursemaid to be fed, Robert scratched under his chin. "Yer wife is a Campbell now, and pretty as a bouquet of wild heather." He gave Brynne a wink. "Sorry, lass, if I offended ye. Having six sons, I tend tae forget tae curb my tongue in polite company."

"That is quite all right," she said, and she meant it.

The Marquess of Kintore was as different from the Marquess of

Dorchester as the light of day was from the pitch of night, but she vastly preferred Robert's–admittedly flawed–character to her father's icy demeanor. It was obvious where Lachlan had gotten his charm from, and while she'd never want to be married to a man whose eye wandered as freely as Robert Campbell's, she was of the opinion that he'd make a fine father-in-law.

Again, she invited him into the parlor, but he declined with a regretful shake of his head.

"Next time, lass. But I'm sure me boy is as eager tae get ye all tae himself as me wife is tae see the twins. She had a bad spell of it, after they were born." Robert tapped the side of his skull. "Something went off, up here. Which is why I suggested she spend a few months in Bath. A change of scenery, and all that. It must have worked, for now she's right as rain and eager tae begin mothering."

Brynne had heard of new mothers who did not bond with their babies right away. A different sort of anxious mannerisms that had left her friend, Lady Wright, in bed for nearly half a year after the birth of her daughter. Thankfully, with time and patience and a good doctor (the first two had been fired after they suggested leeching), she'd made a full recovery and was due to welcome her second child any day, if she hadn't already.

"I am glad to hear it." Kneeling, Brynne gave each of Lachlan's brothers and little Eara a farewell hug. Her chest tightened as she rose, and she averted her gaze as the corners of her eyes stung. She must have touched her face after squeezing the lemons for the lemonade. Or else she'd grown more attached to this rambunctious group of miscreants than she'd thought.

"They'll be happy at Kintore Manor," Lachlan said quietly as he joined her in the doorway to wave a final goodbye. "Spoiled rotten, I am sure, but Lady Heather will have a veritable brigade of governesses at her disposal tae keep them in line. We can visit once they've settled in."

Brynne frowned. "Does she...that is to say, is your stepmother *aware* that your father–"

"Is a lecherous old goat who canna keep his pecker in his pants?" Lachlan said dryly.

Her cheeks suffused with color. "I don't know if I'd put it *that* way."

"Why, when that's the way it is? The way it's always been. Robert Campbell is a man of few vices. He doesna drink tae excess–at least not so much anymore. He's never raised a hand tae me or my brothers when it wasna needed. He honors his bets. But it has never been said that he is a faithful husband. Something Lady Heather well knew before she married him. Especially given that he was still married tae Blaine's mother when they...*met*."

"Then how–"

"If memory serves, me father claimed the marriage was never valid and paid a parishioner tae say the same. Blaine's mother trotted off with a hefty sum for her troubles, and Lady Heather trotted in. Not tae say she hadna already been doing some trotting, if ye understand me meaning."

"I–I see." As her blush deepened, Brynne wondered if she could abide such an arrangement. Affairs were more common in the *ton* than fidelity and if both parties were aware of their partner's indiscretions, as was the case with Lachlan's father and stepmother, then what was the harm? Except she didn't think–in fact, she *knew*–that she'd never want to share her husband with another. Just *imagining* him doing to another woman what he'd done to her...it was impossible. It was intolerable. But it was also something she'd never have to worry about.

While Lachlan had spoken harshly to her yesterday, he'd never hurt her on purpose. Of that, she was certain. She *had* to be certain. Because if he did...if he did, it would take them to a place that they'd never recover from.

She was already clinging by her fingernails. Such a betrayal would wrench her hands free, and then there'd be nothing to do but fall.

Nibbling her bottom lip, she cast her attention to the drive. All of the children–with the exception of Blaine, who hadn't been allowed to bring his snail collection into the carriage–were eager to set off to their new home, and they quickly found a seat in the enormous landau with the twins on Robert's lap. A crack of the whip, and the team of four horses set off in a plume of stone dust.

"Do ye hear that?" Lachlan asked, cupping his ear.

"What?" she said.

"Silence."

It *was* silent.

Almost eerily so.

But instead of finding respite in the quiet, the unease she'd been able to tamp down when Robert arrived resurfaced again. She didn't like this divide between her and Lachlan. This *distance*, even though they were standing side by side. They needed a bridge. Something to close the gap between her insecurities and his doubt. If she had to lay down the first plank, then so be it. Because she hadn't learned how to trap a frog in a silk stocking just to give up now.

"Lachlan–" she began.

"Bry–" he started.

They stopped.

Stared at each other.

"Ye said there were refreshments?" he said gruffly.

At her nod, they went into the parlor, which was really nothing more than a sparsely furnished room with a table in the middle surrounded by mismatched chairs. But the windows offered a view of the fields, and the sunlight trickling in through the glass caught on the tiny pieces of mica in the stone walls, and the air smelled of fresh citrus.

There was beauty to found here, Brynne reflected as she sat across from her husband. It wasn't obvious, or easy to find. It would take work–hard work–to make it shine. For the castle *and* this marriage. But it was possible. All hope needed was a single drop of rain to bloom. And heaven knew they had enough of it sitting around in buckets.

As LACHLAN GAZED at Brynne, her gloved hands demurely folded, her chin bowed, her eyes cast to the side, he felt like exactly what he was.

A great, bumbling lummox.

He'd let his Scot's temper get the best of him…and he'd said things that he shouldn't have. Things that were going to be difficult to take back in the calm after the storm. But damned if he wasn't going to try.

Or at least, that *was* the plan.

Until all hell broke loose.

"PIGS!" Adam McCrery cried as he catapulted into the parlor, splattering mud everywhere. An experienced farmer whom Lachlan had hired on last year to assist him in preparing the fields for sowing and planting, he was a quiet sort who never wasted a word. This was the first time, to Lachlan's knowledge, that he'd ever raised his voice above a thoughtful whisper.

"What?" Brynne exclaimed as she half-rose from her seat.

"*Pigs*," Adam repeated, throwing his arms wide for emphasis. "Twenty of them, maybe more. They got out of their pen last night and ontae the barley sometime early this morning."

Lachlan could *feel* the blood draining from his face. He gripped the arms of his chair to steady himself. "How much damage?" he asked grimly.

"We tried tae herd them off at the high ridge, but–"

"*How much damage?*" he repeated.

Adam hung his head. "All of it, Lachlan. They destroyed all of it."

CHAPTER NINETEEN

L ACHLAN WAS GONE for the rest of the day. Brynne offered to go with him to inspect the fields and see if anything could be done to salvage what the pigs had ruined, but he asked her to remain behind.

"Boars are nasty buggers," he'd told her tersely as he had retrieved his rifle from above the mantel in the drawing room, "and can take down a man if they've the inclination. I'll return when I can. It might not be until tomorrow."

He had given her a chaste kiss on the cheek, and then he'd left, leaving her to fret and wander the castle grounds for what seemed like a small eternity.

At last, unable to sit idly by any longer even though that was precisely what Lachlan had asked her to do, she prepared a basket with bread, cheese, and sliced meats and set off to the distillery to see if there was anything she could do.

She was halfway down the winding trail when she was met by a dark-haired woman with blue eyes and a smile as sharp as the edge of a scalpel.

"Lady Campbell," she said, stopping in the middle of the trail and lifting her lavender-colored skirts in a curtsy. "What an honor tae finally meet ye. I am–"

"Miss Allison Adair. Yes, I remember." Shifting the heavy basket, Brynne was careful to keep her countenance devoid of expression as she addressed her husband's former mistress. "I did not realize you'd be here."

"Once word reached the village of what had happened, we all came as fast as we could tae help. Not fast enough, I'm afraid. All of the seedlings were lost. Lachlan, of course, is absolutely devastated."

Lachlan.

Not Lord Campbell.

The distinction was slight...*but purposeful*, Brynne noted when she saw the gleam in Allison's eyes.

"Is that for yer husband?" the brunette asked, reaching for the basket. "I'm happy tae take it tae him and save ye the trip."

"That really isn't–very well," Brynne relented, automatically falling back upon her manners as Allison all but wrenched the basket from her hands. Well-bred ladies did not fight over chunks of cheese and peppered ham. "I'll accompany you. Is Lachlan in the fields, or–"

"He's resting in the lodge, but I shall make sure tae let him know that ye brought him this." Allison peeled back the blanket Brynne had covered the food with to peer inside. "What a kind wife ye are, Lady Campbell. Lachlan is a fortunate man."

How did Allison know where he was sleeping?

It was an ugly question.

One that she wished her mind hadn't procured.

But now that it had, it circled her head like a gnat, buzzing just out of reach as it searched for a place to draw blood.

"I heard that Robert Campbell came tae visit and take the wee ones besides." Allison arched a perfectly groomed ebony brow. "How did ye manage that trick?"

"It wasn't a trick," Brynne said defensively. "Lachlan's siblings should be in the care of their father, and I..."

I shouldn't be explaining myself to you, she thought crossly.

"Can you see that my husband receives that?" she said, nodding at the basket. "And have someone send word to me when he has awoken."

Allison curtsied again, although there was a detectable hint of mockery in her tone when she said, "Of *course*, my lady."

Brynne smiled thinly. "Thank you."

Against her better instincts, she went back to the castle, and spent a large portion of the night roaming the damp halls, the train of her wrapper fluttering behind her as she paced from one window to the next, searching the inky darkness for sign of a light, or a horse, or even a wayward pig. *Anything* to indicate that her husband was soon to return home.

He'd spent previous nights at the distillery. Too many to count. But they hadn't gnawed at her as they did now. She didn't know whether it was their argument, or her encounter with his mistress, or even the quiet...but *something* was lifting the hairs at the nape of her neck. Something was causing her breaths to shorten and her chest to fill with lead. Something was sending her into a near panic as she fought both sleep and the sly whispers of *"what if?"*

At the first streak of dawn across an ominous red sky, she was on her way to the distillery. Passing fields pillaged by rooting boars, the neat rows of barley torn asunder, the soil churned up, years of hard work utterly demolished in the span of a few hours.

Lachlan would rebuild, because that's who he was.

But as she climbed the steps to the lodge, a rectangular building made of crudely hewn timber tucked behind a line of aspen, she felt the ache of his loss—of *their* loss—as if it were a tangible being.

They'd just have to start over, she decided. Except this time, they'd do it differently. This time, they'd do it *together*. With no secrets or half-truths between them.

She'd write to Weston this day to let him know that she wasn't in Paris, as she had led him to believe, but married and living in a castle in the Highlands. Oh, but to see his expression when he read that letter! He'd be angry with her. Most likely disappointed. But he'd come around when he saw that she was happy. And she *would* be happy. As soon as she and Lachlan had the opportunity to clear the air between them, lay all of their proverbial cards upon the table (no more hiding their relationship from the *ton* out of some misguided attempt at retaining her social standing, no more hiding the truth from her out of some attempt to get the reaction or answer that he wanted), and begin anew.

They would be honest, even when it was hard.

Especially when it was hard.

Because in their hearts, they loved each other. And there was nothing that could tear that love apart.

Except this, Brynne thought dazedly as she raised her fist to knock on the bedroom door and it swung inward beneath the slight pressure of her hand to reveal her husband sprawled on his back in the middle the bed...with Allison Adair draped across the top of him.

She didn't know how long she stood there.

Staring.

Just staring.

At the coverlet thrown on the floor. At the sheets tangled on the bed. Covering some parts of their bodies, but not enough to hide that they were both naked. At Allison's dark hair fanned across his shoulder. At the steady rise and fall of Lachlan's ribcage as he slept, blissfully oblivious to the presence of his wife in the doorway. Or the knife he'd plunged into her heart.

Oh, Lachlan. What have you done to us?

She must have made a sound, a tiny whimper of distress, because Allison's eyes opened and went straight to where Brynne stood frozen; a deer in the midst of a thicket right before the hunter's gun exploded.

"Lady Campbell!" she cried, grabbing onto a corner of the sheet and drawing it over her breasts. "I–I dinna know what to *say*."

Lachlan stirred. His mouth stretched in a yawn that turned into a grimace. He scratched the side of the jaw where a rough shadow of beard had grown overnight and then–while Brynne watched and fought to contain the nausea rising within her throat–reached for Allison.

"This is a pleasant way tae wake up," he said, nuzzling her neck.

"Ye are right about that," Allison purred, rubbing herself against him without breaking Brynne's horrified gaze. "Unfortunately, it seems we've been caught. It was bound tae happen eventually. I'm so sorry ye had tae find out this way, Lady Campbell. But as they say, like father, like son."

"Wait," Lachlan began, his brow furrowing as he set himself up on his elbow and looked down at his mistress. "What–"

"How *could* you?" The words wrenched themselves from Brynne's broken heart. From her very *soul*. With an agonized cry, she spun on her heel and bolted out of the lodge. Picking up her skirts, she ran blindly, forgoing the marked path to plunge into long grass that slapped at her arms and legs. Somewhere behind her, she heard Lachlan calling her name, but she ignored him in her mad dash to escape what she'd seen. Never mind that it was already burned into her memory, never to be forgotten.

Without warning, the grass gave way to the sheer edge of a cliff. Below the rocky embankment, waves crashed against the shore and gulls flew amidst the surf, dodging in and out of the salty spray in a feat of aerial acrobatics.

Brynne's feet went out from under her as she slid to a stop. Her breaths uneven and jagged, her pulse pounding in her ears, she collapsed to the ground. Would have laid right there with her face pressed to the cool soil had Lachlan not appeared behind her.

He scooped her up as if she weighed no more than a bag of goose down, and carried her away from the cliff to a series of gray boulders covered in moss and seemingly carved from the earth itself.

"Let go of me," she demanded, clawing at his hands as if his arms were a steel trap and she were a wild animal hellbent on escape.

"Don't *touch* me."

He released her and stepped back with his hands raised, palms facing outwards. A strong wind whipped across the valley, sending his hair, unbound, across his face. He shoved it out of his eyes. Eyes that were as dark and haunted as she'd ever seen them.

"Bry, ye have tae listen–"

"I don't *have* to do anything," she interrupted. Having reached the bottom of her despair, she was strangely…numb. A ship that had made it to the middle of a hurricane to bob listlessly amidst the waves. Not feeling. Not doing. Just floating in place while it waited for the next surge.

"Ye dinna see what ye thought ye did."

"I saw you naked in bed with your mistress." Her head tilted. "Was that not you?"

He gritted his teeth. "Aye, that was me. But Allison isna me mistress!"

"She was before," Brynne pointed out matter-of-factly.

"Ye know that I ended things between us long before ye and I were married."

"It didn't appear as if things were *ended* when you had your leg on her–"

"I realize what it looked like." He pressed the heels of his hands to his temple. Squeezed. "I do. But I dinna know how or when she climbed intae bed with me. I swear it."

"It is partially my fault, I suppose," she mused, not bothering to give his pitiful excuse so much as a sliver of consideration. Ice had begun to seep into her veins. She welcomed the coldness of it; a frosty balm to soothe the burn of Lachlan's betrayal. "You asked for my loyalty, but you never promised your own. I made an assumption that I shouldn't have, and now I have to pay the price for my naiveté."

Unbidden, she thought of the Dowager Countess of Crowley and what her chaperone had said on the night that Lachlan proposed.

"...at least you will have followed your heart. I shall pray that will be a comfort, when nothing else is."

Yes, Brynne had followed her heart.

But there was no comfort to be found here.

"I am leaving," she said evenly. "Today, if I can arrange transportation. Tomorrow at the latest."

Some women might have stayed. To meekly abide by their husband's command, regardless of the wrongs he'd committed. Or to fight for his affection like a stray cat begging for scraps. She would do neither. Her pride–and the bloody, shattered thing beating feebly inside of her chest–refused to allow it.

Lachlan stared blankly at her, as if she had announced that she'd decided to turn into a unicorn. "Ye canna just *leave.*"

"What possible reason do I have to stay?" she scoffed. "The children are gone, the castle is falling apart, and I am wed to an adulterer. An adulterer who is more loyal to these fields of–of *dirt* than he is to his own wife. You're not married to me, Lachlan. You're married to the damned distillery. There is nothing for me here."

"*I'm* here," Lachlan said softly. His eyes, those gold-flecked orbs that she'd first fallen in love with under a sky filled with stars, pleaded with her to stay. He even held out his hand, fingertips stretched towards hers.

For a moment, she almost relented.

For a moment, she almost forgave the unforgivable.

And that frightened her so much, that she did the only thing she could think of.

She tried to hurt him as much as he had hurt her.

"You are not enough, Lachlan." It was a testament to the depth of her own agony that she didn't flinch when she saw the raw, vulnerable quiver of pain in his gaze.

Coverlet on the floor.

Sheets tossed carelessly over naked bodies.

Touching. Nuzzling. Kissing.

Her chin lifted a notch. Above it, her gaze was as frigid as the Arctic. "You will never be enough. And if you ever loved me at all, you will let me go."

HE DID LET her go. For six miserable months he threw himself into his work at the distillery, doing more in a single day than three men could in two. From sunrise to sunset, he dug posts for fencing and hung barbed wire (a particularly nasty American invention intended to keep out even the strongest of boars) until his palms were blistered and his fingers were bleeding.

Then when the workers headed for the pub, sweaty and stinking and ready to quench their thirst with a pint, he went to the castle and tackled another sort of job altogether.

It shamed him that he'd asked Brynne to live in this place. Having run feral through the halls since before he could remember, he was accustomed to the crumbling walls and the holes in the ceiling and the cobwebs in the corners. Hell, he couldn't even see them anymore. Not until he made himself look at the dark, dingy rooms through the eyes of his wife. And felt a deep, burning embarrassment for having brought her here. For asking her to leave everyone and everything she knew behind, and then taking her to a place where rainwater was collected in buckets. On the *inside* of the house.

He ought to consider himself fortunate that she hadn't turned on her heel and fled back to London the first time she saw her new home. But she'd fought through it for as long as she was capable. Until she came up against a wall that, in her mind, was too hard to knock down and too high to climb. What other choice did she have *but* to walk away?

After the initial wave of hurt and fury had subsided, he was able to understand that. To see it through her perspective. To acknowledge why she'd given up the fight.

And to realize that he never would.

Brynne had been strong for as long as she could. While he'd chased his own dreams at the sake of her comfort, she'd done her best to make a life for them here. A home for them here out of peeling plaster and scurrying mice and screaming children. Until it became too much. Until she had to lay down her proverbial sword. A sword that he'd since picked up, because now it was his turn. His turn to fight for both of them.

He'd given it six months and a stone of his own weight. Probably a pint of his own blood as well, if he counted all the times he'd accidentally sliced his flesh open on that damned wire. But now he was ready to reclaim what was his. To take back what he had lost and take control of what might be. What *would* be, when he and Brynne were back together where they belonged.

If not for the bloody pigs and all that had followed after, they might be there already.

He arrived at Hawkridge Manor on the first night of yet another annual house party. His world may have stopped when Brynne left, but it was apparent that this world–this world of glamour and wealth and prestige–kept spinning no matter what…with Brynne at its center, once again playing her role as the perfect daughter, perfect hostess, perfect lady.

He'd dressed for the occasion in formal attire, even though his invitation must have gotten lost in the mail. Tricky, those Highland roads. No telling when a mail coach was going to turn left instead of right and find itself halfway back to Glasgow before the driver was any the wiser. Might as well dump the letters and start again at that point. Which was as reasonable an excuse as any to explain why he hadn't received a fancy beige envelope with the Earl of Hawkridge's wax seal.

Except when he tried to enter through the foyer and join the rest of the guests in the dining room where they were enjoying a seven-course meal, he was stopped by a portly fellow holding a paper list. A list, apparently, that Lachlan was not on.

"I am sorry, my lord, your name is not here," said the servant. A footman, by the look of him. "If a name is not here, I am not allowed to admit them."

"Give me that," he growled, snatching the list.

The servant immediately paled and took a step back.

It wasn't until Lachlan read to the bottom that he realized why.

Underneath a long row of names, neatly scrawled in Brynne's own handwriting, was a simple, damning instruction.

Should he arrive, Lord Lachlan Campbell is not permitted inside under any circumstances.

She'd known, he thought with a surge of annoyance and sliver of grudging admiration. She'd known that he'd come for her. That there wasn't a bloody thing on heaven and earth that would keep him away. And she had planned accordingly.

How sweet of the wee lass to believe that she'd succeed.

"Are ye tae stop me then?" he asked the footman whom he towered over by at least seven inches.

To his credit, the servant did not move from the doorway. "If I have to, my lord." Then he lowered his voice. "Please don't make me have to."

"I'll go without a quarrel," said Lachlan, holding up his hands.

The servant smiled with relief. "Thank you, my lord."

"Aye." With that, he walked out the way he'd come in...but he had no intention of leaving. Instead, he waited, lurking in the bushes like some sort of besotted Romeo for Juliet to make her appearance. Excluding the part where they died at the end.

Eventually, the dinner ended and the guests took advantage of the warm evening air, venturing outside onto the various walkways and terraces to drink their wine and smoke their cigars while they congratulated themselves on being invited to such an exclusive affair.

The self-important bounders.

There was no one on these grounds, with the exception of Weston, who loved Brynne as he did. Who cared for her as he did. Who saw her–the *real* her–as he did.

These people didn't know her.

They just knew the person she pretended to be when she was around them.

When she stepped out of a doorway and stood with candlelight at her back and moonlight on her face, he was temporarily stunned by her beauty. Six months without gazing upon her countenance and she took his breath as if they'd been apart for six years.

Not another day, he vowed as he cut a silent swath through the shadows.

Not another damned day.

He caught her before she could descend the stairs. Enclosing her wrist between his fingers, he pulled her into an alcove out of sight of those who might wonder what Lady Brynne Weston was doing with the likes of Lachlan Campbell.

"*You,*" she hissed, yanking free of his grasp and causing him to frown.

"Well ye needna say it like I'm the villain," he scowled.

"Why?" Her hands went to her slender waistline, the tips of her gloves disappearing into heavy folds of pale yellow satin. "That is precisely what you are. I was under the impression that I'd made myself clear that we were through, Lachlan."

"Aye, that's what ye *said,*" he acknowledged, and there was a part of him that still ached when he remembered the words she'd used. "But it's not what ye meant. We all say things when we're angry, little bird."

"Look at me carefully." She tapped her chin, drawing his attention to her lovely face. Silky cream with golden brows and the barest hint of rose in those high, high cheekbones. "Do I look angry?"

His first instinct was to say yes. But upon further consideration, he saw that all that white-hot fury from the day on the cliffs had faded and ebbed. In its place...in its place was a quiet, determined resolve that chilled him to the bone. Because it meant that whatever his Bry said now, it wouldn't be spoken out of anger. Instead, it'd come from a place of calculated thought.

And that was much harder to take back.

"Bry–" he began, but she cut him off with a sharp jerk of her arm.

"You need to leave. Right this minute."

"Or what?" he challenged.

"Or I'll shoot you."

She said it so calmly, so matter-of-factly, that he started to laugh.

Right up until she reached inside a reticule he hadn't even noticed she was carrying and withdrew the tiniest, most adorable pistol he'd ever seen. At least it *was* adorable until she drew back the hammer with a loud *click* that made the weapon sound much more deadly than it appeared.

"Are ye going tae kill me?" he said incredulously.

Annoyance flickered in her gaze. "Don't be ridiculous."

"Well that's a relief tae–"

"A bullet of this size would not cause lethal harm." She straightened her arm and, to his horror, pointed the pistol right at the middle of his groin. "But I imagine it's not going to feel very good."

"Bluidy hell! Let's not leap tae any hasty decisions." Holding up one hand to ward her off while the other protectively cupped his bollocks, he retreated a step into the inky darkness. "I came here tae have a productive conversation, Bry. Not tae have me bits blown off. What happened tae a lady's civility?"

A muscle clenched in her jaw. "It disappeared when I walked into that bedroom. I am not going to warn you again, Lachlan. You're not welcome here. I don't *want* you anymore. And you need to leave. Now."

She may not have fired the pistol, but her words cut through him like a bullet. Words that he never dreamed his Bry, his beloved, the girl he'd loved since he was a lad, would be capable of saying. As hurt flared, followed closely by a red-hot flash of rage, he opened his mouth to tell her how wrong she was...but then the clouds over the moon shifted, and silver light illuminated the well of tears in those magnificent hazel eyes, and he gritted his teeth together.

Brynne was hurting, too. Trying her best to hide it, but pain recognized pain. Wasn't that one of the first things that had drawn them together? The English girl ignored by her family, and the Scottish boy tossed out of his school.

"All right," he said stiffly. "I'll leave ye in peace, Bry."

But even as he turned and disappeared into the shadows, Lachlan knew that he'd be back. When the hurt settled and the pain wasn't so fresh and they could have that civil discussion without fearing for his poor bollocks, he'd return.

Brynne wasn't a prize he was keen on giving up.

No matter how much time it took to win her back.

CHAPTER TWENTY

"**I** REMEMBER EVERYTHING." As the past and the present converged to form a lump in Brynne's throat, she swallowed with difficulty and forced herself to look directly into Lachlan's eyes. She owed him that for what she'd said. For her part in the pain they'd caused each other. For her side of the marriage that had failed.

Because it wasn't just him.

It was *never* just him.

And she was a coward for letting herself pretend otherwise for the past eighteen months.

Gazing at him kneeling in front of her, she wished (oh, how she wished) that they'd guarded their words more carefully. That they'd practiced more kindness. Not only with each other, but with themselves. And while she couldn't go back and change the past, she was determined to take responsibility for it.

"I was wrong, Lachlan." She put her hand on top of his. "About so many things. I should never have kept our marriage a secret from my family. It wasn't something to hide, it was something to be celebrated. And I should have listened to you that morning by the cliff. I was hurt, and angry, and I lashed out."

"Ye had good reason tae. Had I walked in and seen what ye had, I would've reacted much the same." His mouth twisted in a humorless smile. "After I broke both of the bastard's legs, that is. But I should have told ye about what ye would be walking intae when ye married me. The *true* state of things; not what I hoped one day for them tae be. The castle, and the children, and the distillery not yet turning a profit."

"Yes," she agreed. "We *both* could have been more honest with each other. We both should have been. But in the end, my most horrible day with you was better than any day spent without you. Over these past eleven years, you've always been where I needed you, Lachlan. When I needed you most. You helped me become a stronger woman, capable of more than I ever thought possible." The corners of her lips curved. "Certainly, I never envisioned myself retrieving toads from the rafters or changing nappies in the middle of the night."

"Aye, and it's a wonderful mother ye will make when the times comes." Again his gaze dropped to her belly, but this time it was with warmth instead of fear. "But ye are wrong about one thing. This isna the end, little bird. It's just the beginning. For ye, and for me. For *us*." He lifted her hand. Kissed the back of it. "We can start again. Knowing what we do now, there'll be nothing tae stand in our way that we canna overcome together."

How tempted she was. But just as she couldn't change the past, neither would she allow herself to forget it...or the lessons it had taught her.

That sometimes loneliness was better.

That pain, even with one you loved, was inevitable.

And that you couldn't lose your heart if you didn't give it away.

It was ironic, really.

Over the course of the house party, she'd urged Weston over and over again to seek out Evelyn Thorncroft because she'd seen the possibility of love between them. She had told *him* to risk everything for the sake of happily-ever-after, and if the letter he'd sent her was any indication, it had worked out splendidly. But she wasn't going to follow her own advice for the same reason that she didn't wear chartreuse despite recommending the color to Lady Nelson.

What worked for one person didn't necessarily work for another. Having pieced together a broken heart once, she wasn't keen to do it a second time.

Logically, she understood that there was no guarantee she and Lachlan would end up destroying each other again. However, there was also no guarantee that they *wouldn't*. Which was why this time…this time, she was going to take the safer path.

"I am having my solicitor go forward with the judicial separation, Lachlan." When he stiffened, she tried to place a comforting hand on his shoulder, but her arm was knocked aside when he surged to his feet.

"Why the devil would ye do that?" he scowled, a shadow rippling across the rigid set of his jaw as he took a step back.

"Because that's what we are." Wanting even footing for what was to come, she rose as well, and took a measured breath meant to both calm any lingering anxiety and reassure herself that she was doing what needed to be done. What was right. What was *necessary*. And while Lachlan likely wouldn't thank her for it now, he'd eventually realize–as she had–that they were better off apart. "We are separated. We've *been* separated. This will just…make if official."

"I dinna *want* tae make it official." He raked a hand through his hair. "I dinna *want* tae be separate any longer. That's why I came here. Tae make amends. Tae sort what needed tae be sorted. And we did. We have. I'm sorry for the mistakes I made, Bry. For the missteps I took. I'm not a perfect man–"

"You don't have to be perfect. That is not what I'm asking."

"Then what *are* ye asking?"

She smiled sadly. "You were always so certain of us, Lachlan. Even when we were children. I used to believe that that certainty meant we were supposed to be together–"

"We are," he cut in roughly.

"–but people who belong together don't hurt each other as we did. As we might again, if given the opportunity. Which is why I am asking you, once again, to let me go. To let us go. I don't *want* to start over. Not if there's the chance we might end up exactly where we are."

"When ye build something magnificent, there's always the chance it will fall apart." He crossed the gazebo. Took her hands. Cocooned them in his. "But if it does, ye build it again."

How simple he made it sound!

And for him, maybe it was.

But not for her.

"I have made my decision, Lachlan."

His eyes flashed. "Well it's a bluidy stupid one!"

When annoyance stirred, she slipped her hands free of his embrace and put them on her hips. "Why? Because *I* am the one who made it? For as long as I can remember, people have made decisions for me. What I ate, what I wore, what I did, where I went–even you, Lachlan. When you proposed marriage, it wasn't so much a question as it was a forgone conclusion. You assumed what my answer would be before you even asked the question."

"Ye said yes, didna ye?" he snapped.

"I did. And now I am saying no."

"Bry–"

"My mind is made up. You cannot change it. I…" When tears unexpectedly threatened, she pressed her lips together until she was able to gain control of her emotions. "I am sorry. I know this isn't what you wanted to hear. The decision you wanted me to make. But it *is* my decision, and I'd like you to honor it."

He went to the edge of the gazebo. Braced his arms on the railing and stared out across the lawn. Gray clouds were beginning to roll in, a preemptive warning of an afternoon storm. But the warning was too late. The storm was already here.

"A judicial separation," her husband said bitterly.

"That's right."

A long, heavy sigh. And then…"What do I have tae do?"

"Sign the papers when they're given to you. My solicitor has told me that we won't be required to present ourselves to the court." *Thank goodness for small favors,* she thought silently. This was terrible enough. If she had to end her marriage in front of a room filled with solemn-faced strangers in wigs… "It shouldn't take long. A month or two, at the most."

"Nearly ten years tae make something, and a month tae destroy it." The wisp of a smile captured his mouth as he looked at her over his shoulder. "This isna where I thought we'd end up, little bird."

Without anger to dull it, the pain of loss sliced through her with all the force of a Scottish claymore. When her knees wobbled and her breath stabbed, she curled her fingers inward so tightly that her nails left crescent furrows on the palms of her hands. *This is what you wanted,* she reminded herself sternly. *It will get easier once he's gone, and everything can return to normal.*

It would have been easier if he'd never come at all, but–for once–she was grateful for his stubbornness. They'd needed to have this time together. To rip bandages off old wounds. To heal old hurts. Now they'd be able to move forward without resentment or regret. Lachlan could return to Campbell Castle to pursue his dreams, and she'd go to London to ensure her brother had his. Then someday, when she had a clearer picture of what she wanted, she would go after her own.

It wasn't happily-ever-after.

But it was close enough.

"If you see the children, please give them my best," she said softly.

"Ye could see them yerself, if ye wanted."

Her hands squeezed tighter. "I've kept in correspondence with Lady Heather. She says they are well, and have enjoyed the presents I

219

sent them for their birthdays and Christmas."

"And there it is." He canted his head. "I never saw it before. Maybe because I didna want tae. But it's as clear as a day now."

"What is?" she asked, self-consciously unfurling her hand to brush her thumb across her cheek.

"Yer father, Bry. Ye're the spitting image of him." With that, Lachlan left.

And Brynne was finally, irrevocably, completely alone.

CHAPTER TWENTY-ONE

"RUNNING AWAY SO SOON?" Sterling drawled as he sauntered into the stable yard to watch Lachlan finish preparing his mare for the long ride to Carlisle, where they'd both board a train that would take them the rest of the way to Glenavon. "I had you pegged for at least another three days. You lost me a bet with the footman, Campbell."

"Maybe ye shouldna be betting with footmen." Lachlan finished tightening the girth, then moved to Aislyn's head to put the bit between her teeth. Brown ears raised and attentive, she lowered her head and stood patiently while he adjusted the noseband and buckled the throatlatch.

It was a good thing he'd tacked her a hundred times before this, for his motions were purely based on muscle memory as his mind and his heart were still in that damned gazebo, going over everything he'd said and where he'd gone wrong.

For surely he had done *something*. Said something. Or not said something. If he could figure out what it was, he could fix it...and he and Brynne could find their way back. They *had* to find their way back. Unless the way back really was letting go. And if that was the way she wanted it...the way it was to be...then the only thing left for him to do was leave.

He'd have liked to *make* her love him. To insist she remain married to him, and to hell with this judicial separation. But then he would just be exchanging one cage for another, and that wasn't how you kept a wild bird.

That was how you broke it.

If Brynne flew to him…if she flew to him, it needed to be *her* decision. Her choice.

He couldn't make it for her.

"Pardon me," he said curtly as he tried to lead Aislyn out of the barn and past the Duke of Hanover, but Sterling refused to move.

"How long have you and Weston's sister been married?" he asked.

That got Lachlan to stop. "Did Brynne tell ye?"

"No," the duke grinned. "But you just did. And I guessed. Watching you two go at it was like seeing my parents all over again, God rest their souls."

As it was apparent that Sterling had no plans to move anytime soon, Lachlan made himself comfortable on a wooden mounting block, knees bent and boots firmly planted, while Aislyn helped herself to a nearby hay bale. "Yer parents hated each other, then?"

Sterling blinked. "Hated? No, they were bloody crazy about each other. It was embarrassing. Always holding hands and gazing longingly. Blech. It was a mercy that when they died, they went together, for I truly don't believe they would have been able to live apart. A boating accident," he explained when Lachlan gave a questioning lift of his brow. "Capsized off the coast with nary a survivor. I was sixteen, my brother barely twenty, our sister Sarah a baby at ten."

"I'm sorry," said Lachlan.

"It will be eleven years ago, next month."

"Does it get easier with time? Losing someone ye love."

"It does…sometimes." Reaching inside his coat, Sterling removed a silver flask. He tipped it back. Took a liberal swallow. "Although I guess it depends on the permanence of the loss. How long have you and Brynne hated each other?"

"We dinna–" Lachlan gritted his teeth. "We dinna hate each other."

"Madly in love, then. Squabbling with that much passion, it's always one or the other." As he took another sip from the flask, the duke's voice took on a dreamy, wistful quality. "Eloise and I would fight like the dickens and then fuck until dawn. Like a pair of temperamental rabbits."

"Who is Eloise?"

"She *was* my mistress. Until I killed her, chopped her body up into little pieces, and fed her to the lions at the Regent's Zoo."

"Ye did what now?" Lachlan asked politely.

"Too gruesome? Too gruesome." At Lachlan's blank stare, Sterling sighed. "Didn't you hear? I'm a murderer."

Lachlan snorted. "Ye're not a murderer."

"How the hell do you know?"

"Because murderers dinna admit tae murdering."

"Maybe I'm just not a *good* murderer."

"I dinna think there is such a thing as a good murderer."

Sterling's brow furrowed. "You're probably right about that." He held out the flask. "Fancy a nip of gin?"

"As I dinna make a habit of drinking horse shite and then riding, I'll pass."

"More for me, then." Sterling drank the rest, grimaced, and slipped the empty flask back into his pocket. "It *is* horse shite, but Brynne locked away the brandy and this was all I could buy off a groom. Where are you riding off to? Back to Scotland, I presume?"

Lachlan gave a brusque nod and rose from the mounting block to gather Aislyn's reins. "Aye. So if ye wouldna mind stepping aside–"

"I take it your wife isn't accompanying you."

"No," he said shortly. "She isna."

"Shame, that."

"Aye."

"But," said Sterling, taking up the entire aisle as he casually stretched his arms out to the side, "isn't there something that can be done?"

"Bluidy hell, man! Canna ye not just get out of the way?" Lachlan knew he shouldn't have spoken to a duke in such a manner, but Sterling was pressing on his last remaining nerve. It tingled right beneath his skin; a tiny boulder suppressing a flood of emotions that he preferred to release in the solitude of his own company.

"When I lost the person that I loved, I'd have done anything to get them back. *Anything.* Except I couldn't, because death is as permanent an ending as this cruel world provides us. You could still have Brynne, if you wanted. Instead, you're just riding away. Damned cowardly of you, if you want my opinion."

"I dinna recall asking for it," Lachlan said bluntly. "I'm sorry ye lost yer mistress, Yer Grace. I am. But a paramour isna a wife. It's more...complicated than that."

"Love is love." Sterling shrugged. "Heartbreak is heartbreak. Do you think that just because I smile more than you I'm any happier?"

For the first time, Lachlan looked at the duke. Really looked. And he saw the dark shadows beneath his eyes from not enough sleep. The flaky paleness of his skin from remaining indoors. The layer of bloat under his chin that came from excess drink. "No, I suppose not."

"I cannot do a damned thing to change my circumstance, Campbell. But *you* can."

His jaw clenched. "She doesna want me. She's made that abundantly clear."

"Then do what all gentlemen of all species have done since the beginning of time when a woman they desired cannot be bothered to give them the time of day."

"And what's that?"

Sterling rolled his eyes. "*Court* her. Flowers, poems, the whole lot. Unless you've tried that already?"

Court Brynne?

The idea had never crossed his mind.

Maybe because, as she herself had said in the gazebo, there *was* a part of him that had always known that she would marry him. He'd expected her to say yes because that was what he wanted her to do. He'd taken her for granted. And in doing so, he had treated her no differently than anyone else had her entire life.

"I gave her a barley stick once, when we were children."

"A barley stick. A *barley stick*." Sterling clapped a hand to his forehead. "Do you know what Eloise would have done if I'd presented her with a barley stick? She'd have shoved it up my–"

"I get the idea," Lachlan interrupted before *that* mental picture could be painted in his head for all of eternity. "So ye're saying I should do what all of ye English blokes do and buy me wife's love with expensive gifts and flashy baubles?"

"I'm saying you put in the effort, you get the reward. That's how it works. And a pretty necklace never hurt anything. The Season is under way. Plenty of balls and soirees and opportunities to impress." The feigned lightness dissolved from Sterling's countenance, leaving him hard, and hollow, and haunted. "Love your wife, Campbell. Love her with everything you have. Because you never know when she'll be taken from you. And what you feel now is nothing–*nothing*–compared to what you'll feel then. If I could have a minute back...hell, a second, I'd grab it in a bloody heartbeat."

Sobering words from an unsober man.

Lachlan led his horse past the duke and, this time, Sterling stepped aside.

"Where can I reach you for that bottle of whisky?" he called out as Lachlan placed his foot in the stirrup and swung into the saddle.

"London," he replied, spinning Aislyn in a tight circle before setting his heels into her sides. "I'll be in London."

"WHAT ARE *YOU* still doing here?" Sterling asked sourly as he entered the library to discover Rosemary reading a book by the window, her head bent in concentration as she followed along the page with the tip of her finger.

It was strange, but in the swath of afternoon sunlight shining in through the glass, her hair didn't appear quite as mousy as before. There were tawny streaks in it he hadn't noticed. Ribbons of gold amidst all that plain brown. And the way she was sitting–curled on her hip, with one leg tucked beneath her and the other dangling off the edge of the settee–allowed him a glimpse at a slender calf clothed only in a sheer silk stocking.

Her leg was far more enticing than he'd imagined it to be, leading him to wonder what the rest of her body looked like beneath the oversized dresses she favored with all of their flouncing bows and nauseating ruffles.

Could it be?

Was Evelyn Thorncroft's cousin actually...*pretty?*

Ordinarily, he had a good sense of these things. Put him in the middle of a crowded ballroom and he could pick out the most gorgeous woman before he tossed back his first flute of champagne. Give him a second glass and he'd have her on the moonlit terrace with her skirts rucked up around her waist.

But boring, bookish Rosemary presented an enigma.

A puzzle he couldn't quite figure out.

At first glance, she was as true a wallflower as any he'd ever seen.

Shy, check.

Socially inept, check.

Blushes easily...double check.

And as a general rule, he did *not* find wallflowers attractive. Avoided them like the bloody plague, more like. But then why had he come to library, the one place he knew that Rosemary was almost certain to be?

"My grandmother is being seen by the doctor tomorrow, and we hope to be able to return home soon after." A frown troubled her mouth. A mouth, Sterling noted, that was far more fascinating than he had first given it credit for.

Top heavy, plump, and with a distracting freckle right below the left corner of her bottom lip, Rosemary's mouth wasn't traditionally beautiful. Some might not describe it as beautiful at all. Why, then, was he–a rogue extraordinaire who prided himself on his collection of gorgeous bedmates–suddenly possessed with the urge to see if it tasted as sweet as it looked?

"I do pray the doctor permits us to travel," Rosemary continued as a little line of worry etched itself between her brows. "I miss Sir Reginald dreadfully, and worry how he is faring without me."

Was the little wallflower *married*?

Even more complexing, was that a spark of jealousy that he felt?

Surely not.

Sterling did not get *jealous*.

He had no reason to.

Women flocked to *him*, not the other way around.

Even when Eloise had tried flirting with other men to get his attention when they'd first met, he'd experienced nothing more than a flicker of amusement, confident that, soon enough, she'd stop her silly games and they would get down to more serious matters. Which they had. Until she'd disappeared, leaving nothing behind but a room covered in her own blood.

Without knowing quite what he was doing–or why he was doing it–Sterling sat across from Rosemary and crossed his arms. "Who the devil is Sir Reginald?" he demanded.

As if it were a question she'd received many times before, Rosemary's countenance was one of resignation when she said, "Sir Reginald is my pet squirrel. I found him when he was a baby and fell out of a tree after a storm. I nursed him back to health, but–"

"You have a rat for a pet?" Sterling was sure it was a nice story, but he'd stopped listening after "pet squirrel". "On *purpose?*"

That plump mouth flattened ever-so-slightly. "Sir Reginald is not a rat. He is a member of the prestigious *Sciuridae* family which includes the American prairie dog and marmot. He is highly intelligent, and–"

"It's a rat," Sterling said blankly. "With a furry tail."

Agitated enough to set her book aside, Rosemary swung both legs to the floor and sat up straight. Pink suffused her cheeks. A loose tendril of tawny gold tumbled over her temple. Her luscious lips parted in righteous indignation. "He is *not* a rat!"

Maybe it was the gin.

Maybe it was the yawning emptiness inside of him that he couldn't fill no matter how much he drank or how many women he slept with. Maybe it was the fact that when he'd talked to Lachlan about losing the person he loved most, he hadn't been referring to Eloise. Or maybe it was a combination of all three.

Whatever the reason, Sterling leaned forward out of his chair, cupped Rosemary's heart-shaped face in his hands, and kissed her.

CHAPTER TWENTY-TWO

BRYNNE LEFT FOR London the next morning and arrived in Grosvenor Square after dinner.

Stately and square, Weston's town residence–hers as well, although she supposed she'd soon need to find new accommodations once Evie moved in–sat back from the tree-lined street behind a towering wrought iron gate, the freshly painted black matching the wooden shutters on the windows. It was three stories with an attic for the servants' quarters, and the high-vaulted ceilings encased in marble tile were one of her favorite features. They loomed above her as she entered the foyer, her footsteps muffled by a thick Axminster rug in a repeating pattern of muted blues and grays.

This manor had always offered a comforting respite from the colorless isolation of Hawkridge Manor. There were paintings on the walls (most selected by her hand). Carpets on the floor. A bust of their grandfather, stern as ever, resting on a pedestal by the grand staircase. Glossy green ferns in glazed clay pots in the corners. It was a space meant to be lived in. And yet...and yet how much had she *actually* lived here?

Afternoon tea in the drawing room. Countless parties in the parlor. Piano recitals in the music room. Balls in the outdoor courtyard. She'd presided over all of them. Lady Brynne Weston, the perfect hostess. Renowned throughout the *ton* for her charm, and wit, and grace.

But what would those same people say if they'd seen her chasing after a snake in the hall? Or juggling bubby pots in the kitchen? Or coaxing a baby goat (courtesy of Callum, little devil that he was) out of the bathtub?

In those moments, she'd wanted *this*. Calm, quiet, elegant surroundings. Ceilings that didn't leak and rooms that had real furniture in them. But as she turned in a circle and absorbed the silence–silence that suddenly felt far too stuffy and formal–she found herself missing the chaos.

Nostalgia, she thought as she made her way to the courtyard where the footman who greeted her at the door had said her brother was entertaining company. *Just simple nostalgia.*

After forcibly preventing herself from thinking about anything that had to do with Lachlan for the past year and a half, it was only to be expected that once those memories resurfaced, they'd shine with a rosier glow than before. Fondness had a way of attaching itself to the past, when in the present she'd be happy if she never saw another snake for as long as she lived.

"There you are!" Evie exclaimed, standing in a swirl of green muslin. "We've been waiting for you."

An automatic smile laid claim to Brynne's mouth as she gazed past her soon-to-be sister-in-law at the other guests occupying the shaded courtyard. Comprised of varying levels made from imported stone, it offered a view of Hyde Park through a living bamboo screen–also imported–and was decorated with a plethora of oversized tables and chairs to encourage lounging on a night exactly like this. Warm with a hint of crisp in the air and a sunset over the Thames that would make a poet weep.

In addition to Evie and Weston, who appeared more relaxed than she'd ever seen him with his cravat carelessly undone, his dark hair windswept and–was that a *real* smile?–there was a bookishly handsome man wearing spectacles that Brynne did not recognize and woman who she'd never met but immediately knew.

Joanna Thorncroft. The secret, illegitimate daughter of her father and his American mistress. A mistress, if Lady Crowley could be believed, that the cold-hearted Marquess of Dorchester had been madly in love with.

If not for that affair, Joanna wouldn't be sitting here.

Weston wouldn't be engaged to Evie.

And Brynne wouldn't have a half-sister.

Two sisters of a sort, she corrected as she abruptly found her arms filled with squealing Americans. Their enthusiastic hug caught her off guard, but after a half-second's worth of hesitation, she responded in kind, tentatively at first, and then with a laughing enthusiasm that Evie and Joanna returned tenfold.

"Your brother came to his senses at last," Evie grinned, holding out her left hand to reveal the ring that she and Joanna had crossed an ocean to pursue. Not with the intention of wearing it as a sign of her engagement–at the time, the Thorncrofts hadn't even known the identity of Joanna's birth father, let alone that Brynne and Weston existed–but it seemed fitting that it had ended up this way. It seemed *right*. A circle coming all the way around to its close.

"The ring is beautiful on you," Brynne said sincerely. She looked over Evie's shoulder. Met her brother's pleased, proud gaze. "Congratulations."

"I have a hundred questions," Joanna chimed in, her blue eyes shining. As slender as Evie but half a head taller and with bright red hair instead of black, she must have resembled her mother as closely as Brynne resembled hers, for neither had inherited any defining characteristics from their shared father.

Which, in a way, also seemed right.

"I don't know if I have a hundred answers, but I'll do my best," Brynne promised.

And over the course of the next three hours, she did.

The man with the spectacles, she learned shortly, was Joanna's husband, Thomas Kincaid. A private investigator, he'd been hired by the Thorncroft sisters after they arrived in London without the vaguest clue of where to begin their search. During the course of his investigation, Kincaid found the ring…and so much more.

It was clear, just from the way he gazed at her, that the subdued, serious-minded detective was absolutely besotted with his bride, and Joanna was equally infatuated with her husband.

Likewise, so too were Weston and Evie enamored of each other.

Which left Brynne noticeably without a partner.

And that was perfectly fine.

It was by her choice, after all.

But as she was quickly discovering, choosing to be alone didn't make you any less lonely.

"…entire summer kitchen went up in flames. To this day, Joanna refuses to take responsibility. But everyone knows it was her fault." Grinning, Evie nudged her sister with her elbow as Brynne blinked and refocused on the conversation at hand.

They'd taken seats around a table with the two men across from each other, the Thorncrofts next to each other, and Brynne by herself on the far side with a wine glass for company.

"I moved the pot!" Joanna protested.

"Not far enough, *obviously.*"

"If we're discussing faults of our past, should I bring up the time you slathered turmeric on your face and–"

"No one wants to hear about that," Evie said hastily.

"*I* do," Weston drawled.

"Orange as a carrot for days," Joanna said with a smirk. "She wouldn't leave her room. Everyone thought she was deathly ill."

Evie smiled brightly at Brynne, and, in a not-terribly-subtle attempt to shift the focus off her beauty mishap, she asked, "Do you have any interesting stories from when you and Weston were growing up? Anything embarrassing I should know about before we're married? No detail is too small."

"Our upbringing wasn't nearly as...entertaining as yours, I'm afraid." Brynne took a sip of her wine, a decadent port that lingered on her tongue. "By comparison, it was rather boring."

Except for Lachlan, a tiny voice whispered.

She ignored it.

"That's disappointing," Evie remarked. "If you should remember anything enticing, you shall have to tell me at once."

"I will," Brynne promised. Then she rose to her feet. "It's nearly past midnight, and I've had a long day of travel. Joanna and Mr. Kincaid, it was wonderful to meet you at last. I am looking forward to getting to know each other even more now that we're all together in London. I take it you'll be at the Duke of Oxford's ball tomorrow evening?"

Joanna's nose wrinkled. "I've found that large social events aren't for me."

"I'll be there," Evie said happily. "We can get ready together, if you'd like."

Although Evie and Weston were engaged to be married, without the presence of a proper chaperone she'd been living with Joanna and Kincaid to uphold the appearance of propriety. Now that Brynne was here, however, she had shared her eagerness to move into the same house as her husband-to-be. In the bedroom beside his, naturally. Never mind that there was a door connecting the two chambers.

"I'd like that very much." Brynne flicked a glance at Weston, and they shared an incredulous smile. Who would have ever thought that they'd be part of such a loud, boisterous family? From somber dinners at opposite ends of a long table to sitting on a terrace with a half-sister, and brother-in-law, and fiancée.

The only person missing was–

No.

Absolutely not.

She hadn't left Lachlan behind to think about him every other moment.

"I shall see you in the morning." Exiting amidst a chorus of "good night" and "sleep well", she went upstairs to find her bedroom precisely as she'd left it. Her lady's maid, a cheerful middle-aged woman named Ira, was already there waiting to help her undress, and doused the candles before she left, blanketing the chamber in rolling darkness.

Through sheer will and determination, Brynne managed to keep her husband out of her head...until that head hit the pillow, sleep wrapped her in its languid embrace, and there was nothing she could do to prevent him from entering her dreams.

"Isn't it amazing?" Evie marveled as their town coach slowed in front of the Duke of Oxford's estate, a spectacular Grecian-styled manor perched high on a hill overlooking the Thames, and joined the twisting black line of carriages reaching all the way back to Harcourt Street.

As one of the largest events of the Season, over three hundred of the *ton's* elite were expected to attend. There'd be dancing, and gossiping, and drinking. Mayhap even a salacious scandal or two. It was the recipe for a perfect evening and Evie, as the newly minted future Countess of Hawkridge, was certain to have a fair share of the spotlight. Which, by all outward appearances, she seemed absolutely elated about.

Once upon at a time, Brynne would have shared in Evie's enthusiasm.

Although for a very different reason.

The Duke of Oxford was a renowned art connoisseur, and over his fifty-seven years he'd amassed a collection that rivaled the Dulwich Gallery in South London. For public events, he opened his private gallery for those who wished to stroll amidst the works of Rembrandt,

Marillo, Canaletto, and even Poussin. Every year, there was something new to find, and Brynne always waited with bated breath to discover what grand painting Oxford had deemed worthy enough to add to his collection.

Now, however, instead of experiencing a tingling wave of anticipation, she just felt…*flat*.

Like a skirt without the benefit of crinoline.

Fortunately, Evie was excited enough for the both of them.

All but bouncing in her seat, the American leaned precariously out the square carriage window, her blue eyes shining in the torchlight. "Do you think we might get there quicker if we walked?"

With a muffled sound of vague alarm, Weston hauled her back in. "We'll be there presently," he said, and Brynne pretended she didn't see the familiar way her brother's hand splayed across the small of Evie's back. "But not if you're a puddle of silk on the ground."

True to Weston's word, the line moved relatively quickly and they were soon able to disembark from the town coach and join the glittering swell of gowns, and cravats, and jewels that spilled between the enormous pillars guarding the front of the manor. But when they were set to enter the massive French doors that led into the ballroom, Weston grasped Brynne by the elbow and pulled her aside.

"Are you feeling well?" he asked with a twin's intuitive concern.

"Fine," she said, tugging her arm away from him and straightening her satin gloves. Ivory with an embroidered hem of Chantilly lace, they complemented her citrine dress. "Why do you ask?"

"You've not been yourself since you returned from Hawkridge."

"I've only been back for a day," she pointed out. "And already attending a ball. Once I've had a moment to settle and unpack, I'm sure you'll see nothing amiss."

But he didn't appear convinced. "You'd tell me if there was something wrong, wouldn't you? Just because I am engaged to be married doesn't mean I do not have time for my sister."

"You're engaged to be married. You *shouldn't* have time for your sister," she corrected lightly. "Have you told your bride-to-be how lovely she looks tonight?"

With the knowledge that eyes would be upon her, some in approval, some in silent judgment, Evie had chosen her gown with care. A deep violet with a chiffon bodice, puffed sleeves, and a wide grosgrain sash that emphasized her petite frame, the dress was as much a work of art as the paintings hanging on the walls.

"She is exquisite, isn't she?" Weston's eyes glowed with warmth and pride as he gazed at his fiancée. It was a noticeable change. Before Evie had turned his life upside down, the Earl of Hawkridge had regarded everything and everyone with a cold aloofness that bordered on contempt. He hadn't only *not* believed in love, he'd actively fought against it. Until a spirited American had thawed all of that ice and laid claim to the heart hiding underneath it.

"*Go,*" Brynne said firmly, giving him a small push. "I'll join you shortly."

But instead of following Weston and Evie through the French doors, she went straight down the massive hallway and then turned right, using the light emanating from polished brass sconces to guide her away from the laughter and loudness in the ballroom to the near-silent solitude of the Duke of Oxford's viewing gallery.

There was no one else in the room, and she hadn't been expecting there to be. People did not attend a ball to look at art. They came to be looked *at*. Which they couldn't be if they were sequestered away in a separate wing of the manor.

Mahogany paneling covered the walls, offering a muted backdrop to the dozens of paintings that comprised Oxford's vast assortment of art. The furniture was minimal; a rosewood chaise upholstered in red velvet here, an armchair in silk brocade there. This was not a place of idle gathering, but of reverence. Hallowed ground to appreciate beauty that transcended time itself.

A sumptuous, hand-knotted carpet devoured the sound of Brynne's footsteps as she wandered from one ornate gold frame to another. Trying to *will* herself to feel something–anything–for works of art that would have usually stolen her breath and left her with a sense of wonder far larger than herself. Wonder she'd only ever experienced when looking at a Rembrandt...and when she was a girl in a meadow, gazing up at her first constellation.

Maybe she *was* ill.

But not with a sickness or disease that any medicine could fix, unless doctors had found a way to mend a broken heart.

For eighteen months, she'd used her anger at Lachlan to bind the pieces of it together. But now that her anger was gone, so too were the bandages that had kept her heart from falling apart. And now it felt as if it were going to fall right out of her chest. Such was her pain from missing him. From missing *them.* The way they'd been when they were good and how they could have been if they'd successfully navigated their way through the stormy seas to become great.

Your choice, she reminded herself. *Your decision.*

Scholars didn't write about the adventurers who remained safely in the harbor, but for every James Cook that discovered a new land, there were a dozen more who never lived past their first voyage.

Maybe she just wasn't destined for open waters.

But that was all right.

It *had* to be all right.

Or else yesterday she'd made the worst decision of her life.

She found the Duke of Oxford's newest addition on the far wall. Small, inconspicuous even, the oil paint on canvas was by an artist whose name she didn't recognize.

"Claude Monet," she muttered, reading the signature scrawled at the bottom.

Whoever he was–or would become–his talent was apparent in every brushstroke. He'd depicted a busy boardwalk in the height of summer, with a dozen different shades of blue between the ocean and the sky. If she stared intently enough, she could almost smell the salt air and hear the call of gulls as they swooped to pick up pieces of bread thrown by giggling children.

"Ye should have a painting hanging right beside it," drawled an achingly familiar brogue from directly behind her.

On a startled gasp, Brynne nearly jumped out of her heeled shoes. *Would* have, had Lachlan not laid a steadying hand upon her shoulder.

"What–what are you *doing* here?" Her hazel eyes as wide as the sky in Monet's beach scene, she whirled around to confront her husband with equal parts disbelief, irritation, and bewildered joy. "You nearly scared me to death!"

"That wasna me intention."

"Then what *was* your intention?"

"Tae see ye," he answered simply. On a low whistle, he stepped back, his gaze slowly traveling from the top of her head to the tip of her toes. "I dinna have the words tae describe what a vision ye are, Bry. A sunset comes close. The colors of it. The way it dances across the horizon as if painted by God's own hand. But compared tae ye, it's nothing but a picture scrawled by a child."

She wasn't going to be charmed.

She wasn't.

She refused.

"Lachlan, if you've come here to win me back–"

"Aye and it's a high opinion we have of ourselves, isna it?" he smirked. "I received an invitation from the Duke of Oxford, same as ye. I didna realize our separation extended tae me being unable tae attend a ball."

"Oh. I thought…" Flushing, she trailed away while Lachlan continued to grin.

Dashingly handsome in all black save the white of his cravat, he was the very picture of a refined aristocrat with his auburn hair contained in a tail at the nape of his neck and his face cleanly shaven. If not for the glint in his eyes and that roguish dimple in the middle of his cheek, she might have almost believed he was a gentleman.

"I figured it would be more awkward not tae seek ye out than tae pretend we didna know each other," he said, arching a brow.

"Yes, you're right." She gave a tiny shake of her head. Pasted a smile on her face. "Of course, you're right."

"And who is it we have here?" he asked, nodding at the painting she'd been admiring before he snuck up behind her.

Taking a deep breath, Brynne pivoted towards the wall and linked her hands behind her back as an irrational surge of annoyance went through her. Why did Lachlan have to be here *tonight*, of all nights? Even though he had as much a right to attend the ball as she did...and this wasn't going to be the first, or the last, time that their paths inadvertently crossed. She pressed her lips together. If this was how he wanted it to be between them–friendly acquaintances, if not outright friends–then she'd do her best to accommodate his wishes. And ignore both the accelerated beat of her pulse and the slick tug between her thighs brought on by his nearness.

A year and a half she'd had to miss him, and *this* was how her body reacted when they'd barely spent a day apart? It was baffling. It was bemusing. It was an outright betrayal. Or maybe it wasn't. Tell someone they had to have something, and they didn't want it. Put it out of their reach, and it was all they desired.

But she couldn't desire her husband.

Because...because she just couldn't.

And that was all there was to it.

"Monet. Claude Monet." She cleared her throat. "I've never heard of him, but if the Duke of Oxford has seen fit to add him to his collection, then he surely is an artist of substance."

"And why is it the duke doesna have one of yer paintings?" Lachlan asked. "I'm sure this Monet fellow is all well and dandy, but it's a beach with some sand and steps. Blaine could do something similar, if he had half a mind tae. But I've seen yer paintings, Bry. The scope of them. The sheer, staggering depth. If anyone deserves tae be in this gallery, it's ye."

"You've–you've seen my paintings?" This was the second time her husband had surprised her this evening. She'd never lifted a paintbrush at Campbell Castle, although she supposed he could have gone through the canvases she had brought with her and kept in a trunk in their bedroom. She just never thought that he *had*, given that he'd never shown any particular interest in her artistic endeavors.

Until now.

"The scene ye painted of our meadow on the hill is me favorite. The colors ye used. The blend of grass, and trees, and stars. Second only tae being there in person."

Her eyes narrowed. "That painting is in my bedchamber. At Hawkridge Manor."

"Aye, so it is," he said cheerfully. "Above yer bed, if I recall."

"You went in my room without my knowledge?"

"I was lost."

"You weren't lost," she said, exasperated–and a tad amused. "Furthermore, it's not *our* meadow."

"Then why is it the first thing ye see when ye go tae sleep and the first thing ye awake tae in the morning?"

Her mouth opened. Closed. "Because I–"

"Who's this one by?" he asked, pointing at a larger painting in a gilt-edged frame.

"William Hogarth, who was renowned for his Rococo style. Do you see how the brush strokes are flowing in nature, and there are high ridges of paint on the canvas?"

Lachlan shrugged. "All I see is that the lady isna very impressed by the bloke who's grabbing her hand."

"This is part of a series titled *Before and After*. This is the Before, and that"–she nodded at the painting beside it, showing the same couple albeit in a much more...*intimate* position–"is the After. It was deemed too risqué for public viewing at The National Gallery, which was how the Duke of Oxford was able to attain it through private auction."

"Aye," said Lachlan, tilting his head. "I can see why he wanted it. From this angle, ye can all but look up the lady's skirts at her–"

Brynne's face heated. "As I said, it is very risqué."

He slanted her a grin. "Ye have tae admire the bloke's persistence. It won him the lady's affections in the end."

"Or maybe," she countered, "the woman acquiesced against her better judgment."

"Dinna know about that," said Lachlan, scratching his chin. "She looks quite pleased with herself."

As Brynne imagined she had worn a similar expression after making love with her husband on the eve of their wedding, she possessed no valid counterpoint other than to move on to the next painting which was, thankfully, a landscape scene.

"This was done by Charles Bernard, a French impressionist who employs primary colors to–"

"Do those hills appear strange tae ye?" Lachlan interrupted.

"Strange?" She frowned at the painting. "Strange how?"

"The way they're shaped. And the single tree on top of each one. Almost makes them look like–"

Breasts.

The hills resembled breasts.

"Over here," she said hastily, "we have another Frenchman, Nicolas Poussin, renowned for his mastery of the Baroque style. As you can see, his paintings are exceptionally detailed."

"Aye, I've never seen more realistic buttocks. Would ye say those are more muscular or less muscular than mine?" He patted his backside. "Ye can feel for comparison, if ye'd like."

If her cheeks were hot before, they were positively burning now. "Is there any painting you won't sexualize?" she hissed.

"Not if it makes ye blush like that."

"You're incorrigible."

"Thank ye." Then he sobered. "Ye never painted at Campbell

Castle. Why? I know ye had everything sent tae ye."

"I did, but..." She hesitated as she searched for an answer to the question that she'd already asked herself to no avail. "I am not sure, to be honest. Had you asked me a month ago, I would have said it was because I was too busy with the children, but that's not completely true. I suppose...I suppose I was lacking for inspiration. Or maybe I didn't want to go in search of it."

"Why is that?"

"Because if I did, I'd have found it." She shrugged helplessly. "Then I never would have been able to leave." When she heard her own words, the blood drained from her countenance. "Lachlan, I'm sorry."

But he only nodded, as if her admission came as no great revelation to him even though it had shocked her to her core. "And there was a part of ye that always planned on leaving," he said matter-of-factly.

"Yes," she whispered. "I'm afraid there was."

In the silence that followed, she stared at the carpet, unable to meet his gaze for fear of the censure she was certain she would see there. But when he spoke, he wasn't angry. And when he took her hand and placed a small, rectangular object in her palm, then wrapped her fingers around it, his touch was gentle.

"I brought this for ye. A token of a time when things were less complicated between us. I love ye, Bry." So soft that she barely felt it, he kissed her forehead, his nose pressing into her hair before he moved away and gave a crooked smile. "Enjoy the rest of the ball."

She waited until he was gone to open her hand and look at what he'd given her. When she saw what it was, what it meant, her breath caught and her eyes stung. Tucking it safely into the beaded reticule dangling from her wrist, she rushed after him in a flurry of taffeta and silk.

But when she reached the hallway, it was empty...and he was gone.

CHAPTER TWENTY-THREE

"I HAVE TO show you something." The next morning Brynne brought Lachlan's gift with her into the front parlor where Evie was drinking coffee and poring over the latest edition of *The English-woman's Domestic Magazine*.

"I'm glad you're here," said Evie without glancing up. "I am trying to decide between these three necklines for the wedding gown I'm having designed. Joanna says they all look the same to her, but her opinion can *hardly* be trusted given that she wore her traveling habit–her traveling habit!–to marry Kincaid. Claimed it was more practical, if you can believe it."

"I can, actually." Forgoing the coffee for a cup of tea–her nerves were already strained enough–Brynne sat down beside Evie and consulted the different dresses that her brother's fiancée had circled with such vigor that dots of ink had splattered across the rest of the page. "You'll be a beautiful bride no matter what you wear–"

"Well *that's* not helpful."

"–but a square cut neckline would complement your décolletage and collarbones the best, I should think. It's a simpler design, but won't distract from your face, which should be the main focus once you lower your veil."

"Weston *does* like gazing at my décolletage."

"So I've noticed," Brynne said dryly.

Evie tapped her pen on the edge of the table, then drew a star beside the dress with the square bodice. "You're right. This is the one. Now I only have to pick the variation of ivory I want, along with the size of the bustle, pearl buttons or gold, and the length of the train. Not to mention–"

"Could we discuss another topic for a moment?" It was either cut in then, or not at all. When fashion was the subject at hand, Evie was capable of going on at great length. Ordinarily, that was something the two women would have in common. But today, Brynne had a much more pressing subject matter on her mind. "Then I promise to give your wedding gown my full, undivided attention."

"That's right. You did say you had something to show me." Evie laid down her pen and linked her fingers together expectantly.

"I also have something to tell you." When she felt her chest beginning to constrict, Brynne inhaled through her nose and exhaled through her mouth. "But before I do, I have to ask that you not share it with my brother. At least not right away. I understand it's a large favor–"

"Is not knowing whatever it is hurting him in some way?" Evie interrupted.

"No. If it were, I never would have kept it from him." She blew out another stream of air, then pursed her lips. "Although he may hurt *me* once he finds out."

"Now I *must* know. And I won't tell him. Weston is going to be my husband, but you're going to be my sister, and both of those relationships are special in their own way. We may not be blood, but you're as important to me as Joanna and Claire." Evie put her hand on top of Brynne's and squeezed. "I want you to know that."

"Thank you. I...thank you." What else was there to say? She was humbled by Evie's willingness to place her upon the same pedestal as her real sisters, even though they'd had an entire lifetime together while Brynne and Evie had just met. But then love wasn't guided by time, or rules, or expectations. It was a river running down the side of a mountain. Diverging into streams and pools, drying up in places and flooding others, all while consistently trickling towards the ocean. And the ocean was–

Me, she realized in a stunning moment of clarity.

The ocean is me.

Not her father. Not Weston. Not Evie.

Not even Lachlan.

The ocean comprised all of the love she should have had for *herself*. Should have, but didn't.

Because along the way, she'd allowed the tide to go out.

Maybe it was when she was diagnosed with anxious mannerisms. Or when Miss Hardgrave discouraged her curiosity. Or her father stopped bothering to even send so much as a birthday letter. Or the girls at Cheltenham Ladies' College had teased her mercilessly. Or the Dowager Countess of Crowley made it clear that a woman's only purpose in life was to marry and marry well.

Her interests, her pursuits, her goals–they didn't matter.

She, as an individual, didn't matter.

All of these little things had chipped away at her self-worth. Her self-love. They'd happened so gradually, so seamlessly, that she had barely noticed. Like a rock being slowly worn down to sand every time a wave washed over it.

Until the rock was gone and her ocean was empty.

And finally, there it was.

The answer she'd been seeking all this time without knowing what question to ask.

She hadn't run from Lachlan because of a supposed affair.

Or because of the children.

Or because of the castle.

She'd left because, deep down, she felt as if she were never worthy of his love. And she had wanted to end things between them before he came to his senses and ended them first. If she was incapable of loving herself, why would she ever expect that a man as good, as decent, as kind as Lachlan could?

"But I was wrong," she whispered as she withdrew the gift he had given her from the handkerchief she'd carefully wrapped it in. "I was so very wrong."

"What is that?" Evie asked, a line of confusion marring her temple.

"A barley stick. My husband gave me one eleven years ago, and this one last night. It's made of sugar, and worth more than all the gold in England."

"Your *husband?*" Evie's jaw dropped. "I had no idea you were married! Who? How? When? *Who?*"

Brynne's mouth curved in a mirthless smile. "Perhaps I should start at the beginning…"

When she had finished, Evie sagged in her chair and shook her head in disbelief. "I cannot believe you managed to hide a *husband.* I cannot believe that all the time we've known each other you have been *married.*"

"Estranged," Brynne corrected as she refreshed her tea and silently wished it was something much stronger.

"What did you wear?"

"Wear?" she said blankly.

"For your *wedding.*"

It was such a silly detail, such a small, meaningless note in the novel that comprised Brynne and Lachlan's eleven year relationship, that she couldn't help but laugh. Which was the point, she gathered from the way Evie's eyes crinkled at the corners. For which she was grateful.

"A green dress that belonged to my mother," she shared. "It was very plain, with only a beige ribbon for decoration."

"It sounds perfect," said Evie.

"It was." She added a spoonful of milk to her tea, but didn't drink it. Her stomach was too knotted to consume anything, even water. "I think I've acted poorly. No, I *know* that I have. Lachlan loved me. He *does* love me, to this day. And I...I have pushed him away. Perhaps irrevocably."

"Never let it be said that loving a Weston is easy," Evie declared with a humorous twist of her lips. "Your brother would have rather jumped off a cliff than admit he adored me. But I won him around in the end."

Yes, she had.

And the notoriously cold-hearted Earl of Hawkridge had never been happier.

"But weren't you afraid?" Brynne asked.

Evie's head tilted. "Of what?"

"Of falling in love."

"If you find the person you're meant to be with, you don't *fall* in love with them." Her blue eyes shining, she smiled gently. "You fly."

THE PRIVATE OFFICES of Mr. Jacobson and his partners were not available to clients, new or existing, without an appointment. Generally speaking, that appointment needed to be made weeks in advance. As the most highly regarded solicitor in all of London, Mr. Jacobson's time was of the utmost value.

And he charged for it accordingly.

But–as with all things–there were always exceptions, the Weston family being one of them. Which was why, when he was informed that the Marquess of Dorchester's daughter had made an unscheduled visit, Mr. Jacobson left his meeting and met her in the grand foyer of the elegantly appointed townhouse without delay.

"Lady Brynne," he said after he'd personally taken her jacket and gloves and ushered her into the adjoining parlor, an informal space meant to put his higher brow clientele at ease. "To what do I owe this unexpected pleasure?"

"Thank you for seeing me on such short notice. Or to be more accurate, no notice at all." Forgoing tea and refreshments, Brynne sat down and neatly folded her hands on her lap. After her enlightening conversation with Evie yesterday, she'd known what she needed to do. What she *had* to do.

"I am always available to you, my lady. Ready to serve in whatever manner you require." Approximately the same age as her father, Mr. Jacobson was tall and thin. The most notable thing about him was his gray moustache, and the way he waxed the tips so that they pointed straight up like tiny barbs. Everything else, from his three-piece tweed suit to the way he kept his hair slicked back (what remained of it, at any rate) with pomade was ordinary. Plain, even. But his intelligence and sharp legal mind were extraordinary, making him the obvious choice when Brynne had sought someone to help end her marriage. And now he was who she needed to see in order to save it.

"I come to you today with a delicate matter, Mr. Jacobson."

"Delicate matters are my specialty."

"You may recall our discussion surrounding the dissolution of my marriage to Lord Campbell," she began. "We settled upon judicial separation as our best course of action, and you had papers drawn up for both parties."

"Indeed," the solicitor nodded. "Lord Campbell has already returned his."

"He–he has?" she said in dismay. "So soon? But he only just arrived in London."

Eighteen months.

For *eighteen months*, Lachlan had held on to hope that their marriage could be saved. And in three days he'd signed papers to destroy it once and for all.

Because of her.

She'd done this.

She'd wanted this.

She'd asked for this.

And now, perversely, it was the one thing she *didn't* want.

"Give them to me," she said wildly. "The papers. I'll–I'll destroy them. Burn them. Throw them in the Thames. It will be as if they never existed, and the judicial separation won't be able to proceed."

Mr. Jacobson frowned. "I am afraid I cannot do that, Lady Brynne. They were filed with the Court of Divorce and Matrimonial Causes this morning. Per your last written directive, that was what you requested me to do as soon as I was in possession of them."

"Yes! No." She clutched her skirt as she struggled to stave off a rush of tears. "I mean, yes, it *was* what I hired you to do. But I've changed my mind. I don't want to separate from my husband. I don't want to separate from him at all."

"Ah," the solicitor remarked, his countenance impassive. "I see."

"I've ruined it."

"Lady Brynne–"

"I've ruined *everything*."

"If I may–"

"Now our marriage is over, and it's all my fault."

Mr. Jacobson cleared his throat.

Loudly.

"I am terribly sorry," she sniffled, dashing at her cheeks. "I never cry, or lose my composure in such an embarrassing manner. It's just that I've handled this all wrong from the very beginning, and I hoped that if I could halt the separation then I might begin to make amends. But I'm too late."

"Yes," the solicitor said gravely. "You are. When I appealed to the courts to begin this filing, I was given a strict deadline of noon today. Lord Campbell met that deadline. You, Lady Brynne, did not."

She gazed at Mr. Jacobson in bewilderment. "I...I don't understand."

"I sent a letter informing you of the impending due date to

Hawkridge Manor, but you and it must have crossed on your way here to London. Simply put, Lady Brynne, your husband submitted the necessary paperwork to file for your judicial separation. But you did not."

"I didn't?"

"No."

"But that's…that's wonderful news!" she cried as she sprang from her chair. "Mr. Jacobson, I could kiss you."

His moustache quivered. "I don't believe I have ever been the recipient of such joy for *not* completing the task assigned to me, Lady Brynne. Can I assume that you do not wish to pursue extending a filing for a deadline extension with the court?"

Brynne swung her head adamantly from side to side. "Please do not take this the wrong way, Mr. Jacobson, but I hope to never see you again."

"In that case, my lady, I bid you farewell…and good luck."

"Thank you," she said with feeling. "I am going to need it."

CHAPTER TWENTY-FOUR

EVERY SEASON, THE Viscount and Viscountess of Denbigh held a dinner party on the third day of the third week. The tradition had begun when they found themselves in need of husbands for their three daughters. The first party had been so successful–with the girls snatching up a marquess, an earl, and a baron, respectively–that like-minded parents with daughters of their own to marry off had begged Lord and Lady Denbigh to host another dinner party, and another after that, and another after that, until it became a staple of the London Season.

Brynne had never put much stock in the claim that a young woman wanting a husband need only attend the Marriage Miracle Dinner (as it was now called) and they'd magically become engaged before the month was out.

But tonight, she was hoping for some of that magic for herself.

The last time she and Lachlan had been together, he'd told her that he loved her. Then the next day, he'd signed papers to complete their separation. That juxtaposition had her sitting on pins and needles all through the five-course dinner and into dessert, a sponge cake topped with powdered sugar and strawberries with a thick middle layer of cream.

Evie and Joanna ate their pieces in a matter of seconds, but Brynne only poked at hers with the silver tines of her fork, her attention focused on the glass French doors at the end of the dining room.

She knew Lachlan had been invited because she'd implored Lady Denbigh to invite him. And while the viscountess had been visibly confused by such a request, she had honored it without question, proving that sometimes it *did* pay to be the granddaughter of a duke.

But Lachlan wasn't here.

At least, he wasn't here *yet*.

Which was fine, she told herself. After the sponge cake was cleared, the party didn't end, but rather spread out to include the parlor, the drawing room, and the rear gardens. As long as her husband arrived within the next two hours, she'd have the opportunity to pull him aside and have a much-needed private discussion, something which she had attempted to do numerous times over the past few days...except she hadn't been able to find him.

He was not, as she'd naturally assumed, renting the same townhouse as he had every other visit to London. Nor was he staying with his brother, Robert, who had been very surprised–and intrigued–to discover a distraught blonde on his doorstep at half-past seven in the morning.

It was, once more, the very height of irony.

Ten days ago, she'd never wanted to see Lachlan again.

And now, she was terrified that she never would.

Her biggest fear was no longer failure, or being ostracized by High Society, or disappointing her family. It was that she'd done enough damage to her relationship with Lachlan to chase him away indefinitely. And while she sat in her seat shredding apart her sponge cake, he was on a train bound for Scotland.

"Are you going to eat that?" Joanna asked. "Or murder it?"

"You can have it if you'd like," she muttered distractedly, sliding her plate towards her half-sister who happily scooped up a large plop of cream.

Evie followed Brynne's gaze to the door. "You're waiting for him, aren't you?"

"Shwoo?" Joanna asked, her mouth full of cake.

"My husband," Brynne sighed.

"YOU HAVE A—"

"*Shhh.*" Evie elbowed Joanna in the ribs as she gave a pointed glance across the wide table to where their husbands (or almost husband, in her case) sat side by side, conversing about some manly thing or another. "It's a secret."

"You have a *secret* husband?" Joanna hissed. "I am going to need more cake for this."

In hushed tones, Brynne delivered an abridged version of the events that she'd told Evie at great length. All three women then departed the table for the parlor where Joanna poured them champagne from a bottle set in a bucket of ice.

"What are we celebrating?" Brynne asked bleakly as they clinked their crystal flutes together.

"To finding our husbands," said Evie.

"To finding ourselves," Joanna added. "No matter *what* path it took us to get here." Then she paused, and something flickered in her eyes. "Brynne, I don't mean to presume, but there is an exceedingly large red-haired man who just entered the parlor and is looking at you as if you were the last piece of strawberry sponge cake. Is that your husband, per chance?"

Fingers reflexively tightening around the slender stem of her champagne glass, Brynne turned around as if in slow motion. When she saw Lachlan standing in the doorway, her breath expelled on a *whoosh* of air and her heart slammed into the wall of her chest.

"Yes, that's him."

"Off with you then," Evie said, giving her a push.

Joanna grinned. "Don't let us keep you."

But Brynne resisted.

"I–I don't know if I can," she said as the dreaded sensation of suffocating in a room filled with air came creeping in. "I want to. But what if I don't fly? What if...what if I fall?"

"Then we'll catch you," said Evie.

This time, she and Joanna pushed her together.

"*Go*," they said in unison.

And so she did.

ONE LOOK AT Brynne's pale countenance, and Lachlan took her by the arm and steered her out of the parlor and through the hall to the library where they could be alone. He closed the door and then leaned against it, hands draped loosely on his narrow hips as he studied his wife in the muted glow of candlelight and a crackling fire.

She looked...different.

Nervous, he decided.

She looked nervous.

An emotion his wife rarely displayed.

Which, in turn, made *him* nervous, given that he'd left the Duke of Oxford's gallery with the impression that they'd taken a stride in the right direction. Since then–although it had pained him to no end–he'd kept his distance, not wanting to crowd her or give her an excuse to bolt again.

It wasn't until Robert revealed that she'd come looking for him that he had accepted the invitation to tonight's dinner. An invitation he hadn't been expecting, given he'd never received one from Lord and Lady Denbigh before. Hadn't even known they were aware of his existence, if he were being honest, given that they'd never been officially introduced.

When the envelope arrived, a little bell in his ear had rung, and he'd thought–he'd hoped–that Brynne had something to do with his name being placed on the guest list. But if her white face and shaking hands were any indication, she'd had no idea he was coming.

"Ye should sit down," he said gruffly, pulling out a chair.

But she remained standing. "You signed the papers."

At first, he didn't know what the devil she was talking about. Then his shoulders stiffened. "Aye," he said. "Yer solicitor was very prompt."

When the skinny bloke with the pointed moustache had popped up in Sterling's foyer like a bloody jester-in-a-box, Lachlan's first instinct was to take the official stack of legal jargon he'd been presented with and tear all the papers in half. To hell with a judicial separation. Then he had reconsidered. If this was what Brynne wanted, then he'd give it to her. Wasn't that what courting entailed? He'd have preferred a bouquet of tulips but, this time, he was trying something different: actually listening to his wife instead of assuming *he* knew what *she* needed.

"You signed the papers," she repeated.

"Wasna that what I was supposed tae do?"

When her eyes filled with tears, he cursed and crossed the distance between them to gather her in his arms. She was slender as a willow, bright as a star, delicate as a rose. And he loved every inch of her. Inside and out. He always would, separation or no separation. Brynne was his and he was hers, their souls twined together in such a way that even if they were to part and never see each other again, a piece of her would exist in him for all of eternity.

"I'm sorry," she said, lifting her damp countenance from his chest to gaze at him with wide, haunted eyes brimming with regret. "I'm sorry, Lachlan. I...I have made a mess of everything. Of us. Of our marriage. I ruined–"

"Aye and it's me duty as yer husband tae stop ye there," he said, tracing his knuckle across her cheek to catch a tear before it could fall. "Ye didna ruin anything, Bry. Or if ye did, then so did I. There's blame tae be handed out in parcels, and we each have our fair share of it, but then that's life. That's learning. That's moving forward even when things get rough. Because seedlings canna grow in fallow soil, and love canna bloom when ye allow yerself tae be trapped in the blame, and the hurt, and the mistakes."

"I made so many mistakes. *Too* many. I–I can't breathe," she gasped, and Lachlan's arms tightened around her in alarm when she began to slip through them.

"What's wrong?" he demanded as fear coursed through his veins. "Bry? Bry! Can ye hear me?"

Her eyes were closed. Her face waxen. Her breaths quick and shallow. She made no sign that she heard him. No sign that she was even cognizant of him holding her.

Frantic, he ripped at the buttons running the length of her gown. Found the metal teeth securing her corset and tore those apart, too.

He was about to shout for help when her lashes trembled, and her eyes slowly opened.

"Lachlan," she said weakly.

"Aye, I'm here. I've got ye." *And I'm never letting ye go again,* he thought grimly as he carried her to a chaise lounge and gently laid her down, then sat beside her and took her hand, her fingers ice cold in his. "Do ye need water?" he asked. "Or a doctor?"

"You." She struggled to sit up, then sagged against him, her head resting in the crook of space beneath his chin. "I need you."

"Ye have me, little bird." He pressed his lips to the top of her head. "Forever."

"That doesn't seem nearly long enough."

He wanted to ask her what had happened. The old Lachlan would have. Would have pushed, and prodded, and demanded until she gave him answers whether she wanted to or not. But the new Lachlan–at least, the new parts of him that he was trying on, rather like a coat at the tailors–reminded him to be patient. To wait. To let Brynne choose when she was ready. In the meantime, he'd enjoy the simplicity of just holding her. Stroking her back. Listening to her heartbeat as its erratic rhythm gradually slowed and evened out.

"The doctor called them anxious mannerisms," she said finally. "I had my first when Weston left for school. The doctor said they were very rare, and I was only the second case he'd ever seen. He was going to write a paper. I don't know if he ever did."

Lachlan's hand continued to follow the line of her spine. Up and down. Up and down. "What does it feel like?" he asked. "When it happens."

"A shortness of breath, as if all the oxygen has been sucked out of the room but I'm the only one who seems to have noticed. Sometimes my head swims, as if I was underwater, and dots dance in front of my eyes. I call them Episodes. I had them frequently as a child...and several since you came back to Hawkridge Manor."

He recalled the gazebo where she'd gone as pale as a ghost and he'd assumed she was with child. "Is there any treatment? Or medicine tae take?"

"No, not that I've found. The doctor suggested I merely tell myself not to have them."

Aye, Lachlan thought sourly, and why didn't this doctor ask a patient with a broken leg to will themselves better? Admittedly, his knowledge of the medical field was sorely lacking. But even he recognized that an illness brought on by someone's own mind was no less severe than an injury or disease of the body.

"The doctor sounds like a bluidy useless prat."

"I never saw him again. Mrs. Grimsby, the housekeeper, who was only a maid then, helped me learn how to breathe through them when they happened. I came to realize they were tied to my emotions. If I was upset, they occurred with more frequency."

Which meant he was to blame for the Episodes she'd had recently, and wasn't he a bastard for causing her such suffering?

"Bry," he said hoarsely, "I never meant–"

"It's not your fault." Here, she raised her head to stare him in the eyes. Her own were dry and remarkably clear. "It's not mine, either. It took a long while to understand that. To accept it. To love myself for who I am, and not what others expect me to be. I never should have agreed to your proposal, Lachlan."

A knife twisted in his gut. "If that's how ye feel—"

"I never should have agreed to it," she said steadily, "because I wasn't ready. I didn't know who I was yet, let alone who I was supposed to be as a wife. But your coming here has forced me to reflect on some difficult choices. And I've had to ask myself some difficult questions. About who I am, where I want to go, and what I deserve."

He angled his body so that they were facing each other and bent his head to hers, their foreheads lightly touching as their hands linked together. "What answers did ye find?"

"That I love you, Lachlan Campbell. That I've always loved you. You're the boy who showed me the stars. The man who gave me my first kiss. The husband who broke my heart...and mended it back together again, stronger than it ever was before. I am yours, and you are mine." She hesitated, and her gaze lowered. "If you'll have me, that is."

For a second, he could only stare and wonder if this was a dream. If it was, he never wanted to wake up. But it wasn't a dream. It was life. Hard, and messy, and imperfect. With swells and rough water aplenty. But through each storm, he and Brynne had managed to find their way back to each other. And while the only thing certain about the future was that it wouldn't be easy, there was no one he'd rather navigate those rough seas with than the woman sitting in front of him.

"*If* I'll have ye?" he said, near bursting with love as he cupped her face between his hands and gently coaxed her to look into his eyes. "Bry, I never let ye go." Then he frowned as a cloud slipped across their bright, beaming sun. "But the judicial separation—"

"I never signed them," she said on a breathless laugh. "My papers. I never signed them."

Four of the most beautiful words he'd ever heard.

But not as beautiful as these.

"Kiss me, little bird."

And so she did.

BRYNNE DIDN'T KNOW for how long she and Lachlan lost themselves in each other. In soft caresses. Slow, lingering kisses. Whispered words of love and devotion and just a little wickedness.

Long enough for her dress to find its way onto the floor, leaving her clad only in her chemise and drawers and partially unbuttoned corset.

Long enough for the stars to light up the night sky.

And long enough for Weston to come searching for her.

A loud knock on the door, and then it opened as she and Lachlan broke apart and she frantically reached for her dress to cover herself.

"Brynne, are you in here? I…" Weston froze in the doorway. Surprise was the first emotion to register, followed by a wave of rage so strong that it knocked Brynne back a step even before he stormed across the library and grabbed hold of Lachlan by the lapels of his jacket.

"You son of a bitch," he snarled, his countenance taut with fury. "How dare you lay a single bloody *finger* on my sister!"

"Wait, you don't understand," Brynne said desperately. But when she tried to tug on her brother's arm, he didn't spare her so much as a glance, such was his focus on Lachlan.

Who, devil take him, wasn't exactly helping matters.

"I've laid a lot more on her than that," he smirked, seemingly unperturbed by the fact that Weston's hands were *literally* at his throat. "Isna that right, Bry?"

"Lachlan," she groaned. "What are you *doing?*"

"Having a bit of a laugh."

Weston's face reddened. "You won't be laughing when you're dead on the floor."

"You can't kill him!" she exclaimed.

"Why the hell not?" her twin demanded.

"Because–because he's my *husband*."

Triumph gleamed in Lachlan's eyes.

Confusion glimmered in Weston's. "You…and Campbell…are…?"

"Married, yes! For more than a year and a half. It's a very long story, and if you release him unharmed, I'd be more than happy to share it with you."

"Lachlan Campbell is your husband," Weston said slowly.

"*Yes.*"

"Well, in that case, I don't feel bad doing *this*." Drawing his arm back, Weston punched it forward in a blow that caught Lachlan completely unprepared on the side of his chin and sent him stumbling sideways into a table.

"*Weston!*" Brynne cried, shocked and dismayed.

"It's all right, Bry." Wincing and working his jaw back and forth, Lachlan staggered to his feet. "I deserved that."

Weston snorted. "You're damned right you did. Now, pour all three of us a glass of brandy, let's have a seat, and discuss how it is I'm just now learning that I have a Scot for a brother-in-law."

They sat and they talked. At some point, they were joined by Evie, who took one glance at Brynne and Lachlan sitting side by side on the chaise lounge holding hands while Weston glowered at them from his chair like an overprotective father, and all but hopped in delight.

"See?" she said, flitting across the room to stand behind her husband-to-be. "I knew you would fly!"

Weston turned his head to slant his fiancée a narrow-eyed glare. "You knew about this?"

"Only for a few days," she said with an airy flick of her wrist.

"A few…" Growling something indecipherable under his breath, he shook his head. "You should have told me. I'm going to be your husband."

"Yes, but *she* is my sister." Evie grinned at Brynne, who smiled back.

How fortunate she was. A husband who loved her, two sisters who supported her no matter what, and a brother who adored her (just as soon as he recovered from finding out one of his best mates had married his twin).

They were like individual stars that made up the same constellation, she thought. Separate but always connected, even when they didn't know it yet.

And Lachlan, well, he was her North Star.

Pointing her to home, and hope, and happily-ever-after.

EPILOGUE

"LACHLAN, IT'S...IT'S *BEAUTIFUL*." Stunned, Brynne traced her fingertips across an antique tapestry as she wandered through the newly renovated foyer of Campbell Castle.

Her husband told her before they left London that he'd begun to work on his childhood home, but he had neglected to specify just how much work he had done.

The old stone floors had been ripped up and replaced with kiln-dried oak harvested from the forests behind the castle. The wide planks, sanded smooth and polished with beeswax, brought a much-needed warmth to the room. As did the tapestries hanging on the walls and the removal of the cobwebs from the ceiling beams. Even the roof had been patched, with nary a bucket in sight. The parlor was done as well, and the sight of it stopped her in her tracks.

"Lachlan Campbell," she said. "Is that *real* furniture?"

Crossing his arms, he rocked onto his heels and grinned at her. "Aye."

As Brynne gazed at the beautiful set of matching chairs in striped silk and elegant settee and mahogany sideboard, it occurred to her–somewhat belatedly–that her husband had taken this task upon himself well *before* their reconciliation. He'd done this for her without having any true confirmation that she would ever return to see it and, once again, she found herself humbled by his faith in her.

His faith in *them*.

Lachlan had always believed.

Even when she hadn't.

When she *couldn't*.

And how she loved him for it.

Which was why, at the dinner party where her brother had clocked her husband in the side of the face (a story, no doubt, that would be retold at many a family gathering), she'd discreetly pulled Lady Theresa aside and casually let her marriage to Lachlan slip. Not to prove her love, but to show how proud she was of it.

Oh, to have been able to capture Theresa's expression!

The shock, the awe, the sheer *delight* of being handed the juiciest piece of gossip to hit the *ton* since it was discovered that the Marquess of Dorchester had an illegitimate American daughter.

Brynne had made certain to ask Theresa not to tell a soul, all but guaranteeing that the news would be printed in the *London Caller* come morning. And while it hadn't gone quite that far, it wasn't long before everyone knew that Lady Brynne Weston had married the barely titled second-born son of a Scot.

More than that, she was *happy* about it.

Blissfully so, as anyone with eyes in their head could see as she and Lachlan proceeded to finish out the Season in London before taking a short holiday in Edinburgh, and eventually making their way back to Campbell Castle. In two weeks, they'd return to Hawkridge Manor to celebrate Christmas with Evie and Weston, Joanna and Kincaid.

Sterling as well, if he hadn't moved out by then.

But in the meantime, Brynne was looking forward to being alone with her husband. Not to make up for memories they'd lost out on by being apart, but to create new ones for the future they were building together.

Already, they'd discussed how they would divide their time be-tween here and England. With the distillery at long last turning a profit, Lachlan would need to be here, at Campbell Castle, more than anywhere else to oversee the day-to-day management of his fledgling business, while the rest of Brynne's family was divided between London and Hawkridge. Then there were Lachlan's siblings to factor into the equation…but they'd already made a plan for that.

Beginning this June, all of the children–Callum, Blaine, Tavish, and Eara–would spend their summers here at the castle. In September, Brynne and Lachlan would travel to Hawkridge Manor where they'd stay through the annual house party and then go on to London for the beginning of the Season, before returning to Glenavon and Campbell Castle before the first snow fell. Spring would be for planting, and then they'd repeat it all again, adjusting things here and there as necessary.

"Come upstairs to our bedroom," Lachlan said, taking her by the hand. "There's something else I want tae show ye."

Our bedroom.

How she loved the sound of those two words side by side.

Despite her laughing protest, he covered her eyes at the top of the winding staircase and guided her down the hall to their private chamber. She heard the creak of the door on its hinges as it opened, and then he slowly lowered his hands.

At first, she didn't know what she was looking at.

Unlike the foyer and the parlor, the bedroom appeared unchanged.

Then she saw it on what had once been a span of empty stone wall, and her heart all but melted into a puddle at her feet.

"Lachlan. I…this…*how?*" she managed as she ran across the room and stopped short in front of the Monet painting that she'd last seen hanging in the Duke of Oxford's gallery. "How did you get it?"

Grinning smugly, Lachlan came up behind her and looped his arms around her waist. Tucked her snug against his chest. "I can be very persuasive," he murmured in her ear.

Yes, he certainly could.

"And who knows?" he went on between kissing his way down her neck and across her shoulder. "Maybe it will be worth something someday."

Maybe it would. But even if the painting's value never exceeded a single pound, Brynne would treasure it. Always and forever. Just as she treasured the man who had given it to her. The man who had just scooped her off her feet and was carrying her over to their bed.

"*Lachlan*," she squealed as he dropped her onto the coverlet.

Bouncing down beside her, he lifted himself up on his elbow and arched a brow. "Aye?"

"It's the middle of the day! Hardly past noon."

"And?" Bending his head, he lightly grasped the edge of her bodice with his teeth and gave it a sharp yank downwards, spilling her breasts into his waiting hands.

On a sigh, Brynne let her head fall back onto the pillow as a contented smile curled her lips. "And I suddenly forgot what I was going to say."

THE END

About the Author

Jillian Eaton grew up in Maine and now lives in Pennsylvania on a farmette with her husband and their three boys. They share the farm with a cattle dog, an old draft mule, a thoroughbred, and a mini-donkey—all rescues. When she isn't writing, Jillian enjoys spending time with her animals, gardening, reading, and going on long walks with her family.

Made in the USA
Middletown, DE
15 October 2021